BOOKS BY DANA MASON

Accidental Groom
Accidental Lies

Accidental
SECRETS

DANA MASON

bookouture

Published by Bookouture in 2019

An imprint of Storyfire Ltd.
Carmelite House
50 Victoria Embankment
London EC4Y 0DZ

www.bookouture.com

ISBN: 978-1-78681-859-1
eBook ISBN: 978-1-78681-858-4

PROLOGUE

Rachel

Fourteen years earlier

I know it's a wasted effort, but I have to do it. I have to get this letter written and get the words out, if only to save my own sanity. This secret I'm being forced to keep—this lie—is so much more than my parents make it out to be. I have no clue where their sense of right and wrong has gone. I don't understand how they can be so cruel. People don't do this sort of thing in real life, do they? It's so soap opera-like, so callous.

If I thought I could do this on my own, I'd leave right now. I'd call Mike and pack a bag and get the hell out of here. But I can't. I don't have anywhere to go, and neither of us is ready to be parents on our own. Unfortunately, I can't trust his parents to help us in any way either.

I have no choice but to fold under my mother's demands that I keep this from Mike. With that heavy thought, I put my pen to paper and write the words that I know will haunt me forever.

Dear Mike,

I'm so sorry for disappearing. I know you must be worried and hurt and utterly clueless about where I am and why I left, but I want you to know that nothing has changed. Our love will never change or diminish for me. This love, you, are everything to me. I don't know how I'm going to do this without you, and I wish there was another way, but right now, I can't find one.

I stop writing to wipe my tears. My eyes are raw, and my face is swollen from all the crying. I've been like this since we left for the airport this morning. I can't help it. I don't want to be here, I want to go home, back to Portland… and Mike. I hate my mom for what she's done.

I take a deep breath and get back to my letter.

What you don't know is I missed my period. I didn't even realize it until my mom pointed it out. She made me take a pregnancy test, which was positive. She's livid and insists that I've ruined my life. Worse than that, she forbids me from telling you about our baby. She brought me to California to live with my dad.

I don't know what to do, Mike. I'm scared, and I miss you.

She's watching my every move. She even stood guard while I packed my stuff to keep me from calling you. I'm writing this because I know I owe you an explanation. You've done nothing wrong except shown me warmth and love where I thought it never existed. You thawed the coldness I've been raised in. This image-driven, self-important, frigid family I come from isn't good enough for you, and isn't good enough for our child.

I hate what's happening. I hate that I can't call you and that I'm never going to see you again. I hate that I was careless, and that because of my carelessness, I had to leave you. I love you more than you'll ever know, and this is breaking my heart. But I'll do what I have to do to protect our child, even if it means giving you up. I just don't know what else to do. My mom is crazy, and I'm afraid of what she'll do to us and our baby if I don't go along with her plan.

I'll make sure to raise our baby in a warm home full of light. I promise our child will feel loved every day. I swear with my whole heart.

I love you,
Rachel

I close my journal, knowing I can never actually send this letter. But at least I can get the thoughts out of my head. I need to keep my mom happy to protect myself, Mike, and the baby.

CHAPTER ONE

Michael

I'm not sure what to do. I stare down at my phone and reread the email I just received.

To: mmurphy@crossfitforlife.com
From: shouldbemurphy@email.com
Subject: A secret

I think you're my dad.

That's it. Five words. Five of the most unsettling words I've ever read. I lean back against the sofa cushions in the office of the Oakland CrossFit and reread the email… which is stupid. It's not going to change from one moment to the next. I try Googling the address, but nothing comes up that matches explicitly. I'm not sure what I was expecting from an email address like *should be murphy*, but I thought it was worth a try.

Gavin smacks my arm, bringing me out of my haze. "Dude, why do you look like you've seen a ghost?"

I hand my phone to him, and moments later, his mouth gapes. "Oh shit, Mike. You have a kid?"

"No, I don't." I point to the phone. "It's got to be a prank, but I can't figure out who did it." I give Gavin a long calculating look and say, "Are you messing with me, asshole?"

He draws back with an amused chuckle. "Nope, not me." He hands back the phone and says, "Just ignore it if you really think it's a prank. Nothing gets under people's skin like being ignored."

"That's true, but I want to know who the hell sent it."

He settles down into the office chair. "So, respond to the email and see what happens."

I hit reply and sit there, finger poised to type. What should I do, ask questions? Tell them to screw off? Play along with the asshole? Whatever, I don't need to overthink it, I just need to start typing.

To: shouldbemurphy@email.com
From: mmurphy@crossfitforlife.com
Subject: RE: A Secret

I don't have a kid. Why would you think I'm your dad?

Before I can change my mind, I hit send. "Alright, it's done. We'll see what happens."

"Good. Let's get back to work." Gavin pulls out the color samples we've been considering for our new CrossFit location in Sacramento. "I'm thinking, keep the walls dark, like Oakland. Navy blue with a lime green stripe all the way around the main gym. For the Pilates studio, we can add a wall of windows here, to divide it from the open gym."

"Right, but I want to keep that room light. I like the contrast."

Gavin writes down the colors then taps his pencil. "I like that too. How about the logo on that far wall?" He points to a photo of the room.

"Yeah, that's a good spot." My phone pings with a new email alert. I pick it up and tap the screen until the message pops up. It's a reply:

Because my mom dated you in high school about nine months before I was born.

My pulse kicks up, and my mind immediately scrambles with the faces of the girls I dated in high school. One specific face comes to mind. *The* girl. Rachel Williams. The girl I lost my virginity to. The only girl who was capable of breaking my heart. But there's no way she could have had my kid. I'd know it. She would have told me.

My mind lingers over the memory of the last time I saw her. We'd been hanging out at the park, throwing the ball for my golden retriever, Bart. Just a normal day... I had no idea it'd be the last time I'd see her. She just stopped coming to school and disappeared. After weeks of showing up at her house and pounding on the door, her mom finally answered and told me she'd moved to Boston to attend a private school. I didn't believe her, not at all, but after weeks of trying to find her with no luck, I had no choice but to give up.

I sit back down and try to remember those last few months together... and then the misery I felt after she left. I started my senior year in such a funk because of her. That was the summer I became obsessed with running and working out. Physical exertion was the only thing that cleared my head, and I've been addicted ever since. I eventually started dating other girls and got over it, but I still think about her often. I always wondered what happened to her and why she didn't tell me she was leaving. Hell, she could've at least called to say goodbye. I was broken hard over that girl and really pissed at her for a long time.

"Mike, what's up, man? I thought we were deciding on this shit today."

"Sorry." I shake my head. "I just got another email from this prankster saying they're my kid."

"No way!" He leans over to look at my screen. Then he says, "So what if you did date the mom? That doesn't mean she had your kid."

"Yeah, I know, it's just creepy."

I quickly type out another email.

Where did your mom go to high school?

Just as I hit send, Gavin says, "You dated a lot of girls in high school, didn't you? Weren't you some local football hero? Maybe you should ask them to narrow it down a little."

I lean forward and rest my elbows on the desk as I wait for a reply. "I mean, yeah, I dated a lot my senior year, but I didn't sleep with a lot of girls."

"Right, but this person doesn't know that."

"True." When my phone pings, I tap to open the email and read it.

The same high school you went to, Hogan High.

I hold my phone up to Gavin. "They know which school I went to."

He snatches my phone and says, "And like I said, you were a local football hero, lots of people know that. It might even be in your bio on our website. Let me try something." Gavin starts typing, and after I hear the swoosh of an email being sent, he hands it back to me. I read what he wrote.

It's easy to get information like that. What's your mom's name? If you're serious about this, tell me something that isn't public knowledge.

Well… at least he didn't type *fuck off.*

Again, my mind lingers on Rachel Williams. I'd like to say I haven't thought about her in a long time, but memories of her drift through my thoughts more often than I want to admit. We met when we were thirteen and fourteen and slowly became friends. Then as we got older, we got closer. By my junior year of high school, we were one hundred percent committed to each other. I loved that girl hard.

Loved her hard enough for her disappearance to have a huge impact on me… But I don't have time to think about that now so I shake away the funk and get back to work.

Gavin and I decide on the color scheme and design then take the time to type it into an email for Wesley, our third partner. When we dreamed up this business, we wanted to open three CrossFit boxes. One for each of us to run. This Sacramento box will be mine, but the decisions are still majority vote. We're all three still partners in each location.

Next year, we're going to open the third location. We've been discussing West Sacramento, but since it's where Gavin has to settle, he's not totally sure he wants to stay in Sac.

When my phone pings, I grab it and open my email.

I know that you lost a front tooth trying to do tricks on your skateboard while drunk.

"That's pretty specific," I mutter. "They know my front tooth isn't real."

Gavin glances up from the laptop and says, "Most of your friends know that, Mike. It's a prank. Delete it and move on. Don't let that crap get inside your head. We have work to do."

I blow out a breath and nod. Gavin is right, I need to get my head in the game. We open in a few weeks, and we don't even have paint on the walls yet. "Okay, you're right." I put my phone down and get to work.

Once we've decided on almost everything, I close my laptop and say, "I'm heading to Sac. When are you coming up?"

"I'll be there to help by the end of the week. I have three personal training sessions and a class tomorrow."

"Great! That gives me time to get all the painting supplies picked up. I plan to be ready to start painting on Monday."

"Perfect. I'll be there Monday morning."

As I'm heading out to my Chevy Tahoe, my phone dings. I lift it to glance at the screen, then click the notification. It's a text from my mom.

Mom: *Hey, Mikey! Look where we are.*

There's a picture with the text, and it's my mom and my dad with the Hollywood sign behind them.

Mom: *We're with Diana and Olivia. Tomorrow we're going to Disneyland. Wish you could join us.*

I'm a little surprised. My parents haven't traveled in years. Since losing my little brother Bradley in a drunk-driving accident, they've been mired in grief. Diana and I have both tried getting them out of the house more. I've even offered to pay the airfare for them to visit me, not that they need my money. They'd never come, but I'm glad to see they're doing something at last. I'm happy they're finally building a relationship with my niece Olivia.

Diana got pregnant with Olivia by accident, after a brief affair with a marine. By the time she found out she was pregnant, he'd been deployed. Unfortunately, he was killed three days after arriving in Afghanistan. Diana never even got the chance to tell him she was having his baby.

My parents were pissed off at her for a long time. They even threatened to disown her. Fortunately, they didn't take it that far, but they made it clear that they thought she'd ruined her life. Olivia was born a few months before Bradley's death and it was only the beginning of our rocky relationship. Since Brad died, things have just gotten worse. It's been seven years and I'm starting to feel like maybe there's an end to the dark tunnel they've been living in.

Me: *Sounds like you guys are having fun. I'm busy getting the Sacramento CrossFit box open. If it wasn't for that, I'd join you. Give Olivia and Diana a kiss from me. Love you.*

Mom: *So proud of you, Son. Love you too, and I hope we get to see you soon.*

Aw, Mom. I feel a little flutter in my chest when I read that. They always wanted me to play football, and were very disappointed when I was injured and gave it up entirely. Since then, they've never once said they are proud of me. Not even when I graduated from college. But she makes it hard for me to be mad when she sneaks in little nuggets like that.

Feeling a little lighter, I load a couple more boxes into the back of my car. I'm slowly moving my stuff from Oakland to Sacramento. My East Sacramento apartment is a massive upgrade from the shithole in Oakland I've been living in. I can't wait to get settled. It was my old friend Kelley who helped me decide to move to Sacramento and open the new location there. She helped me research the neighborhood and find the property. She's also one of the reasons I don't have a good relationship with my parents.

Kelley was engaged to Bradley when he died. She was actually in the car with him during the accident and was severely injured herself. My parents blamed her for everything. *Publicly* blamed her, and it's partly their fault she lost her professional dancing career. Of course, none of it was her fault. She was a victim of Bradley's reckless behavior—he was the drunk driver and essentially killed himself and nearly killed her too. It wasn't until a couple of years ago that she started to bounce back from what happened. Now she's married and very happy.

I just can't fully forgive my parents until they make an effort to apologize to her. They were wrong for what they did. They blasted her to the media as the reason for my brother's alcoholism. They even actively worked against her, and *with* the dance company who dropped her after the accident. Those aren't easy actions to forgive.

After getting everything loaded, I hop into the driver's seat and thank God we only have a few more weeks until our second location is open. It feels good. I feel good about life in general. Work is great, my family is finally getting back to normal, and everything is falling into place for me.

Just as I'm about to start the engine, my phone pings with a new email.

To: mmurphy@crossfitforlife.com
From: shouldbemurphy@email.com
Subject: RE: A Secret

I'm not ready to share my mom's name yet, but I will soon.

"What the fuck?" Persistent little shit. I hit reply and type out:

Sounds like you're full of shit. Don't email me again.

I go back and change *shit* to *it*, just in case this is some confused kid, then hit send and get on the road. I don't have time for this nonsense. But even as I try to put it out of my mind, I can't help feeling unsettled. As much as I want to believe it's a prank, what if it isn't?

CHAPTER TWO

Raegan

I take several deep breaths, trying not to panic. I wasn't expecting him to ask my mom's name. God, Raegan, you're so stupid. Of course, he's going to ask her name. It's so obvious. Why would he believe some random email without proof, and what was I expecting him to say? Jeez—at this point he probably thinks he's being blackmailed or something stupid like that. I'm not trying to make him defensive… The whole point of this was to make him ask questions about me, to look for *me*.

I toss my phone on the couch and look around Uncle Mitch's living room helplessly. I've been researching Mike but I need something better. How am I going to get that kind of information out of my mom? I slide her yearbook out from my backpack and flip through it again. I look at every picture of every group, club, and team, but I need something else. Anyone can have the information in this book. I need something more personal.

I get up off the couch and walk down the hall and poke my head in my uncle's office. "Hey, Uncle Mitch."

"Hey, hey, little Rae." He grins up at me over the rim of his reading glasses. His white hair is standing on end as if he's been running his hands through it repeatedly. "What's up with you?"

"Nothing, but do you mind if I go play on the pool table in the garage?"

"Oh, hon, I can't play with you right now, can you wait a little while?"

"Yeah, cool, but can I go practice while I'm waiting?"

"Sure, sure, go ahead. Just give me about half an hour to finish this blog post."

"Thanks, Uncle Mitch." I rush away and head to the garage. Mitch is my grandma's brother, so technically, he's my great-uncle, but he was also my grandpa's best friend before Gramps died.

Before Uncle Mitch retired, he wrote for prominent newspapers like *The New York Times*, the *Washington Post*, and the *San Francisco Chronicle*. Now he runs a popular blog about the current state of affairs in California. And when I say all that, what I really mean is he runs a blog that criticizes the state government. He doesn't usually have anything good to say. I think that's why he was such good friends with my grandpa. Gramps was a politician before he died… even the Mayor of Sacramento for a long time, before being elected to the State Assembly. They could sit around for hours and argue about politics.

My grandma owns this house, it was where my gramps lived before he died. Now my uncle lives here to take care of the place. I stay here after school so I don't have to be home alone. I'm too old for the after-school programs, and I'm glad about that.

Uncle Mitch pretty much leaves me alone, it's his housekeeper Annie who has the eagle eyes. I can't get anything past that woman. Thankfully, she's not here today or I'd never be able to do what I'm planning.

Once I'm in the garage, and the bright fluorescent lights are glaring down on me, I head over to the third garage stall, where he keeps his golf cart. This house is near the golf course and 'The Club' as my uncle calls it. His usual mode of transportation in the area is this little golf cart. Sometimes he lets me drive it too. The space behind the golf cart is where my mom keeps some of her old things. When my grandpa lived here, my mom and I lived in the guesthouse out back. These boxes are full of the stuff she left behind when we moved. Our house is pretty small, and this place is huge, so she just stores this stuff here. You'd think she'd get rid of it, but lucky for me, she never throws anything away. I've seen her in here, searching through the boxes a few times. I'm hoping I can find some proof about my father.

My stomach flips a little when I think about Mike Murphy. I know he's my dad, but I just can't confirm it for sure. In the past, when I've asked my mom about my father, she wouldn't talk about him, but I didn't want to push too hard. I get the feeling she was hurt pretty badly and I don't want to upset her, but now I think it's time she told me more. Especially if I can't get Mike to take the emails seriously.

I deserve to know who my dad is. Mike deserves to know he has a daughter. I thought if I sent him a few cryptic emails, he'd start doing his own research. I wish I knew what happened between them all those years ago. I wish I knew why he isn't in our lives. Why he doesn't seem to know I exist.

Occasionally my mom will lower her guard and tell me something about my father, but not often and she never tells me anything concrete—nothing I could use to prove it's Mike. The last time I asked her about him, she completely avoided the subject. From what I've gathered, she hasn't seen him since before I was born. Lots of things can happen in that time.

I scan the boxes in a grid pattern so I don't miss any. Most of the boxes are labeled by date so it doesn't take long to find a couple labeled with the years she was in high school. I pull two from the stack then restack everything so nobody can tell they've been moved.

I squat on the floor next to them and slap my hands together to get the dust off me. Then I lift the first lid with bated breath. I can't wait to see what's inside. Once the top is off, I frown at the folded baby clothes inside. Little dresses that make my eyes roll. Pathetic.

I know this is my grandma's doing. Grandma wanted a prim and proper granddaughter, but she ended up with me instead. I laugh at that because I'm not a girly girl. I'm not even sure Grandma thinks girls should wear pants, she's that backwards. Most of my family is like that, but thankfully, my mom isn't. Grandma is a complete prude, though. I can see why Mom avoids her so much. I search the box for anything else, but it's mostly clothes.

I put the lid back on it and lift it to add it back to the pile. Then I pop open the next box. There's an old cheerleader uniform, a couple of photo albums, some old school work... why would she keep that? Then I see it. A journal. I grab it and put it aside. Then I find a zipper makeup bag full of little folded-up pieces of paper. What are these? It looks like sad attempts at origami. I unfold one, and my eyes widen. Score! They're notes from friends. I take the entire pouch out and then lift out one of the photo albums. I flip through and snicker at what life must have been like before digital cameras... before the instant gratification of taking a picture and having it available on your phone.

When I come across a series of photos of my mom with a guy, I stare hard at them. After seeing Mike's Facebook profile, I know it's him, but I can see the difference between then and now. He's younger and not so big in the pictures. He has more of a baby face, and his brown eyes seem like he's laughing at something. His eyes... they're like mine. I can't pretend they're not and I'm not just trying to get my hopes up. He definitely looks like me. When I come across an empty spot, I know that's where the original photo is from.

A week ago, I found a photo in my mom's desk drawer of this guy. It was dated the summer before I was born and it said Michael Murphy on the back. Anyone who can do simple math can calculate nine months. I was born in April, but I was three weeks early, so I know my mom got pregnant in July or August.

This photo is what prompted me to search for Mike. I started with my mom's old high school yearbook, which was stored on the bookcase in her home office. Mike was a year ahead of my mom in school. So, if she was seventeen when I was born, he must have been eighteen, or close to it.

I pull a few more of the pictures out and then replace the album before I put the lid back on the box and return it to the stack.

My heart is pounding so fast I feel like it might explode. I grab the notes and the journal and quickly carry them into the house to hide them in my backpack.

I take a breath and try to rest my hammering heart. Just as I start to relax, I hear the front door open then my mom's heels on the tiles. A moment later, she's in front of me. I know she can't possibly know what I did, but I still have to fight the sense of guilt as she smiles at me.

Her smile fades, and she says, "What are you up to?"

I try to act offended. "Why do you always think I'm up to something? I'm just sitting here, minding my own business."

One side of her mouth twists up as she stares at me. "Really? Just sitting here? And why is that?"

"I was waiting for Uncle Mitch to play pool with me."

Thankfully, my uncle picks that time to come into the living room, rubbing his hands together. "So, did you practice? Ready for me to beat you?"

I lift a brow and look over at my mom. "See."

"Hey, Uncle Mitch. What are you up to?"

She walks over and kisses his cheek. He wraps an arm around her shoulder and says, "I wrote a post about the new gas tax. People just don't get it. The tax is a good thing. We need the money to fix infrastructure."

My mom tilts her head in irritation. She's several inches shorter than Uncle Mitch, but he's at least six feet tall. My mom is super pretty, with dark hair and thick, long black eyelashes that frame her sea-blue eyes. I always wished I had her eyes until I saw a picture of Michael Murphy. Now I'm glad I have something of his.

Mom's super-hot for a mom too. She's always making cracks about looking like a soccer mom, but I see men stare at her all the time. She has a perfect hourglass figure, which means all her clothes look good on her. I glance down at my small chest and I'm kind of glad they're small. It's hard to play sports with big breasts. I have friends who are already in C cups.

"Well, I'm not too pleased with the higher gas prices either," Mom says. "So I understand the frustration."

"Oh, now, Rachel, don't you worry your pretty little head about it. I know you don't understand much about things like infrastructure, but we'll sort it out for you."

I watch as my mom's face turns red, then she sort of drifts out from underneath Uncle Mitch's arm and says to me, "Are you ready to go?"

My mom and uncle don't always agree on politics, but more than anything, she hates when he *mansplains* things to her. She's not stupid, not at all. My mom is one of the smartest people I know, she's just too quiet, and she doesn't really stand up for herself. It bugs me that she doesn't, but when I think about some of the things her parents have said to her, it's no wonder she picks her battles so carefully. Some things aren't worth the aggravation. "Yep, I'm ready. Let's go."

"Hey hey, Rae, we'll get that game of pool in tomorrow. Okay?"

"Sounds good." I give him a big hug before following my mom out the front door.

Once we're settled in the car, she starts in on her usual questions about school, Uncle Mitch, and how I spent my afternoon. I watch her as she talks and I wonder if this conversation ever bores her like it bores me. I feel like we never have real conversations. At thirteen, she still considers me a child. She has no idea how wrong she is.

"Mom, what's my dad's name?"

Her head whips around, her blue eyes wide. Then she turns back to look at the road. "Why are you asking me this?"

"Because I want to know who my father is. I think it's time." I don't understand what's so unreasonable about wanting to know about the man who shares my DNA. When she doesn't respond, I try again. "Seriously. I want to know, and you don't have a good reason for not telling me."

She tucks a strand of inky black hair behind her ear and says, "Maybe I do, and I'm just not sharing it with you."

"Then you should at least tell me what that reason is."

"Raegan, I'm not sure this is something you're ready for."

"No, you mean, *you're* not ready for it. Because if you told me, I might want to spend time with him and you'd have to share me with someone other than Uncle Mitch."

"You seem so sure this man will want to be a dad." She glances at me and says, "How do you know I'm not trying to protect you from getting hurt—protecting you from rejection?"

"So, it's true that he doesn't know about me."

Her head shakes instinctively. "I didn't say that."

"Then he does know about me."

"I didn't say that, either."

"Mom! Say *something*. It's time, and besides, I can handle it, and I want to know." I shrug and say, "What do you think? That I'm some fragile person who can't handle bad stuff? I can, Mom, you have to give me a chance."

"Raegan…"

"I don't need you to protect me. If he rejects me, we'll deal with that."

She throws her hand up, shaking her head. "Spoken like someone who's never been rejected. Spoken like someone who's never dealt with heartache—who's been given everything in life and never needed or wanted for anything."

"But I have, Mom!" I didn't mean to shout at her, but she acts like it's so easy to not have a dad. As if dads don't matter. "I've lived my entire life needing and wanting a father. That's a pretty big need."

I see the hurt on her face, and I feel bad about it, but not bad enough to stop pushing her. "I'm not saying you're not good enough. Don't go all sappy and guilt-trippy on me. This isn't about you. I love you, Mom, but what if I have siblings? Besides that, I deserve to know where I come from."

"You come from *me*, Raegan. I'm the one who gave you life. I'm the one who changed your diapers and lost sleep for years and goes to every one of your school events."

"Mom, I'll ask Uncle Mitch if you don't tell me."

She laughs at this. "Even if Mitch knew, he wouldn't tell you, *I promise.*"

"Just tell me. I want to know who my dad is. Tell me now, Mom!"

"I'm not telling you anything when you speak to me like that. You need to remember who you're talking to."

"I'm talking to the woman who won't let me have a dad. The same woman who's been lying about me for fourteen years."

"Is that what you think?" She waves a hand around and says, "You think this is something *I* don't want you to have? Like I'm purposely depriving you of having a father. Is that really who I am to you?"

"I don't have a choice. That's all I can think when you won't even have a conversation with me about it."

"Interesting." Her eyebrows raise when she says, "You want to have this all-important adult conversation, but you're acting like a child with all your demands and shouting." She points a finger in my direction. "You know, Rae, my day was bad enough without having to come home and take abuse from you."

"I'll leave you alone if you just tell me his name."

"Right, give you his name so you can jump on the internet and start searching for him without considering the consequences."

"But I thought I was some dumb thirteen-year-old who couldn't take it."

"You and I both know what you're capable of. And just because you know your way around a computer doesn't mean you're ready to take on real-life problems. Not to mention, why should I tell you anything when you're acting so nasty to me?"

"You can't protect me forever." I put my earbuds in and ignore everything she says after that. I don't understand why she won't tell me. Is she trying to protect me, or is she just trying to protect herself?

CHAPTER THREE

Rachel

Once we're done eating, Raegan retreats to her room, and I'm almost relieved. I sit down at the table with a large glass of wine and rest my head in my hands. Jesus, what am I going to do with her? She's so curious about everything. Why this sudden interest in knowing her father's name? Just thinking about him makes my stomach somersault. It's been years, and I still remember every moment I spent with him. He was so different from the other guys in school. So thoughtful about everything. So on task and so sure of what he wanted. I was never like that. I never knew what I wanted to do until I got my first position at The Sutter… and then it was a letdown to my parents. To hear my mom say the word *hospitality*, you'd think it was a dirty word. I sigh and lift my head to sip my wine.

Not that I care about my parents' approval. My dad went to his grave disappointed in me. Even though he said he was proud of me, a daughter knows. My mother has never tried to hide her disappointment or her discontent at my lack of scholarly achievement. She and I don't have the same opinions about success. If I can't manage in a career of her choice, I should find a husband—*excuse me*—a suitable husband, whatever the hell that is. But that's ridiculous. My ambitions circled more around being a suitable and loving parent to Raegan. Especially since I was her only parent, thanks to *my* parents.

Besides, I love my job. I love what I do, even though it's never been good enough for my mother. I've never had an interest in politics or academia. I want to have my own life. I want a job that makes me happy, and my daughter.

When did I stop being enough for her?

She looks so much like him. Those eyes and the way they look at me… or through me. Jesus, we were just kids, but still, it felt so real. When I think about Raegan, I know it was real. Mike and I made her, and that means something. But how can I tell her? How can I tell him after all these years? He's going to hate me. If he didn't hate me for not telling him fourteen years ago, he'll hate me now for throwing his life into upheaval. It's no small thing to show up on someone's doorstep with a teenager.

I refill my glass then walk into the guestroom, which doubles as my home office. After opening my laptop, I tug open the drawer to take out his photo. The picture is from the summer I got pregnant, weeks before I left town. I shift things around and lift the pen tray, but no photo. Crap. What did I do with it? I pull open the other desk drawers, but I can't remember where I left it. The damn thing must be in my bedroom.

I sigh as I stare at the screen. I could try to find him. I don't have to tell Rae, but I could look him up, see what he's doing. See if he has a family and kids. I didn't have any luck the last time I tried, but that was years ago. Now, with the popularity of social media, he might be easier to find. I set the glass down and type his name. It's a pretty common name, but if I'm careful, I can find the right search terms. I know his brother's and sister's names too.

I hit enter, but I get so many results. I know it's useless. So I include the University of Oregon in the search terms. I know he went to school there on a scholarship for football. Once I add this, I find him pretty fast. My heart lurches in my chest. I'm bombarded with memories of high school and how popular he was. I click on a couple of news articles from back then and read about him. A local hero who kept his talents in Oregon. Then I go back to the search results and see a local connection.

I click on it and stop breathing. It's a photo of him with two other men. He's incredible. Mouthwatering, even. Big, healthy, and inked. The words tall, dark, and dangerous come to mind. He's got a layer of stubble on his chin, just enough to make it look like he doesn't keep it on purpose. He looks so… cool, and that reminds me that I'm a mom, which is about as far from cool as it gets. I read the article and slowly exhale.

CrossFit entrepreneurs to open a chain of CrossFit Gyms in Sacramento.

CrossFit is a high-intensity workout that incorporates circuit training, weightlifting, and cardio. Founded in California, it has gained popularity over the years with people looking for a tribe with similar interests in health and wellness. These three men are trying to focus on that community as a way to be accountable for each other. They consider themselves a family and their clients aren't just clients, they're friends, or brothers and sisters.

I finish the article and rest back in my chair. Mike's in Sacramento? That can't be right.

I Google his name with the term 'CrossFit', and there he is, in the first search results. Oakland CrossFit. I click the *About* link and Mike's picture and bio pop up. God, he looks good. He's big—outright buff—and so hot. His dark, whiskey-colored eyes are smiling at me, and it reminds me of when we were in school. He was smaller then but that face is the same, his expression relaxed and looking like he just told the funniest joke. His dark brown hair is cut short and stylish, combed to a faux hawk on top of his head. He has a small mole on his right cheek… I remember I used to kiss it every day. God, we were so good together. I know people say nobody finds real love at that age, but damn, it felt right… until I got pregnant and my mom shipped me down here to live with my dad.

And I just left. No note. No explanation. I just left him. The loathing I feel about myself for doing that is unmeasurable.

My mom had booked tickets that morning without even giving me the chance to call him. Within hours, we were in Sacramento with my dad. She threatened to take the baby away and put her up for adoption and said she'd never forgive me if I tied myself to 'that boy' for the rest of my life. My dad said he'd throw me out if I told anyone in Portland about the baby. Mother even threatened to tell everyone that Mike had taken advantage of me. Said she'd ruin his reputation, which would have destroyed his future football career.

I believed her too. She'd done something similar to a former teacher of mine. His first mistake, in my mother's eyes, was failing me in pre-calculus. Mother was livid. Then when he didn't let me join the debate team, she really lost it. She blamed him, even though the calculus class was too advanced for me, and I was never debate team material. I didn't belong on that team and everyone knew it but my mother. She didn't consider any of that when she got revenge on the poor teacher. Of course, she never outright admitted to it, but I know she's the one who went to the school administration and told them she'd seen him making out with a student in his car at the mall.

Soon after that, the school board received an anonymous letter with the same accusations. Within a few days, it was all over the news. I'm sure she did that too. When I asked her about it, she denied it, but she denied it with a gleam in her pale blue eyes and a knowing smile.

Poor Mr. Gardner never saw it coming, and even when nobody could find proof, he still lost his job because of the media coverage. Of course, after watching this debacle and seeing the wrath of my mother's revenge, I believed her when she said she could ruin Michael's life.

There were so many threats to force me to keep a secret that I'm still keeping. So many threats to a scared sixteen-year-old girl who didn't know any better. And God, was I scared to death. Even once I was in college, I still didn't try to contact Mike. It wasn't until after we both finished college that I really tried looking for him. At that point, I didn't think my mother had any power over us. Of course, then I couldn't find him. It was as if he'd disappeared. I know he never got drafted into the NFL, but I don't know why, or where he went after he graduated.

After a couple of years, I became more afraid of his reaction if I told him than I was afraid of what would happen if I didn't. I knew he must hate me for the way I left. Not to mention that he had a life, he'd moved on. My life eventually got too complicated. Too many things had happened that drove a wedge between me and my dream of reuniting with him, and between me and my dream of Raegan finally having a father who would love her, even if he didn't love me. One of those complications makes me shiver… and that one has kept me from searching for Mike for the last several years. But I need to stop letting it hold me back.

I think about what Raegan said in the car and I know I need to do something. She's right; it's time. As frightened as I am, I know I need to move forward with contacting Mike. As much as I fear his reaction and his anger, I want Raegan to have a father. She deserves that and he deserves to know about his daughter.

I sign into Facebook and try looking him up. It doesn't take long, and I'm happy to see most of his posts are public. Of course, most of them are promos for the CrossFit gym, so that doesn't help me learn anything about his personal life. My heart nearly stops at the sight of him. He's certainly grown and matured. He's not the boy I remember. He looks like one of those insanely hot fitness models you see on the cover of health magazines. Looking at him causes a stir I haven't felt in a *very* long time. I can't help it, he's incredible, and God, I miss him so much it makes my stomach hurt.

As I search his photos, I'm relieved when I don't find any that look like they're with a family... or a wife. He has lots of him surfing and rock climbing. Several workout videos too. I get up and close the door so Rae doesn't hear, then I click on the most recent video. It's Mike climbing a rock face, and the guy holding the camera is making fun of him. Mike's laughing at him as he climbs the rock like a spider monkey. He's in such great shape and damn, that makes me feel fat and ugly. The muscles in his arms and calves are flexing as he climbs and it nearly makes me groan. The next video is an interview about the new Sacramento CrossFit location. Mike's answering questions with the broadest smile... oh God, the sound of his voice! It's the same mostly, just a bit deeper. He looks so happy, and I'm glad he's happy, but it makes me sad that he's moved on, done something with his life and I'm still in the same place I've always been. But now... he's here.

In Sacramento.

When I get the urge to cry, I switch back to the photos. What I'm searching for, I don't know. It's masochistic, what I'm doing, but I need to know about a girlfriend or wife. There are some photos with different girls but most look like they're in the gym. I click through the few to see if those girls have lots of pictures of him, but none do.

As I'm searching, I get a notification that my mother has commented on one of my photos. I click the notification and read: *Really, Rachel, do you think it's wise to wear such a low-cut blouse to work? You should try to set a better example for your employees.*

I glance at the selfie of Isla and me having lunch on the east-wing patio of The Sutter. I remember the day because we were discussing making changes to the wrought-iron wedding arch used in this particular space. It was a beautiful day and a really productive working lunch for us both. I look at my cleavage in the photo, and I'm not sure what my mother expects me to do about it. I have large boobs. I can't help that. No matter what I wear or how I wear it, I'm going to have cleavage showing.

It's something different with her every day. She doesn't even need to be in town to criticize me. She can now do it daily on social media from Portland for the entire world to see. I never should have accepted her friend request.

I try to shake off her rudeness and get back to looking for more information about Michael. I Google his sister and nothing comes up, but when I Google his brother's name and *Portland, Oregon,* I get a slew of results.

"Oh my gosh!" I place my hand over my mouth as I read an article about his brother's death in a drunk-driving accident. Poor Mike. That must have been terrible.

After reading all of that, I close the windows on my computer and clear my search history in case Rae gets nosey, and then I close my laptop. Never again. My heart can't take it. My brain can't take it, and for sure, my relationship with my daughter can't.

How strange that a feeling can linger for years and years without fading. I can remember the feel of Mike's touch, how gentle he was with me—but I can also remember another man's touch, and not a gentle one. I remember a hand over my mouth, telling me to be quiet. I remember rough hands and terrifying—paralyzing—fear.

I think about that single horrible memory from four years ago and know I'd rather never be touched again than have to relive that moment. I shake it away, trying not to let that memory take hold. My thoughts turn again to Michael.

No one has been able to make me feel the way Mike made me feel. Again, I get the urge to cry. Did I really peak at sixteen? Am I seriously destined to be just a mom for the rest of my life without any pleasure for myself? Is that what motherhood is? Not that I don't love being Raegan's mother. I love her and I treasure our close relationship, but I can't help feeling like so much is missing from my life. Is that why my mom was so harsh with me for so many years? Was she jealous that I had someone to love—that he loved me just as much? Was she lonely enough to resent the love I shared with him… Resentful enough to take it away?

I remember how Mike smelled after football practice. That manly athletic, sweaty smell, covered with scented deodorant. I remember the heat of his body when we slept next to each other. The firm grip of his arms around me. As painful as it is, I'm so thankful I remember every minute.

If only I knew what kind of a man he is now and whether he's capable of being a father to Raegan without hurting her. And, God, I wish I knew what prompted Raegan's new fascination with knowing who her father is. What's made her so curious all of a sudden? And what should I do about it?

CHAPTER FOUR

Raegan

Once I'm sure my mom has a glass of wine poured for herself and is distracted, I take the chance to flip through the journal I found in the box from my uncle's garage. After opening it, I realize it's more of a sketchbook than a journal—or at least a mixture of both. The first few pages are colored pencil drawings of butterflies. Then there are sketches of dogs, or of a specific dog. A golden retriever, from what it looks like. I try to remember her telling me about pets she had growing up, but I'm pretty sure she didn't have any. I actually remember her complaining about my grandma being allergic. Below the drawing of the dog is a caption that reads *The Tales of Bart Murphy*. The name Murphy jumps out, and I wonder if this was Mike's dog. I flip the pages and then come across portraits, and I know right away: this is him.

I've studied the picture I took from my mom and have his face memorized. The next few pages are of random birds, but nothing particular to help me with my mission. I knew my mom could draw pretty well, but I had no idea she was this good.

I put the book into my backpack and take the zipper pouch out, but before I open it, I check on my mom. I can hear her typing on her laptop, so I go ahead and close, then lock, my door. Settled on my bed again, I open the zipper pouch and sort through the letters. I open one, dated April 21st.

Hey babe,

I can't wait for this weekend. I can't believe we lucked out the way we did. My parents leaving for the weekend and your mom agreeing to let you spend the weekend "camping" with Carly's family. I owe Carly bigtime for backing us up like that. It'll be just the two of us. We can veg out in front of the TV and hang out with Bart. No interruptions and no family obligations. We can just keep to ourselves, or we can invite a few people over on Saturday if you want to barbeque. I don't care as long as you're there too.

Love you, Mike

That didn't tell me anything new. I sort through again, opening them one at a time. They're all from Mike. I expected a few, but I thought she'd have some from other friends as well.

After reading several, I start to get discouraged. There's nothing in here that I can use to prove I know more about him that can't be Googled. I open another, and it looks like the type of note written during class between two people.

The first line reads: *You think you're funny, but you're snot.* With a hand-drawn frowny face, and it makes me laugh.

The next line is written in what's probably my mom's handwriting. It's a little curlier than she writes now but similar enough.

Oh, but that was hilarious! How's your nose feeling? And she added a little hand-drawn heart.

Mike replies: *I don't know what you mean??*

Mom: *LMBO! You know exactly what I mean. It's surprising you didn't knock out your new tooth. Hard to believe you're such a great athlete with your clumsiness.*

Mike: *I'm not clumsy, you brat! Not everyone can have my grace—and the nose and tooth are fine.*

Mom: *Oh, I wish I had a camera! Hahahaha! Lucky for me, other people saw it, otherwise you'd deny it to the point of making me feel like I imagined it. I guess we're gonna need to tell the janitor to stop cleaning that glass door so well, otherwise it might kill you. I'll go ahead and mention it to Coach since it's in the gym.*

Mike: *Again, I don't know what you mean—don't you mention anything to Coach—and if you do, I'll tell him you're off your meds, and that's why you're acting so crazy.*

Mom: *Ur so cute.* And there's another heart with a smiley face.

Mike: *Shut up.*

I can picture this in my head and to be honest, he does seem a little clumsy between walking into a glass door and falling on his skateboard.

I'm smiling when I open the next note. This one is dated May 15th the year before I was born.

I love you so much, Rachel. I hate that your mom works so hard to keep us apart. I don't understand why she hates me. Am I that bad? I miss you, and I'm tired of sneaking around. I don't understand what I did to her. Have you told her something that would make her hate me? Does she know we're having sex? You wouldn't tell her that, would you?

Bingo! This note is dated eleven months before I was born. I find it highly unlikely she moved on from Mike and had sex with a different boy in two months. Impossible, right?

I get up to see what my mom is doing, and I find her sitting in her office, writing. I stand there and stare at her, and the longer I watch, the angrier I get. Why won't she talk to me?

"Mom, what are you doing?"

Her head pops up quickly, and she gently closes her notebook shut. "I'm working. What are *you* doing?"

"Is that a journal? I didn't know you kept a journal."

"It's a work journal. I'm writing about my day and what happened. Why are you being so nosey?"

"Can we talk? I want you to tell me about my dad."

She drops her head back with a heavy sigh. "Raegan, why are you suddenly so interested in this person you've never met?"

"He's my father. Mom, why is this so hard for you to understand? Is it because you had such a bad relationship with Grandpa?"

"If only," she says.

"I'm not going to stop asking. I want to see my birth certificate. Is his name on it?"

Her eyes narrow at me, and her face flushes with anger. It's the strangest thing I've ever seen. She goes from calm to not in seconds. "You don't seem to understand that I'm the parent, and I make the rules. You don't get to step into my office and make demands of me. Do you understand that?"

"This isn't about *who's the boss*, this is about my DNA. My family history. I'm not trying to demand things from you, I'm trying to figure out who I am."

"You're Raegan Elizabeth Williams. My daughter. What more do you need?"

"A dad, Mom! I need a dad! Stop being so unreasonable. Stop being like this. I don't understand, were you raped or something, is that why you won't tell me?"

Her face goes really red now, and it makes me think I'm spot on, but then she says, "Don't even think such a thing." Her expression grows hard as if she's offended by the idea that my father was a rapist.

"Then tell me!" I shout, now just as angry. Why is she so stubborn? "How would you feel? Huh, Mom? How would you feel if someone kept a secret like this from you? What if your mother did this to you?" I see a flash of something in her blue eyes, then she slides the journal into the drawer of her desk before looking back up at me.

"You think I'm a bad mother? Is that what you're trying to say to me?" She stands and walks over to the bed before dropping down on it. "Be careful, Raegan. Some things, some words can't be unsaid." Her voice is quiet now. Soft, unlike the anger. I probably hurt her feelings, but I can't seem to stop myself.

"What kind of mother keeps the father a secret? I can't even understand because you won't tell me why. And you should follow your own advice. You can't give me years back with my father. Once they're gone, they're gone. Does he even know about me?"

Her face pales a shade, and she shakes her head as if at a loss. "You're too smart for your own good, Raegan." She sounds like she's about to start crying and I'm torn between being glad I'm getting a reaction and feeling bad for making her cry.

"Mom, I think you should try to understand how I feel. Just once… but I guess you can't because you're too concerned with how *you* feel. You're too selfish to get past your own issues to let me have a dad."

I half expect her to get up off the bed and approach me, but instead she keeps her eyes on the ground, and a tear slips out from between her long lashes. I feel bad, but I still meant what I said. It's true. I know I'm being harsh, pushing her, but I need to be like this to make her see it from my perspective.

She reaches for a tissue and wipes her face, then nods. "You're right. I don't want to get hurt, but more than that, I don't want *you* to get hurt. Do you understand that? It's not selfishness to want to protect you."

"Mom, I can take it. I promise." I walk over and sit across from her on the bed. "I know there's a chance he won't want anything to do with us. I get it. I'll accept that, but I want to try. God, Mom, do you know how hard it is to answer questions when people ask about my dad? Can you imagine what that's like? What it's like not knowing where I get my brown eyes from? I'm the only one in the family with dark eyes. Why am I so tall? I'm already taller than you and Grandma. Gramps wasn't tall either. And what am I supposed to say when my friend's parents say, *wow, Raegan, your mom works at The Sutter, that's so cool, what does your dad do?* I have to stutter through an explanation about how I don't have a dad. I never know what to say. *Gee, thanks for asking but I don't have a dad. I don't know my dad. I've never met my dad.*" I lift my hand then drop it to my side and say, "And the looks they give me, they're always a little torn between pity and curiosity."

Mom looks up at me then, and her expression is so sad, but I feel like she's finally listening to me. "I'm so sorry. You're right, I've been too selfish to realize how hard this is for you."

"Don't be sorry… talk to me."

"I never meant to hurt you. I've been afraid of so much for so long." She scoots back on the bed and crosses her legs, and my heart's fluttering in excitement. She's finally going to talk to me. I scoot back too and mirror her position so that I'm facing her.

She picks at the comforter nervously. "I fell in love when I was your age." She stops suddenly, and her gaze lingers, but then she says, "At least, I thought it was love."

I roll my eyes and say, "Stop. You don't have to lie to protect me. I'm not going to go out and get pregnant because you did."

She chuckles through her tears and says, "All right. Honestly, I did love him. I was thirteen, and he was fourteen. We had met through some mutual friends, but I was never brave enough to talk to him until we ran into each other at the local public pool.

He sort of saved me when I got a cramp and couldn't get to the edge of the pool."

I already have so many questions, but all I can do is snort. "You're the best swimmer I know, how could that even happen?"

She grins, and I see a little gleam in her eye… that really makes me believe that she loved him once. "I was faking because I liked him."

"Mom!"

"I know, but I was sure of what I wanted… sort of like you are now." She rests her elbows on her knees and says, "He helped me to the side of the pool and then helped me sit up on the ledge."

"You should drink more water, that'll help avoid cramps."

Of course, I already know this, but I nod and say, "Oh, okay. I'll do that."

"I brought some water bottles, you can have one." He hops out of the pool in one leap and walks away. A moment later, he's back with a bottle. He twists the cap and hands it to me.

I take it and thank him before taking a few sips. I point to the girl next to his little cooler and say, "Who's that? Is she your girlfriend or something?"

He laughs hard and crinkles his nose. "No! That's my sister, Diana. I don't have a girlfriend."

"Oh, sorry." I sip the water, a little embarrassed now that I openly asked about his girlfriend.

"Do you have a boyfriend?" he asks, and my cheeks get hot.

I shake my head, afraid my voice will squeak if I talk.

"Doesn't your family have a pool? Why do you swim here?"

"I like to get out of the house and away from my mom. She drives me crazy."

"How old are you?" he asks.

"I'm almost fourteen. I'm starting Hogan this year."

"Wait… your parents are letting you go to public school?"

I stare up at him for a moment. How did he know they didn't want me to go there? "Yeah, but I had to beg them to let me. How do you know that?"

"I didn't, really." He shrugs then says, "Your family doesn't seem like the public school type. I thought you'd go to a private high school."

"It took me a while to convince her, but once my mom researched the school, she agreed. It's a pretty good program and still a charter school. You go to Hogan too, right?"

"Yeah, I'll be a sophomore this year. My sister's a senior."

"Cool. Don't you have a brother too?"

"Yeah, but he's younger."

"A dancer, right?" I look around for him, but I don't see him here. "He's terrific, too."

He shrugs as if reluctant to give his brother credit. "How do you know?" he finally asks.

"I took a dance class with him. I wasn't very good, so I quit."

This makes him laugh. "I can't dance at all. Somedays, I can barely walk straight."

I laugh because I feel the same way about myself. "That's okay, we can't all be graceful."

"I'm going to the movies tonight with a group of friends, do you want to go?" I meet his dark eyes, and he looks a little nervous as he asks, but he can't be nearly as nervous as I am.

"Yeah, that sounds like fun."

"He was a year older but not a douche like all the other guys. You know what I mean? He was a nice person. Helping me to the side of the pool was a natural reaction to him… I guess I already knew that when I pretended to need help."

"You know, Mom, he probably could tell you were faking."

I laugh because I'm sure she's right. "He might have, but not calling me out on it is another example of how nice he was."

"If he's so nice, why can't I meet him?"

She sighs and says, "The situation is very complicated, Raegan. So, so complicated… but I'll tell you what, I'll try to find him and when I do, I'll reach out to him. Once I've checked him out, I'll see if we can set something up."

I jump into her arms and squeeze her in a tight hug. I don't want to cry, but I can't help it. The lump in my throat keeps me from being able to thank her. She pulls back from me and wipes my face. "I'm sorry I didn't realize sooner how important this is to you. All this time I've been worried about you getting hurt… And now I see I'm the one hurting you. I'm sorry, but Raegan, you have to let me do this, okay? Don't try getting ahead of me. Don't go out and start your own search. Just be a little patient and trust me. Okay?"

"Okay," I croak. There's no way I'm going to tell her I've already found him. If I'm careful, she won't find out. "I hope you know I don't want you to get hurt either, Mom."

"I know you don't, and I'll be fine. Don't worry about me, okay?"

I nod and squeeze her again. I'm so happy and so nervous at the same time.

CHAPTER FIVE

Rachel

Dear Michael,

Our baby is a year old today. I can't believe it. She's so strong and so smart. You'd be proud of her, of course you would… if only you had the chance. She looks so much like you, and she's stubborn like you. Busy and always moving. Aside from sleeping, I don't think she's been still for two minutes together since she was born. She's curious and sweet and the most beautiful little girl I've ever seen.

I wish you could see her…

I wish I could see you…

I miss you so much. Watching her grow is lonely, fulfilling, heartbreaking, and rewarding all at the same time. It's the most incredible experience, and I so badly wish I could share it with you.

Every time she makes me laugh, I wish you were there to laugh with me, and every time she makes me cry, I wish you were there to wipe my tears.

You'll be happy to know, I'm back in school… sort of. I'm homeschooling with a tutor. I've also started looking at colleges, although I don't know why. My only real option is the community college or Sacramento State. It's not like I can leave my dad's. Raegan is a full-time job. I can't raise her on my own while trying to support myself and go to school at the same time. Dad said I can stay in the guest house as long as I'm in school. I feel like it would be stupid not to take advantage of that. Speaking of school, I've seen some of your U of O games. You're still the best player on the field. I'm so proud of you. I hope you're doing well and I wish you all the happiness.

My plan is to contact you once I'm sure my mother can't hurt you or your reputation. I'm scared of your reaction, but I know it's the right thing to do. I have to wait until... well, until I know she can't spread hurtful rumors about you and ruin your career.

Here's a fun fact: Raegan cries whenever we sing "Happy Birthday". She did it on my birthday, Dad's birthday, and again today for her birthday. What do you think that means?

I love you,
Rachel

CHAPTER SIX

Michael

I walk into the cool darkness of the building; over five thousand square feet of warehouse space, including the open gym, Pilates studio, and the yoga room. I click the lights on and then open the roll-up doors. When people first learn about CrossFit, they're often confused by the warehouse space. We don't put huge TVs up for them to mindlessly run on treadmills. And we don't have rows and rows of machines. No, we prefer that people talk to each other. We prefer standing in a circle and facing each other while we work out. We do class workouts specialized for individual needs and strengths.

Our philosophy revolves around building a community. I designed this box for the vast space, with four huge warehouse stalls with high ceilings and roll-up doors. I want open space that leads to an incredible outdoor area for workouts, and even cookouts when the time comes.

We've started painting, so I open all the doors to encourage fresh air to clear out some of the paint fumes. Once the space is lit, I inspect the work that's been done. One more coat of paint and then we can start fitting the stall flooring and installing the rigging.

Just as I get everything opened, Gavin arrives in his paint-stained clothes. "Ready to get to work?" he asks, as he heads into the office to get rid of his backpack.

"Of course… but *I* was on time. You're the one who's late."

He sneers at me but then gets to work opening paint cans and laying out tarps. Once we're ready, we both start on the second coat. The music is blaring from the computer, and we're both working, but as I reload my paint roller, I see this kid outside on a bicycle. She keeps circling the parking lot and peeking inside at what we're doing.

When she stops in front of the open roll-up door, I give her a little wave. "You okay?" I ask, not sure what else to say.

She nods then points her finger in a circle. "What's this going to be?"

"We're opening a CrossFit box."

With a strange look, she says, "Box?"

I bob my head and say, "That's what the CrossFit gyms are called. Boxes. It refers to the open warehouse style."

"Oh, okay… so like a weightlifting type of gym?"

"Yeah, and circuit-style training." I grin at her and say, "You interested in joining a gym?"

She shrugs and says, "Do I have to be eighteen?"

"Nope, you just need to get a consent form signed. Do you play any sports?"

"Not anymore, but I like basketball, and I used to play soccer." She gets off her bike and comes closer. "I like the colors. Did you pick them? Are you the owner?"

"I am, but I have two partners." I point to Gavin and say, "Here's one of them. This is Gavin. I'm Mike. What's your name?"

"R-Raegan." She crosses her arms over her chest awkwardly and looks around. "Can I help you paint?"

"How old are you?" I ask, not sure I can let her help.

"I'm thirteen."

"Do you live around here?"

"I stay with my uncle after school. He doesn't live far."

"You're not out of school for summer yet?"

"No, my last day is next week."

I glance over at Gavin, but he just shrugs.

"Your parents gonna get pissed if you come home with paint on your clothes?"

This time she shrugs. "I doubt they'll notice if I do."

This makes me feel bad, but maybe that was part of her plan. I give her a long look. She seems pretty mature for her age. "All right, you can help, but wait a second." I walk into the office and pull a t-shirt out of my bag and toss it to her. "Throw this on over your clothes just in case."

She grins at that and tugs the shirt on over her head. It hangs down below her hips, and I'm glad. Now she's pretty well protected. I get a roller and show her how to dip it in the paint and the best way to roll it on the wall.

"Why are you painting over the same color?"

"It's called a second coat. If you compare this wall to that wall," I point to the far wall, "you'll see the difference."

"Okay, cool." She gets to work, and so do I. After a while, she starts asking me questions about the gym and the workouts. She's pretty curious, and I'm happy to see a kid who's interested in something other than phones, video games, and computers.

When I ask her questions, she's a little evasive, but I can't blame her; I'm a stranger, and she doesn't know me. Every once in a while, her gaze scans beyond the roll-up doors to make sure there are other adults in the area. I'm glad to see she's watching out for herself, but she probably shouldn't approach people so easily. She got lucky we're not predators.

When the other warehouse tenants around us end their day, and the parking lot starts to clear out, she coolly makes her exit with a couple more questions. "Will you be painting again tomorrow?"

"I hope not," Gavin says. "We need to finish tonight."

Her shoulders slump. "Oh."

"We'll be here," I say, "but we won't be painting. You can hang out if you want. We'll be working so we can't entertain you, but if you want to watch us set up the rigging, you're welcome anytime, Raegan."

That gets a smile out of her. "Cool. Thanks!"

She rushes over to her bike and says, "I'll try to come back tomorrow or the next day."

"See you later."

She waves as she rides away. I watch to see which direction she goes, just to keep an eye out. Seems odd no one's checked on her in the last couple of hours, but what do I know about kids? Then again, at thirteen, she isn't really a kid. I was riding my bike all over Portland at that age.

Rachel was thirteen when I first met her. We were both on summer break and hanging out at the local swim center. Although at the time I didn't know why she bothered when she had a pool in her backyard. But when I remember what a bitch her mom was, it's no wonder she wanted to get out of the house as much as possible.

Rachel and I were friends at first. We didn't really start dating until school started that fall, but we were joined at the hip after that. Of course, at thirteen and fourteen, dating meant we held hands at lunch and talked on the phone all night, which meant sneaking the house phone into our rooms since kids our age didn't have cell phones back then. Thinking about that twists my gut. Maybe if we'd had our own phones back then, Rachel would have called to say goodbye before leaving.

"Just because the kid is gone doesn't mean you get to stop working," Gavin says.

"Right, I know." I walk over and pick up my roller. "Maybe we should have hired someone to do this shit."

"Don't be lazy. We're almost done anyway."

An hour later, the painting is finished, and we're cleaning up. I look over the schematic of the open gym layout and then up at the corner we have planned for the kids. We're going to build a half wall with plexiglass sides so the kids can watch their parents while they work out. I'll provide a small picnic table and some toys, but I think that's all they'll need since they all have devices to keep them busy. The opposite corner will be the lifting corner. We'll hang climbing ropes down the center beam. Picturing it in my head makes me eager for opening day.

The next morning, Gavin and I get an early start. We've got less than three weeks before the grand opening, and there's so much to do. We're planning an all-day open house where people can stop by and check the place out. It'll be like an all-day party. That means I have a ton of shit to do before then.

Our programmer is here working on the database, which is so far over my head. Thank God we found him in Oakland. He keeps our memberships and class schedules in great working order. We can display the class workouts on the two screens we have installed in the gym, and we also have a computer set up for people to sign in as they arrive. The damn thing syncs with our accounting system too, which is terrific. I'm so excited about this place, I can't wait to start training new clients.

As Gavin and I are working on installing the rigging, I look down from my ladder to see a friendly face. "Hey, Kelley. What are you doing here?"

"I came by to check the place out. What a huge floor plan! Are you getting nervous about your opening?"

I step down and give her a big hug, lifting her off her feet. "Not really nervous, just glad to get the place finally open. Are you and Mac planning to be here for the opening?"

"Yeah, Mac didn't tell you?"

"Tell me what?"

"He's coming down here with a broadcasting crew to promote it on the radio."

"Shut the hell up! You're kidding!" That'll give us a huge boost. People in this town love Mac.

"No, not kidding. He's already worked it out with his boss. I can't believe he didn't mention it to you."

"That's so awesome!" I see movement in my peripheral and look over to see Raegan riding up. She stops hesitantly and parks her bike. "I need to come up with a way to thank him for that."

"He's happy to do it. He's also looking forward to being a member. He doesn't like the standard gyms in the area, so he's glad you're here. I'm thrilled to have you close by too."

"Aw." I give her another hug. "I'm so glad to be here."

When I release Kelley, I glance over at Raegan again and say, "Want to meet my first Sacramento client?"

She draws her brows together and glances over at Raegan too.

"Kelley, this is one of our neighbors, Raegan. She helped Gavin and me paint yesterday."

"Oh, that's cool. Hi, Raegan."

Raegan nods at her with a wary eye. "Raegan, this is one of my oldest friends, Kelley Thomas. She owns a dance studio in town… just in case you're interested in learning how to dance."

Raegan waves and I can tell she feels a little awkward. "I don't think dancing is for me. A little too girly, you know?"

Kelley and I both laugh at that. "Dancing is a sport, like football and basketball," Kelley says. She gives Raegan a thoughtful look and says, "Have we met before? You look so familiar to me."

"No, never," Raegan blurts, and her eyes cut to me as if for confirmation.

"Oh, okay." Kelley takes another long look around, then says, "I have to get going, but I'll see you at the Grand Opening, right, Mike?"

"Yeah. Hey, before you leave, I wanted to give you a heads-up." I lift my hand to scratch the back of my head, not sure how to approach the subject. "My parents... they're trying to... they've been—" I roll my eyes, irritated with myself. "What I'm trying to say is, they may be contacting you to apologize."

Kelley stares at me for a long time, and I can tell she's looking for the right words without hurting my feelings. She lets out a long breath and says, "You know, I don't really need an apology from them, Mike. I've moved on, and I don't want to live in the past like that. I'm no longer killing myself to gain their approval. I don't need it, and I don't want it."

"I totally understand that, but *I* need the closure. I don't know if I can get close to them again without it. Do you know what I mean?"

She gives me a soft smile. "Thank you, but you shouldn't let what happened with me get between you and your family."

"First of all, you're my family too. Second, it's too late for that, and you know it."

She nods in understanding. "I'll tell you what, if they feel like they want to apologize to me, ask them to send me a letter. A handwritten note or card would be great."

"That's a really good idea. I'll work on it."

She lifts to her tiptoes and gives me a big hug, then drops back on her heels and turns to go. As she leaves, she glances over and says, "It was nice meeting you, Raegan."

Raegan simply nods to her and as soon as Kelley is gone, she says, "Is that your girlfriend?"

My brows lift at the intensity of her tone. "Um, no. Kelley is an old friend. Why do you ask?"

Her shoulders lower a little but then lift in a shrug. "Just curious. She doesn't seem like your type."

My mouth quirks into a grin. "Really? And what is my type, do you think?"

Her eyes lift to the sky for a moment, then she says, "Someone a little older than her and not so skinny. Maybe someone who likes to wear business clothes instead of what she was wearing."

I laugh at this and wonder if she has someone specific in mind. "Kelley was wearing a dance leotard because she's a dancer. If she worked in an office, she'd wear business clothes."

"I guess so. What are you working on today?"

I gesture toward Gavin on the ladder. "We're installing the rigging. What are you up to?"

"I gotta go play golf with my uncle, but I thought I'd stop by and say hi. Is it okay if I get the consent form to join the gym?" She looks over her shoulder and says, "I think I can get my mom to sign it."

"Sure, step into my office."

She follows me into the office and stares hard at our programmer, Aaron, who's working away on our new system. "Is that JavaScript?"

My head pops up. "How do you even know what that means?"

"I know computers! Jeez, do I look like an idiot?"

Now I feel stupid. "Do *I* look like an idiot?"

"No," she mutters.

"Well, I don't know crap about computers, but it doesn't mean I'm stupid, does it?"

She watches me as if she wants to argue my point, but she doesn't.

Aaron grins over at her and says, "Yeah, it's written with JavaScript. Do you know it?"

"Yeah, a little, I'm still learning though." She looks at me and says, "You should learn more about computers. Everyone should know a little."

"I know a few things, but none of that shi—stuff." I correct myself. "I don't need to know more, no thanks. Spending too much time on a computer will only widen your butt. I'll stick to the gym, thank you."

This makes her giggle, and it's nice to see her smile. It makes me wonder what her home life is like since she always seems like she's brooding. I reach into the desk drawer and take out two forms. "Here." I hand her the first one and say, "This is the membership questionnaire and this—" I hand her the second form, "This is the consent form that needs your parent or guardian's signature."

"Awesome! I'll bring them back after my mom signs them." She rushes off, and before I can say anything else, she's riding away on her bike.

CHAPTER SEVEN

Rachel

I told Raegan I'd try and find her dad, but I still wish she'd never brought it up. Now I can't get Michael Murphy out of my head. I can't resist the urge to drive by the CrossFit gym, and by the time I get to work, I have the shakes. I didn't see him, but the sneakiness of driving by makes me anxious. I can't believe we're in the same town. How did that happen? I groan as I get out of my car and head into the hotel.

The Sutter House was opened in 1972. It's a converted Victorian mansion built by a prominent Sacramento family, the Rowlands, in 1892. After sitting empty for decades, the family sold the property to the current owners in the hope that it would be restored. Eight years ago, the Ander-Radcliffe Hotel Group hired me as their assistant wedding planner. It was my first real job, and I hadn't even graduated from college yet. I remember feeling so privileged to get the opportunity to work for such an elite wedding venue.

A year after I was hired, the wedding planner retired, and I was promoted from assistant to full-time planner. I'd recently finished school and was thrilled to jump right into my new role. I loved that job, and I'd still be doing it if they hadn't offered me the hotel manager position five years ago. I quickly hired my own replacement, and now Isla Young handles the weddings with a little help from me. She has her own team, but I love event planning so much she allows me to help out with big events. Isla also happens to be one of my best friends.

Isla is the polar opposite of me. Where my hair is black and my eyes blue, her hair is strawberry blonde with that hint of red throughout. Her eyes are brown, like dark chocolate. She's also super petite and barely weighs a hundred pounds. Me, ha! Well, my hips are substantial. I hate it, but pregnancy wasn't kind to me, and there's no possible way of getting back narrow hips once they've widened—trust me, I've tried. I'm also several inches taller than Isla. She's full of spark, and I guess that's why I like her so much. Nothing dampens her mood. Nothing rattles her, which is why she's so good at her job. Nervous brides and anxious grooms always fall under her spell.

When I step inside the hotel, Howard, our oldest, most reliable desk clerk is there to greet me. "Morning, Ma'am." He nods and says, "Coffee's ready."

"Good morning, Howard, and thank you. It's good to see you this morning, how's Maya?"

"She's happy school's almost out. Thank you for asking."

"Yeah, only a couple more days. Raegan's pretty happy about it too."

Howard's granddaughter is a year older than Raegan, and they attend the same school. Once in a while, they hang out, but Raegan's too much of a tomboy for Maya. Maya's into makeup and boys, but Raegan isn't there yet. Thank God! I head toward the back of the building and into the administrative offices and run directly into Isla's smiling face. "Morning, Boss! Coffee's hot. Howard is so wonderful, isn't he? If I were thirty years older, I'd be all over that man."

"I know, he's such a dreamboat, *and* he makes great coffee." I get my office door open and turn the light on before setting my bags down. Then I immediately head to the coffee pot.

As I'm pouring, Isla sidles up to me and stares me down. "So, what's up?"

I glance over at her. "What do you mean?"

"Why the mood? You've been like this all week, it's not like you."

"Ha." I sneer. "It's exactly like me. Where have you been for the last five years?"

"No." She points, and her finger gestures up and down my body. "This isn't. *This* is different."

I carry my fresh cup of coffee into my office and say, "You're barking up the wrong tree. There's nothing wrong."

"Are you fighting with Raegan?"

I purse my lips, irritated that she knows me so well. I shake my head. "It's nothing." I close my eyes, feeling a little guilty about how easily that lie comes out. I wish I didn't have to deal with this, but she's given me no choice. Life is so much easier when I can poke my head in the sand and pretend this thing with Raegan isn't *a thing* at all, but this isn't the first time she's asked about her father.

"So, you gonna talk to me?" Isla asks.

My eyes drift open and I lean sideways to peek around Isla to make sure nobody else is in earshot of our conversation. "Raegan is asking about her father."

Isla gives me a confused look. "Wait, her father? I thought he wasn't in the picture."

"He isn't... which is why this is a problem."

"Where is he?" She sits down and sets her coffee on my desk. "Do you know? I mean, I know you had Raegan at seventeen, but did you stay in contact with him at all?"

"No. Not at all. I didn't even tell him I was pregnant." I lean forward and rest my face in my hands and remember the photos of Mike from Facebook. "I did an internet search for him and found out he recently moved to Sacramento. I had no idea."

"Oh... shit, Rachel." We sit in silence for a moment, and then she says, "What are you going to do?"

"I don't know, Isla. I'm so afraid to face him… I had plans. I was going to contact him years ago, but…" I pause when my voice wavers. "Things got so weird when my dad got sick… then I just dropped it."

Isla tilts her head and gives me a strange look. "Rachel, it sounds like you got lucky he moved to town. Having him nearby is a gift, if it's anything. You can give her something she's never had." She lifts a hand to keep me from interrupting. "I mean, I get this is going to be difficult, but it's difficult for everyone. Especially Raegan. Imagine what it's like for her now?"

"I know. We had a long talk about it, and I get it. You're right, she's right. I'm the one who needs to get over it and go see him… but it's so hard to face him after all this time. It just got away from me… time and Jesus, *life* got away from me."

"Forgive me for saying this, but you need to put your big girl panties on and get on with it. You made some bad choices when you got pregnant, but you're a grown woman now. You need to do the right thing."

Feeling heat in my face and the vehement need to defend myself, I say, "Don't misunderstand, Isla. I didn't get to make any choices when I got pregnant. My mom forced me to keep Raegan a secret from him. She packed me up and shipped me down here without even allowing me to call Mike and tell him I was leaving. It's not like I chose to leave—I didn't choose to keep Raegan a secret."

"Honey, I'm sorry your mom was so brutal, but that was a long time ago. Raegan's asking, and he's here."

I laugh sardonically. "Heh, yeah, I'll just show up and say, *hey, Mike, it's good to see you after all these years! By the way, you have a thirteen-year-old daughter. She looks just like you, and she's been dying to meet you.*"

"Well, yes, something like that. You're not going to be able to keep Rae from him forever. Eventually, she'll take the choice out of your hands."

"I know. I had the same thought, that's why I agreed to look him up. That was last week. I've been putting it off and I'm sure she knows that, but she doesn't know I already know where to find him."

Isla's face breaks into a surprised smile. "Oh, that's great! She's going to be so happy."

"Yes, but remember, I left town without a word. He might not even see me. Not to mention, what if he rejects her? What if he breaks her heart?"

"Is he that type of guy?" She leans back in her chair and crosses her legs in front of her. "What was he like when he was young? Was he a bad guy?"

He was incredible. "No, he wasn't. He was good to me. I was… in love with him. We were really good together—but we were kids then."

"Oh, I see. So that's what you meant. You're avoiding him because of your feelings for him, not because of Raegan."

I shake my head vehemently. "No, that's not true. If it were only my heart at risk, I'd take the chance, but I can't risk Raegan."

She stares at me for a long moment and then quietly says, "If you say so."

Changing the subject, I say, "Let's get back to work. What's on the agenda for today?"

"I have a meeting with Toshi Meyer about her July wedding. We're deciding on linens and tableware. I have three showings this afternoon but guess what! On Monday, I'm meeting with a new bride I recently signed. Guess who the groom is?"

"No idea. Someone we know?"

"It's that hot KQCC DJ Mac Thomas—from the morning show. They've decided on us, but the bride wants to go over a few things. I'm sure she's worried about security. They really want to have a local wedding, but they're concerned about their privacy."

"I can't say I blame them. When is the wedding?"

"They've picked November ninth. It's Veterans Day weekend. They're planning a whole weekend of events so we'll be doing the rehearsal dinner here and brunch the morning after the wedding." She sucks air through her teeth and says, "I was hoping maybe you could step in during our meeting and give a little added reassurance while they're here."

"Wait… I thought Mac Thomas was already married."

"They are." Isla snickers and says, "Over a year ago they had a drunken wedding in Reno, but now they're planning an actual ceremony so they can invite their families."

"Oh, right… I remember hearing about that." I nod in agreement. "I can stop in, just add it to my calendar." I boot up my computer as she finishes her list and say, "Is that all?"

"Yeah, that's all I have this morning. How about you?"

"I have a group coming in from Canada. They're in the boardroom tomorrow. Will you check with their Canadian handler to make sure we're all set on that? I have the meals arranged with Gerard already. They're also having happy hour on the roof deck. They're a small group, and it's supposed to be warm tonight, so I thought that would be best."

"Sounds good. I'll give them a call. Anything else?"

I glance at my calendar and shake my head. "No, that's all I have for now."

She slowly gets to her feet, and when she turns, I stop her. "Isla?"

She turns back with a hesitant smile. "Yeah?"

"I know you're right. I am going to contact him… I just need to figure out how first. I don't want to react thoughtlessly. I need a plan."

"I think a plan is a good idea. Let me know if you need any help. You know I'm here for you."

Her words nearly bring tears to my eyes. I don't think I'll ever get used to having someone's unconditional support. I've never had that. I've never had anyone on my side... Someone who just wants to be here *for me*. "Thank you, Isla. I appreciate that. I'll let you know."

CHAPTER EIGHT

Michael

I've almost got all the arrangements for the grand opening in place. With Mac's help, we're going to have a huge crowd. I turn in a circle in the middle of the open gym as my eyes catch on the little details. I'm afraid I've forgotten something. I'm sure it's paranoia, but I can't shake the feeling that something important is missing.

When I hear a noise behind me, I turn toward the open roll-up door. Raegan is riding up on her bike. She parks and cautiously steps inside.

"Hey, what's up?" I ask, wondering why she's hesitating.

"What's up with *you*? You look weird."

"I'm trying to figure out what I've forgotten." I look around and then shake my head. "I know there's something missing."

"Well…" Raegan puts a hand on her hip and glances around too. "It's awfully quiet."

I snap my fingers. "That's it! Speakers!" I sigh in relief. "Thanks, kid. I'm glad you stopped by."

"Um… you're welcome."

"What are you up to? You got that parental consent form so you can join?"

"Well, no, not yet, but um…" She dips her head and says, "I don't think my mom will pay for the membership fees."

"Oh, I see. Too high, I guess."

"Yeah, I don't think she'd pay for that."

I watch her for a moment, not sure what to say. Before I can respond, she says, "Do you mind if I hang out still?"

"I'll tell you what, I'll agree to it, and maybe even let you work out a little if you help me out around here once you're out of school. I could use a little help cleaning up after my classes, but you still need to complete the two forms I gave you." I point to her and say, "I can't let you do anything without the parental consent form. And don't tell anyone, especially your friends. I can't give all the neighborhood kids a free ride."

She grins at me and says, "Really? You would do that?"

"I said maybe. I'm not negotiating until I get a signed form. You know, I was thinking about doing a couple of classes for twelve to eighteen-year-olds over the summer. Maybe you can help me figure out a good workout plan."

"I would love to help," Raegan says, her brown eyes lighting with excitement.

"All right, get that form back to me and we'll work something out." I glance at my watch. "I have to go pick up some speakers so we have music." I nod to her bike and say, "You need a ride home? I can throw your bike in the back of my Tahoe."

"No, thank you. I don't take rides from strangers."

This makes me smile, and I wink at her. "Good girl. Keep thinking like that, and you'll do okay, kid."

I lock up the gym and hop in my truck. Once I'm in, I realize I have no idea what kind of speakers I want. I grab my phone and text Gavin, asking him to send me the information on which ones we installed in our Oakland gym.

Once I get to the electronics store and park my truck, I open my email, hoping Gavin's sent what I need. I quickly scroll through but then stop on the last email I received from that prankster claiming to be my kid. I completely forgot about this jerk. It's been over a week and I haven't received anything new. I'm glad to see they took me seriously when I said to stop emailing me.

I can't help but think about Rachel again, and out of some masochistic curiosity, I go to my Facebook app and type in her name. The results are massive. I scroll through the list and when I see her, I almost gasp. I click on the profile picture, but her account is totally private. Like, on lockdown. I can't even look at her friends list or interests. She looks fucking hot as hell in her profile picture, though. The idea of contacting her makes my heart jump in my chest. I stare at her photo and remember how hurt I was when I realized I wasn't going to see her again. For months and months I waited for a letter to come in the mail but it never came. I get it if her mom shipped her off to keep her away from me, but she could've at least written to me. I got nothing from the girl after years of being together. Nothing but a broken heart.

I put my phone down and close my eyes, and take a moment to think about her.

"What do you think?" I ask.

"Think about what?" She glances up from her book.

I swat at the book and say, "You weren't even listening to me, were you?"

She tilts her head and bats her eyelashes. "I'm sorry, babe, but I just got to the good part." She leans over and rests her head on my shoulder. We're on my bed, propped up against the headboard, and she's reading while I'm looking through college pamphlets.

"I said, what about the University of Oregon? Do you want to stay in Oregon?"

"I want to be where you are, and if that's Oregon, then yes! Also, if you choose Oregon, you won't be so far away next year. Eugene is less than two hours away."

"That's true. Closer than the University of Washington." I kiss her forehead. "It's going to be a long year without you."

"I know… I'm not sure how I'll survive my senior year alone."

"So, where would you prefer? I don't want to decide for both of us. For all I know, you want to go to school back east to get away from your mom."

"Hmm… I want the University of Wherever Mike Murphy Is." She chuckles and says, "Really, I don't care. I don't even know what my major's going to be. Just as long as it's a university, so my mom doesn't have kittens."

"I don't think it's going to matter. Your mom is going to hate your choice regardless. It's in her DNA."

"That's true. And all the more reason to pick what you want and I'll follow."

I shift so that I can get a good look at her. I meet her hooded eyes, judging if she's being honest or trying to placate me. "My parents graduated from U of O, they'd really dig it if I went there."

"My parents graduated from UCLA, but it still doesn't matter." She lifts a single eyebrow and says, "I really mean it, Mike. I'm not like you. You're already sure of what you want. I'm not. I'll figure it out when I get there."

"I know I want you, if that's what you mean."

She leans in and kisses me deeply. Deeply enough to give me a hard-on. "I'm sure I want you too, which is why I'm going to follow you anywhere. So…pick the school you want."

That was the summer before my senior year. A month later, she was gone, and I was left wondering what the hell happened.

God, she was the closest thing to perfection I've ever had. I wonder if she's married. Has kids. Lives in Boston still—that's if she ever lived in Boston. On Facebook, she's still using Williams as her last name, but nowadays, most women don't change their names when they marry. I tried searching for her for a while when I was back east, with no luck. But honestly, I never tried that hard. It hurt too much to think about what she'd done. It hurt to think that she could walk away from me so easily.

I lift my phone and look at her picture again.

Should I send her a friend request? I lean my head back, not sure I'm ready for that. I'm not so sure I can forgive her for what she did. But God, I'd kill to touch her again. I'd wrap my hands around her hips and hold her close. My teenage mind still wants her. It's the grown-up version that knows it's a bad idea. I don't need to go through that again. It took me a long time to get over her. In a lot of ways, I'm still fucked up from it. Just ask all of my ex-girlfriends since her. Every one of them would say I held back, that I was afraid of commitment or emotionally unavailable. It's true, I keep women at arm's length because I don't trust them—with the exception of my friends. Brianna and Kelley, to be specific. There's never been anything romantic between me and either of them.

When my phone pings with Gavin's email, I try to shake off all thoughts of the past. I have a gym to get open, I don't need to worry about shit I can't control. Shit that's only going to distract me from the job I need to get done.

CHAPTER NINE

Raegan

I park my bike by my uncle's garage and hop off, dropping to the ground and taking several deep breaths. I can't believe he actually asked me to help him with workout plans! I take a couple more deep breaths, then get to my feet. I have to figure out a way to get the permission slip signed. I can probably get my uncle to do it if Annie's not here. He's always so distracted, I doubt he'll even read it. I enter the house and put my backpack down in the living room. Then I head into his office.

"Hey, hey, little Rae, what are you up to?" He looks up from his computer and smiles at me.

"Where's Annie?"

"She had to run an errand. Do you need something?"

"No, but have you heard about the new CrossFit gym that's opening? I checked it out today."

He gives me a sideways look and says, "Yeah, I saw when they had a crane hanging the sign. You rode your bike there? I'm not sure that's such a good idea."

"It's not far. Less than a mile and that's an easy distance on my bike, and there's a trail most of the way."

He examines me, then says, "What were you doing there?"

I lower myself down on his couch, trying to act as natural as possible. "It was an accident, really. I was riding to the frozen yogurt shop with Maisie, and we noticed it, so we stopped to check it out." I shrug like it's no big deal, then I say, "They're doing a promotion for the next two months. They're offering a few free memberships to teenagers who want to join. It's their way of getting kids to stop looking at screens and learn to work out during summer break when school's out."

"Free? Are you sure about that?"

"Yeah, I talked to the owner myself. He said they need to build memberships and by offering a few spots to kids, they're hoping word will spread. He's really nice and has this whole workout plan for kids who are interested."

"Wow, really? That sounds like a great idea. You kids do spend too much time looking at your phones and computer screens, and what else are you going to do while school's out for summer?"

"I know, right," I say, agreeing with him. "It's only the second day of break, and I'm already bored. But I need the permission slip signed. Will you sign it for me?"

His brow furrows when he says, "Are you sure you want to work out at a gym, though? You don't want to get all bulky like a guy, do you? Maybe you should try yoga or dancing… something like that. It doesn't sound like it's a great place for girls."

"They have a yoga studio too… and I like this place. It's not just for boys." I let out a heavy sigh and say, "They only have a few free spots."

"All right, hand it over."

I hop up and go to my backpack for the slip, fist-pumping the entire way. When I return, he reads the form over much more carefully then I was expecting.

"This looks pretty standard, but it doesn't say anything about the membership being free. Make sure you don't sign anything else from them without me looking at it. I don't want you to be obligated to anything."

"I will, Uncle Mitch. Maybe you can check the place out and start working out with me." I know he won't, but I'm trying to be as transparent as possible.

He laughs and says, "I'm a little too old for a place like that." He points to me. "Make sure you let me know when you're supposed to be there. I want to know when you're there and how long for."

"Cool. I will! And, hey, Uncle Mitch, would you have been worried about me riding my bike that far if I were a boy?"

He scrunches his nose up and says, "Probably not."

I scrunch my nose up and say, "Then you should probably start pretending I'm a boy." I wave the signed form in the air. "Thank you for this. I'm gonna go watch TV and wait for Mom." Then I leave his office, fighting to hide my smile.

I almost feel bad for manipulating him… *almost*. It's not like I totally lied. Okay, so Maisie wasn't with me for one, and she doesn't know about this. But she's such a goody two-shoes, she'd never let me get away with it. And, yeah, the CrossFit gym isn't offering free memberships, but Mike did say we could work something out. So why shouldn't I get to know my dad when given a chance? And why should I be upfront and honest with the adults in my life? It's not like they're upfront and honest with me!

I do feel bad for lying to Mike… and a little guilty that I haven't told him I'm the one who sent him those emails, but at least I stopped. I told my mom I wouldn't look for him, and even though I already knew where to find him, it seemed fair to stop emailing him. I'm just hoping my mom connects with him soon before I have to tell any more lies to them both. I asked her again this morning if she'd contacted him, but all she did was mutter that she hadn't done it yet. I don't know why she's dragging her feet. It's not like he's hard to find. The gym is only a few miles from our house. If she doesn't move forward with it soon, I'm gonna have to give her another push.

CHAPTER TEN

Michael

With the speakers installed, we're almost finished. I'm working with Brianna in the yoga and Pilates room, trying to get her set up. There's not much left to do now that the equipment is in place, but we need to get the rooms cleared of the paint smell. Not very Zen, as Bri put it.

"I think if we set up a fan here and another over there, it'll help carry the smell outside."

"Good idea." I lift the fan and carry the enormous thing over to where she pointed. "When is your first class?"

"Tomorrow morning. I've got some candles to light, that will help, and I'll add some air fresheners."

I plug the fan in and hit the power button, then head back over so she can hear me. "I think it'll be cleared by then."

Bri nods toward the entrance, and I look over to see Kelley coming inside. "Hey, what's up, Kell?"

She gives me a big hug, then looks around. "Wow! Guys, it looks incredible!"

"Do you smell paint?" Brianna asks.

Kelley lifts her nose and sniffs around the room a little. "Not too bad."

"Good. We're trying to get it aired out before the first yoga class. It's tomorrow morning," I say.

"Hey, Kelley, you should leave some business cards for the dance studio. We're setting up a board where members can advertise their businesses," Brianna offers.

"Oh, great idea! I'll bring some next time."

Brianna points a thumb over her shoulder and says, "I need to finish sorting out the equipment. See you two later."

Kelley gives her a wave goodbye, and as she does, the smile falls from her face and I know something is up.

"What's wrong? I get the feeling this isn't a friendly visit."

She shakes her head, clearly frustrated. "I know you're super busy getting ready for your opening, but I need to ask a favor."

"Dude! Don't be stupid. You know you can ask me anything. Let's go into the office." Once we're in the office, away from the noise of the large fans, I say, "What's up?"

"Mac's been obligated to a gig on Monday afternoon, and we were supposed to meet with our wedding coordinator. It took me weeks to get this appointment, and I really don't feel comfortable by myself. I'm sure this isn't your sort of thing, but I could really use some back-up. I don't want to be pressured into spending more than I've budgeted, but I have a hard time saying no. I need someone there to keep me and the coordinator on track. Do you think you can come along?"

I laugh at her. Not because she's asking me to come along, but because she was so hesitant. "I don't mind. I don't know much about wedding planning, but I can be there."

"Thank you so much! I don't really need input for the wedding stuff. What I really need is someone to be the asshole and say no when I can't. It's usually Mac, and he's great at it." She rolls her eyes and says, "Although, it's usually because the women fawn over him, so his 'no' doesn't seem so much like a rejection. Anyway, I suck at hard-lining, and I need a strong presence to help me. I would ask Lexi, but she's as soft as I am."

"Kell, I'll come, and I'll be the asshole you need me to be."

"God, Mike, you're a lifesaver. Thank you for getting it." She laughs again and gives me a long look. "Have I told you lately how happy I am that you moved to Sac? Really. I'm so glad to have you here."

"Believe it or not, I like Sacramento. I'm a little afraid of the hot-ass weather I keep hearing about, but it's been nice so far, and the people in the neighborhood have been great to us."

"I'm so happy," she says and sighs out a deep breath. "God, thank you so much! I need to get going, and I know you have a lot more work to do. When do you start your personal training sessions?"

"I already have. I had two today. I have a few more tomorrow."

"That's so great!"

We both stand and walk out of the office. I glance over and see Bri dancing and singing to the music as she works on the yoga room, and that makes us both laugh.

Kelley nods in Bri's direction and says, "She's going to be so much fun to work with. Where did you find her?"

"She relocated with me. She was one of the best coaches we had in Oakland. She followed me so she could be the lead here."

"So…" Kelley says. "Are you two…" Her finger bounces between Brianna and me.

"A couple, you mean?" I shake my head vehemently. "No! She's great and all, but I don't date co-workers. It's a strict rule. Besides that, we're just friends—and I'm her boss. That doesn't work."

"Oh, right. I guess that makes sense. Probably better that you don't." She lifts a brow and says, "Does that mean I can fix you up?"

"Hm… I don't know that I've got time for a girl right now." I run a hand through my hair and say, "I'm not sure I'm interested in the trouble."

Kelley laughs at that. "Okay, I can respect that, but you're going to get old fast if all you do is work. I hope you know that."

Chuckling, I say, "Yeah, well, let me get settled in first. Once I have my new clientele through their PT sessions, I'll be less frantic. I also need to hire a few more coaches."

She nods and purses her lips. "Okay. In six months, if you're still single, I'm hooking you up with a friend." She tilts her head and says, "Maybe even Lexi."

"Okay, Kell, get the fuck out," I say, straight-faced.

That really makes her laugh. "She's great. You'd be lucky."

"I'm sure you're right, but I don't need those thoughts in my head while she and I are helping you with the wedding."

"Alright, I'm out of here." She wags a finger at me as she turns to leave. "Six months, though."

CHAPTER ELEVEN

Rachel

Dear Michael,

I know you don't want to hear this, but I need to tell someone. I started dating again. It's crazy, really. There are no words to explain what it's like as a single mom in college trying to navigate life and dating. But I'm trying. He's a nice guy, and I really like him, but I'm not sure I can ever love him.

Honestly, I don't know if I can ever love anyone but you. I'm pathetic. I bet you've had a hundred different girlfriends since I left. You should. You deserve to be happy. Me, I'm not relationship material. I'm a mom. That's my life.

I've been casually dating this guy for a few months, but last night we decided to make our relationship exclusive. It's laughable, really. I was already exclusive… but I guess that's not normal for women my age, so I acted like it was a big thing.

Me and Raegan. That's the only thing I'm sure about in life. Is that sad?

Here's a fun fact: Sometimes Raegan looks at me, and all I see is you. It's beautiful and agonizing all at the same time.

I love you, and I miss you… still.
Rachel

CHAPTER TWELVE

Rachel

Happy hour. It's aptly named. Although maybe happy *hours* would be better. At least, I plan on making several of them happy, not just one. Raegan is spending the night at a friend's house, and that means I get the night off. A break from her brooding. I thought we'd talked it all out. She even agreed to my plan of finding her dad and checking him out first. Then she went right back to being angry. Apparently, I'm not moving fast enough for her. I know I need to fix it and I know it's going to be hard, but I must. Maybe after this night off, I'll have the energy to come clean with Mike and Raegan. Maybe after a good night of drinking away my problems, I'll be able to face him.

Isla and I are heading to the Public House, and I'm so glad I can relax and have a few drinks without having to worry about being home at a specific time. Uber. It's another happy in my life this evening. It's a beautiful thing when you want many drinks.

Isla and I pick a great spot on the outdoor patio. We met at my house before heading downtown, which gave me a few minutes to freshen up and change into a spaghetti-strapped, bright blue summer dress. I left my hair down and traded my studs for some fun, beaded drop earrings. The weather couldn't be more perfect, it's such a beautiful evening. Once the sun dips below the horizon, I'll need to add the light sweater I brought, but right now, the temperature is comfortable. When summer's in full gear, it's going to be too hot to sit outside and have a drink so we're taking advantage while we can.

The Public House is known for the pub food, and we order the most unhealthy dinners we can find and Moscow Mules. With drinks in hand, Isla and I both start to giggle. She looks at me and says, "It's a vodka type of night, right?"

I lift my glass and say, "Amen." I take a drink then say, "Raegan's been so cold to me all week, it's nice to get a break from her."

"Have you moved forward with your plan to talk to her dad?" she asks in a relaxed tone and I know she's trying to approach the subject without making me defensive.

I stare into my drink. "I already told her I would find him, but that's not good enough for her."

"You told her that, but then you didn't do it. You're dragging your feet, and she knows it. The girl is no dummy."

"I know, I know." I let out a heavy sigh because I don't have an excuse. I'm just scared. "I promise, I will go see him next week."

"I think that's a great idea, Rachel. It will be difficult at first, and you're going to be on the receiving end of anger from both of them, but it needs to be done."

I nod and purse my lips. "I know that. I need to find the right time. I've been doing some research, and I know he's got a lot going on with the new gym. They're planning a big grand opening party and growing pretty fast. Every time I look at the website, they've added more coaches."

She sips on her drink and then looks at me through lowered lashes. "I think the longer you wait, the harder it's going to be. Honestly."

"I don't know if anything would make this harder." Our food gets delivered, and I'm suddenly not so hungry for fish tacos. "He already hates me for leaving. I'm sure of that. Dropping this bomb on him isn't going to win me any points."

"Maybe he'll understand, Rach. Give him a chance."

"I will. I know I need to. I owe him an explanation, and I owe Raegan a dad. It's important I make things right with her. At this point, I know I'm not behaving any better than my mother."

When fresh drinks are set down on our table, we both look up at the server, confused. She smiles and says, "From the two guys…" She points and says, "Inside, at the bar."

The Public House has large sliding-glass doors that open to bring the outside in. Where Isla and I are sitting, we can hear the crowd from inside and the music. It's a Friday night, so the place is pretty busy.

We both look over to where she's pointing and see the two guys sitting at the main bar watching us. Isla lifts her glass toward the guys and mouths a thank you.

I give her an incredulous look. "Woman, do not invite those guys over here. We don't need strange men wanting to sit with us."

The waitress leans in and says, "They're safe." When I turn sharply to look at her, she says, "The drinks and the guys. I know them. One of them is a regular here, and he's super nice. The other moved to town a few weeks ago, but he's really cool too."

"Thank you," Isla says with a huge grin.

I give her a hard stare and say, "But still…"

"I know. I get it. Jeez, it's not like I'm going home with them. Just accepting a drink."

"I'm not in the right frame of mind to stutter through forced conversations with someone I'm not interested in talking to, and I'm certainly not interested in hooking up with a strange guy."

"Haha!" She laughs… too hard. "Are you kidding me? You've been the good girl your whole life. That is, if you forget that whole teenage-pregnancy thing." She rolls her eyes and says, "You've been a mom for practically your entire life. You're way overdue for a good hook-up."

This makes me laugh because she's right about the mom part. "Okay, you may have a point. Being a single mom was never my life goal, and it's all-encompassing, for sure."

I think about what she said and scan the room until my gaze lands on the two guys who bought us drinks. As I start to turn back toward Isla, my eyes drift to the table behind them, and the couple sitting there. "Oh, hell," I slide down and spin so my back is to the bar. "Oh, hell, Isla!"

"What is your problem?"

"He's here. Jesus. I can't believe it. Raegan's father is here. He's sitting at a table with a girl near the bar. I need to get out of here."

Her head whips around. "Which one?"

I slide some cash across the table and say, "Pay the bill, I'll meet you by the—"

"Hey, ladies..."

I freeze when I see the two guys from the bar approaching the table. One of them is wearing a San Diego Padres ball cap, and he's got a massive smile on his face. I narrow my eyes at him because he looks so familiar.

"Rachel Williams?" he asks, as he gets closer.

"Yeah, I'm Rachel. Do I know you?" I say this as quietly as I can. I don't want Mike to hear my name, not that he could from here, but just in case.

This guy's pretty damn hot and nicely built, dressed in jeans and a long-sleeve Henley, with broad shoulders and light, startlingly blue eyes. It's the eyes that really get my attention. I know those eyes, they're pretty hard to forget. I stare at his smile and wonder how in the hell this could happen twice in one evening.

He removes the ball cap, and that's when I sputter, "Adam Wright?"

"Yeah, what's up? You don't recognize me?"

"Oh my God. Yes, of course I do, now that you're closer. How are you?" I whisper-shout, still crouching in my chair.

"I've grown up a lot since senior year at Sac State. How are you?" He gestures to my posture and says, "Everything okay?"

I nod, pursing my lips. "Yep. All good, just avoiding an ex who's sitting near the bar."

Isla laughs a little too loudly at that.

"It must be a night for exes," he says with a chuckle.

"You, I don't mind, but I really don't want *him* to see me."

He nods toward the street and says, "Want to get out of here?"

"Oh my God, yes." I get to my feet, keeping my back to the bar, grabbing my sweater and purse. "Where are we going?"

"We were planning to head over to the Dive Bar on K. Do you want to join us?" Adam's friend asks. "It's a short walk over."

"Absolutely!" I say, a little too enthusiastically. I glance at Isla and she's nodding in agreement. "How about now?" I grip Adam's arm and let him lead me from the patio. Thankfully, he's a big guy, and I'm pretty hidden from where Mike's sitting inside.

Once we're clear of the bar, I nearly melt in relief. "Thank you so much for getting me out of there."

He chuckles. "No problem. How have you been?"

"Whew," I say, then I laugh. "I've been fine. Busy working and raising my daughter."

"How is Raegan? Wow, she must be a teenager by now." He snaps his fingers and says, "Thirteen... fourteen?"

"Yeah, good memory." I turn to see Isla and his friend exiting the Public House and heading in our direction. "She recently turned thirteen."

"Yeah, that's right, you were so young when you had her."

Thankfully, they approach at that moment and save me from responding.

Isla looks at Adam and says, "Thanks for the drinks."

"Sorry, Adam, this is my friend Isla. We work together at The Sutter."

"This is Henry," Adam says. I shake his hand. He's cute. Not in a hot, drooly sort of way like Adam, but still attractive. His brown hair flops over his forehead, and he has a friendly, genuine smile, with golden eyes and perfectly white teeth. His graphic tee says, *Stand Back I'm about to do Science.*

"The Sutter?" Henry says, "Like the hotel?"

"Yeah," Isla responds. "Rachel manages the hotel, and I'm the wedding planner."

"That's cool. My brother got married there a few months ago. It was a lot of fun."

I see Isla's expression light up as he says this and she rests her hand on his arm. "That's so nice to hear. I love when people say they had fun at one of our weddings."

Crap. I see the look in her eyes, and I know that means we're not going to make our apologies and leave without them.

We all start walking toward K Street, and as we fall in step, Adam looks over at me and says, "How's life been treating you since college?"

"Oh, fine. How are you? How was San Diego? Did you just get back to town? I can't believe this is my first time running into you since then."

"Yeah, I got a job right out of grad school and stayed there for a few years, but I moved back here a couple of weeks ago."

"So, what are you doing now?"

"I took a job with the Sacramento Sports Commission. I moved into an apartment in Midtown. I really like it there."

"Yeah, Midtown is an up-and-coming neighborhood for sure. Very hipster these days."

He lifts one brow. "You're not calling me hipster, I hope."

I laugh at his expression. "No, and no offense. Just sharing my observations."

"None taken… I think." He waves toward the Public House and says, "So, what's the story with the ex at the bar. Recent history?"

"No, not recent. Ancient actually, but awkward nonetheless."

"So, the Dive Bar?" Isla asks, with scrunched eyebrows.

"Wait—isn't that the bar with the mermaids?" I ask, now realizing what they were talking about. I've heard of the bar but never been inside.

"Yeah. You've been?" Henry asks.

"No. Never. Do they actually have people dressed as mermaids in a tank?"

"Yep, they do a show every hour or so." Adam glances down at his phone. "We should get there in time for the eight o'clock show if you want to see it."

"How fun! I think we should do it, Rachel. I want to check out the mermaids."

"Um, yeah, I guess that's alright. I don't know how long I'll stay though," I say.

"Why not? Raegan isn't home, you have time."

I turn to glare at Isla when she says this. "True, but it's been a long week."

As promised, we arrive at Dive Bar to find a massive aquarium over the long bar. The place is impressive with dim chandelier lighting and exposed brick walls framed in dark wood beams. The seating is large leather wingbacks that feel like a comfy hug when you sit in them. The music is pretty loud, and a few people are dancing. After settling in, Adam leans over and says, "Moscow Mule?"

I get close to his ear and say, "I think it's my turn to buy."

He shakes his head and says, "No way!" Then he's off to the bar to get a round of drinks. Before he returns, Isla and Henry get up to dance. They look so cute together.

I close my eyes for a moment and wonder what the hell I've gotten myself into. I wanted a couple of drinks with my friend and a relaxing evening with a strong buzz. Now I've got to avoid the strong buzz so I can be on guard. Not only because I know Mike's in the neighborhood but because I'm essentially hanging out in a strange club with a guy I haven't seen in years. A guy I dated for a while but broke up with because I couldn't manage school, motherhood, and a boyfriend. At least, that's what I told him when I broke up with him. He was a great guy, and we had a good time, but I was still so hung up on Mike, I just couldn't commit.

When Adam returns with the drinks, we try to chat over the music. He's obviously interested but fortunately not super pushy, which is a good thing because I don't do pushy. I actually don't *do* dating… or guys at all. I haven't dated in years… not since my last attempt went so badly.

"How about a dance?" Adam says with a huge smile.

"Ah, no, sorry. I'm not up for dancing tonight. I'd rather relax." As I say this, the tank above the bar lights up, and large tail fins appear in the water. "Wow. They really have mermaids in that tank. That's not strange at all," I say, fighting not to be sarcastic.

A moment later, a woman and a man dressed in mermaid costumes start swimming back and forth. They're waving at the crowd and posing for photos.

"This is insane," I say.

"Yeah, it's not your normal type of live show you'd see at a bar," Adam agrees. "I'm not sure what I was expecting."

After the show, Henry and Adam leave us to get more drinks. Once they're gone, I lean over to Isla and say, "I'm so sorry. This really wasn't my intention."

She flashes me a huge grin and says, "It's okay, I actually really like him. Don't you?"

"Henry? Yeah, he seems great."

"How do you know Adam? He's pretty damn hot, Rachel."

"We dated in college."

Isla laughs a little too much at this. "Wow! Quite a night for you, honey."

"I know. Actually, I think I'm going to take off. Do you want to stay with them and hang out?"

She nods with a slight wink. "Yes. Don't worry about me, I can get myself home." Just as she says this, they return with fresh drinks.

I don't want to be rude, so I sip at my drink a little longer, chatting with Adam about his new job, but after another ten minutes, I get to my feet and say, "Well, I think I'll grab an Uber and head home."

Adam stands with me. "But we just got here."

"I know, I'm sorry, but I had a very long week and I'm not up for a late night."

Still the gentleman, he says, "I'll walk you out."

Again, I'm thankful not to get any grief. Most men would have tried to talk me out of leaving.

I hug Isla and say, "Have fun but make sure to call me when you get home. Otherwise, I'll worry."

"You know I will. Bye, Rachel."

I let Adam lead me out of the bar, and once we're out in the quiet, I say, "Thanks for the rescue and the drinks."

"So, can I get your number?" he asks, tapping on his phone.

I'm surprised, but not opposed to giving him my number. "Sure."

We swap numbers and then I call for an Uber. Adam waits with me. "Sure you don't want company for the ride home?"

I can't help it, but I laugh at that, then lay a hand over my mouth and say, "Wow, smooth. You've learned a few things since college."

"Oh, ouch." He chuckles and says, "Sorry… but you can't blame a guy for trying."

"Thank you." I give him a sincere look and then a big hug. "You're so sweet, but you always were."

He holds onto me a little too long. "Too bad it didn't keep you from breaking up with me."

I try to pull away, but he doesn't release me and that makes me extremely uncomfortable. "Adam… I'm sorry, but…"

"I'd be willing to give it another go. What do you think?" He grips my rear with both hands and says, "Round two?"

I break free from his grip and push him an arm's length away. "No, I don't think so."

"What? Are you too good now, Rachel?"

"Yeah, no. Sorry. I'm not interested. Too bad, though, I really was having a good time, until now." I step away from him to get a little more space and when the Uber stops at the curb, I'm so thankful I could cry.

He waves dismissively and says, "Whatever, no hard feelings… You have my number if you change your mind."

Once I'm safely inside the car, I quickly go through my phone and block his number. Jesus! What is it with men these days? It's no wonder I've been single for so long.

CHAPTER THIRTEEN

Michael

Just as I'm locking up the gym, I hear someone behind me. I turn quickly, and Raegan nearly runs me over with her bike. "Hey, Raegan, can't hang out. I'm running late for an appointment."

"But I brought my signed permission form and the questionnaire. So, I can join now, right?"

I take the papers from her and scan the release form for a signature. Then I take the questionnaire. "I'll have to look at this later. Can you stop by this evening or tomorrow morning?"

"I can tomorrow... probably."

"Good deal." I wink at her, glad she was able to work it out with her mom. I slip the forms into the mail slot and say, "I have to get going. Need a ride?"

She grins at me. "Thanks for asking but you're still kind of a stranger."

"Aha! Good girl. I'll see you tomorrow. Be prepared to work out."

She waves as she rides away on her bike. I rush to my truck, now late for meeting Kelley at the wedding venue.

When I get to the hotel, Kelley's at the entrance waiting for me. "I'm so sorry. Am I too late?"

She brushes a hand at me and says, "No, you're fine. I just got here too. I thought I'd wait for you. I really don't want to do this by myself."

"Let's do it then."

We enter, and the older gentleman at the check-in counter says, "Checking in?"

Kelley approaches and says, "I actually have an appointment with the wedding planner. Her name is Isla."

He looks down, then back up with a smile. "Yes. Mr. & Mrs. Thomas. Let me show you to the conference room."

I leave it to Kelley to correct him, but she doesn't bother. As we're walking, he turns and says, "It's not often we get couples planning a wedding after they've already gotten married. I bet there's a story there."

We both laugh, and she says, "Oh, yeah. A fascinating story, I'm sure, I just don't remember it because I was drunk. And this isn't my husband. He's my… what are we calling it, Mike? Man of honor?"

This makes me laugh. "You can call it whatever makes you comfortable."

The man looks over at me then back to Kelley. "We're seeing that sort of thing more and more these days. It's a nice change from tradition."

He steps to the left and into a hall of double doors. "You probably already know, but the ballroom is at the end. This here is our conference room. Miss Isla will be with you in a few minutes. We have refreshments set up for you. Please help yourselves." He places a hand over his heart and says, "I'm Howard. Feel free to let me know if you need anything at all."

Kelley gives him a big smile and says, "Howard, thank you so much."

He does a slight bow and we both nod at him as he leaves us alone.

Once he's gone, Kelley turns to me. "Thanks again, Mike."

"So, what's the deal? Have you decided on this place for sure? Have you paid a deposit? What upsells are you worried about?"

Kelley ticks a list off on her fingers. "Deposit is paid. Small-ish wedding in the garden. Reception in the ballroom. I don't want to up my guest count. I'm mostly worried about security. I want to do my own invitations, and I don't need the little extras. Like… chocolate-dipped strawberries on all the tables." She rolls her eyes when she says this. "I don't want to upgrade to a full bar—especially since there will be several AA members coming. We only want the beer and wine bar." Her gaze wanders, as if trying to think of something else. "Oh, and I *do not* want to serve any kind of seafood. *At all.*"

"Okay, you seem pretty sure… so, why am I here?"

"I give in too easily. Seriously. It's a problem. Oh, and I don't need more than ten guest rooms. They want me to buy out the hotel at sixteen rooms."

"That could be fun, though. Renting out the entire space. It would also be better for security."

She gives me a thoughtful look. "That's what they said."

"Makes sense," I say. "I'd definitely take a room. That way I wouldn't need to worry about drinking too much and getting my ass home—and it is only six more rooms. Also, aren't you planning an entire weekend of events? Why not buy the place out?"

"All right," she says, "I guess I'll give it more thought."

Before I can say anything else, the door opens and a petite woman steps inside. She's smiling widely, her blonde wavy hair dancing around her head, and teetering on the highest and spiki-est heels I've ever seen. Balancing on those shoes is a talent and nothing less. "Kelley, so good to see you again, and—" She freezes when she faces me. "Sorry! You're not the groom, are you?"

"Mac couldn't make it," Kelley says.

"It's okay," I say. "I'm used to the disappointment when people see me instead of Mac." My joke gets a chuckle from the pretty blonde, so I say, "It's a hard image to live up to."

"I don't think a man your size has much trouble in that area," the wedding planner quips as she looks up at me like I'm the Tower Bridge. "If you don't mind me saying."

That gets a hearty laugh out of Kelley. She grips my arm and says, "This is Mike. He's my best friend and my man of honor—*and he's single*. Mike, this is Isla. She's the planner." I see the look in her conspiring green eyes and quirk my mouth into a crooked grin.

"Oh, awesome," Isla says. "So, no maid of honor, but a man. I like it. We've seen a lot more of that recently."

I smile and say, "And the best man is a woman, so we're a pretty confused group."

"Mac's partner is the best man… er or woman," Kelley stutters.

"I have a feeling this wedding is going to be a lot of fun. Let's have a seat and get started." She waves to the conference table. Kelley and I sit with our backs to the door, facing a wall of windows that looks out over a patio and beautiful garden. I can see why she waved us to this side of the table. We can see the area where the wedding will take place. It's a great sales tactic even though Kelley and Mac have already decided to use this venue.

"It's so beautiful, isn't it, Mike?"

"Yeah, I see why you picked it." Wisteria lines the pergola above the patio, framing the scene perfectly. The sun is bright outside, making the green lawn pop with the lining of colorful flowers.

Isla opens the file and says, "It's time to finalize some of the arrangements: we need to set a schedule, decide on the start times and start talking about the dinner menu. That doesn't need to be finalized today, I just need some ideas for the tasting with Gerard." She hands us both a set of menus. "He's our chef, and he's fabulous! We can also sample cakes and maybe even talk about signature cocktails."

"We actually don't want a full bar," Kelley says.

"Oh, okay. Are you sure? It's not much more and—"

"Mac is a recovering alcoholic," I say, trying to interrupt her in the kindest way possible. Kelley glances over with a thankful expression. "They both feel it's not appropriate. They also expect to have a few other AA members at the wedding, and so they don't want to highlight the alcohol. Just beer and wine," I emphasize.

Isla smiles politely and agrees. "Okay. That's settled. What about hors d'oeuvres during cocktail hour? You have a choice of one to four circulating. I always feel that one is too little, but four is too many."

Kelley nods in agreement. "I think at least two, but I would like to wait to decide until the tasting."

"Great," Isla says, and a knock sounds on the door behind us. "My manager said she'd stop by to say hello and talk about security."

I hear her footsteps as they drift across the carpet, but I don't turn. It's her scent that gets my attention. It's a citrusy orange fragrance I'm so familiar with but haven't smelled in so long. My mind immediately drifts to my high school days. I look up, and the first thing that catches my attention is her raven hair, falling in waves over her shoulders and down her back. When she turns to say hello, her smile falters slightly.

I'm stunned. Completely speechless. I can tell she is too. We stare at each other for a long time. I look her up and down to find an hourglass figure hiding behind her fitted suit jacket, but the cleavage above the buttons stands out as a blush of pink sweeps up her chest and into her cheeks. Her eyes are the brightest blue, and they're locked on me. Her hand is frozen on the back of the chair she was about to pull out. Instead, it looks as if she's using it for support.

"Rachel?" I say, still not totally sure I believe what I'm seeing. A tingle spreads through me, heat, anger, confusion... and something akin to anticipation. I feel it all... all at once.

"Oh," Isla says. "You two know each other."

The blush drains from Rachel's face as she stares at me. Her eyes turn glassy, and she says, "Wow, Michael. I… wasn't… I'm so surprised to…" She stops trying to talk and glances over at Isla. At the same time, Kelley looks at me and whatever she sees on my face makes her own grow paler too.

"Yeah, I'm surprised too," I say, and it comes out gruff. Not on purpose, but the one emotion I'm having trouble containing is the anger. I look her over again, catching every detail. Her full, pink lips, the glint of blue from the earrings she's wearing. The slight shake of her perfectly manicured hand. She's incredible, and as this thought crosses my mind, I realize she's more than incredible. She's fucking stunning to the point of pissing me off. "I had no idea you were in Sacramento—California even—but then how would I know?"

She nods, and the raven waves bounce around her face. She frowns a little as she stutters, "Yes. I, um, live here." She turns toward Isla again. "It looks like you have things well under control so come get me if you need me."

Then she retreats from the room. Fast. I stand up to follow her but don't. My heart is pounding out of my chest. So much so that I need to sit back down. I can't fucking believe she's here. Right fucking here. I lean forward and rest my head in my hands, taking several deep breaths. I feel Kelley's cool hand grip my arm, so I turn my head to look at her.

"You okay?" The expression on her face shows her concern.

"Yeah." Nodding, I say, "Just taken by surprise. I'm fine."

The meeting is a complete blur after this and I know it's not just me. Isla and Kelley seem off too. In the end, Kelley makes another appointment and adds a date for menu tasting to her calendar. I can't fucking concentrate, and I really want to go hunt down Rachel, but I'm second-guessing that instinct too. I'm pissed at her, but fuck, I want to touch her so bad. Every pent-up emotion I've been holding onto for the last fourteen years is wanting to break free.

We say our goodbyes to Isla and leave the conference room. We wave to Howard before stepping out into the parking lot. I walk over and lean against my truck. Kelley is watching me, and I finally look at her.

"What's happening, Mike? Who was that?"

"You don't remember Rachel?"

Her head tilts as she considers that, and it's as if I see the realization hit her. "The girl you were with in high school. The one who left town the summer before your senior year?"

"Yep. The one who left without a word." I run my hands through my hair and say, "Her mom told me she went to Boston to boarding school."

Kelley gives me an intense calculating look. "Michael… is that why you moved to the East Coast after college? Did you go there looking for her?"

"No, not really." I shrug, fighting to seem indifferent. "But I sought her out when I spent some time in Boston… I didn't have any luck."

"Oh, shit."

"Yeah… but here she is." I snap my fingers. "Just like that, Kelley."

"What are you going to do?"

I shake my head, defeated. "Come on, I'll drive you home."

"No, no, no. I don't need a ride. Don't you need to go talk to her? She owes you an explanation."

"I'm not so sure I'm ready for that." I drop my hands to my sides and say, "I'm too angry. I'm not sure I can be objective."

"You have every right to be angry with her—and you obviously need closure. Go get it."

I shake my head, unable to talk.

"Either you talk to her or I will, dammit." Kelley reminds me of an angry kitten when she's mad. It almost makes me laugh. "Are you going back in there?"

I think about that for a minute, then say, "No. I don't want to cause her trouble at work. I'll wait until she comes out, then I'll approach her."

Kelley watches me for a moment and then says, "Okay, but don't be all stalker-ish. Waiting for a woman in a parking lot is not always the best idea, so if you decide to hang around, you need to be… very non-aggressive when she comes out. Do you understand that?"

"Right. Yeah, you're right. I'll be cool. I promise."

"Okay, all right. I'm going to take off—mostly because I don't want to intrude. Are you going to be okay?"

"I'm fine. Go home. I'll call you later and tell you what happens."

She reaches out on her tiptoes to give me a hug, squeezing tight. "I'm here when you need me, okay? Maybe stop by the house when you're done talking to her?"

"Thank you," I mumble in her ear.

When she's gone, I settle in to wait. I'm not leaving until I talk to Rachel. I don't care if it looks bad that I'm waiting for her in the parking lot. I refuse to let her get away this time.

CHAPTER FOURTEEN

Rachel

Dear Michael,

My dad has cancer.

Whew. It feels good to tell someone and get it off my chest. I've been keeping it in, and it was starting to tear me apart. I miss having a best friend. I miss you. I need you. I need a friend and a shoulder. Sorry. This wasn't meant to be about me... I'm just so drained... empty, really.

My dad has cancer, Mike!

He's dying, and I can't do anything about it. All I can do is stand by and let it eat him up from the inside out. I hate that Raegan has to watch him die slowly. It can't be healthy for kids to see this sort of thing, but then again, it's the circle of life, so I'm even torn about that. At six, Raegan is a smart kid, too quick sometimes. Trust me when I say nothing gets past her.

Dad's been sick for a few months, but now that we have an actual diagnosis, we can move forward with treatment. He's a fighter, and I'm trying to fight as well, but all I can do is be here for him. Since the diagnosis, my mom has been living here. I know she brings my dad comfort, but she's making me insane. She seems to constantly need my companionship. I think she's doing it on purpose.

She criticizes everything about me, and she does it in front of Raegan. My mother has zero respect for me, and I'm utterly incapable of pleasing her. She hates my hair, the clothes I wear, she hates my job, and she's always telling me I wear too much makeup. She tells me I'm fat—and how I'd better hurry and find a husband before I become so ugly no one will want me. I'm trying really hard not to fight with her, but she continually baits me. Fortunately, she's very kind to Raegan. If it wasn't for Raegan and my dad's illness, I'd tell her to go straight to hell.

Seriously, though, I'm trying to be a grown-up and set an example for Rae. I don't want her to see me fight and argue with my mom—but Mom is making it so hard!

Mom's not strong enough to really help Dad, so I have to be there all the time. It makes me feel terrible that I don't want to be with him during this; I'm afraid of losing him, but I can't even enjoy time with him because of her. Why does she make it so hard to love her? I hope and pray that Raegan and I never have such a contentious relationship.

Raegan is playing soccer. She seems to really like it. Did you play soccer as a kid? I don't remember. I didn't. My mom said sports weren't for girls. Ugh.

Here's a fun fact: Raegan fell off her skateboard and chipped a tooth. Crazy, right? I told her the story about you breaking your tooth. This was probably a bad idea because now she's full of questions.

To be honest, I'm full of questions too. Where are you? How are you? Do you miss me as much as I miss you? I wish you were here.

I love you,
Rachel

CHAPTER FIFTEEN

Rachel

When Isla steps inside my office, I quickly wipe the tears from my face. She closes the door behind her.

"Is it safe to assume that's Raegan's dad?"

I nod, using the tissue to wipe my nose. I can't talk, and if I could, I'm not sure what I'd say. I'm stunned. Stunned into silence. So ashamed and so heartbroken at the same time. How could I wait all these years to tell him about his daughter? God, she looks so much like him. He looks so good. So healthy and vibrant… and pissed. He's still pissed at me and who could blame him? I deserve his anger. I know it.

Another sob escapes, causing Isla to circle my desk and crouch down to face me. "Rachel, honey, I'm sorry. Maybe you should call it a day and go home." She sighs as if looking for a better answer. "Get some rest, then come up with a plan to talk to him about Raegan."

I shake my head because I can't face Raegan. How can I? "I'm so sorry," I stutter through my sobs. "Isla, is he getting married? Was that his fiancée?"

"Is that why you're so upset?"

I shake my head and say, "I'm so shocked, and I'm just so ashamed I didn't try to contact him sooner."

"Rest easy. That's not his fiancée. Remember, I told you it was Mac Thomas and his wife coming in? That's why I wanted you to step in. I wanted to reassure them about the hotel's security. Mac couldn't make it, and Mike stepped in to help."

"Oh, God, that's right." I lay my head in my hands, relieved. "I'm sorry it all went to hell."

"I think he was just as shocked as you. He actually stood to follow you out of the room but stopped himself." She inhales deeply and says, "We didn't get much accomplished, but that's okay. I'm meeting with the bride again another time, but I'm sure Mike's going to want to talk to you. I wouldn't wait any longer to tell him."

I rest my head against my fist and say, "I'm not waiting. If I've learned anything today, it's that keeping secrets doesn't pay. God… did you see the look on his face? He's so angry with me, and he doesn't even know the truth yet."

"Maybe he'll be more understanding once you tell him everything."

"I doubt it."

"Go home, Rachel. Get your head together and figure out what you're going to tell him. There's no point in sticking around here. You're not going to get any work done." She lifts from her crouched position and says, "I have another meeting in the conference room in five minutes otherwise I'd drive you home."

I glance at the clock and realize that if I leave now, I'll have a few hours to get my act together before I have to pick up Raegan. I agree with a nod and slowly get to my feet. I stop at the mirror and try to clean up my face. It's clear I've been crying, but there isn't anything I can do about that right now.

I pick up my purse and give Isla a big hug. "It's okay, I'll be fine. Thank you for being here for me. I don't know what I'd do without you."

"Fortunately, hon, you'll never have to find out."

I hike my bag up on my shoulder and head out. As I'm leaving, it occurs to me that I should just do it. Do it now. Go straight to the CrossFit gym and tell him before I lose my nerve. I wonder what the chances are that he went back to work.

Once I'm in the lobby, I slow my progress when I see men's boots sticking out from around the corner. I take another step and his huge frame comes into focus. He's resting in a small armchair in the little reading nook near the front door of the hotel, across from the front desk. I stop and glance at Howard and then back to Mike. His hands are steepled in front of him, and he's watching me. Waiting.

He's all dark and brooding, sexy, and… angry. A thrill of frightened anticipation touches my spine. That and a wave of affection… a longing I can't ignore. I've missed him so much and it makes me wonder if he's *only* angry or if somewhere, inside of him, he's missed me too.

I walk toward him, praying this doesn't turn into a scene in front of Howard. I swallow back my nerves and fight to push out an audible greeting. "Hey."

"We need to talk."

I lower my chin, trying not to be hurt by his tone and remind myself that I deserve this. "I know…" I clear my throat and try again. "This isn't exactly a great place to—"

I hear a faint click and turn. Howard's stepped into the reception office. I look back at Mike and gesture for him to get up. "Quick, follow me."

I rush past the front desk and through the door to the service stairs. I run up and open the door on the second-floor landing and step out with Mike on my heels. I'd rather not have one of my employees see me sneak into a room with him so I'm trying to hurry. I yank my key card from the side pocket of my purse and open the door to suite 108, which I know isn't occupied.

I hold it open for Mike, and once he's inside, I follow, letting the door swing shut behind me. I can tell by the lingering scent of the hotel's cleaning supplies that the suite was recently made up. Mike doesn't enter the room all the way; he stops a few steps inside, and when I turn, we're facing each other in the dark foyer of the suite. The entry isn't pitch-black, thanks to the partly open curtains in the seating area behind Mike. It's light enough that I can see the hard stare in his dark, brooding eyes and as I take them in, I'm wondering if this was a bad idea. The old Mike would never hurt me, but the old Mike was always smiling. This Mike hasn't smiled at all.

His body is like a wall between me and seating area, and this little entry hall feels very crowded. I take a step back so that I'm against the door. He takes a step closer—close enough that his musky aroma overpowers the clean scent of the suite. He smells so good I want to bury my nose in his neck and breathe him in. I want to remind myself what it felt like when he was mine and I was his. I want to relive a simple time when all that mattered was the two of us together. Even as close as he is, it's not close enough… I wonder if it'll ever be close enough to fill the gap between us.

He's so tall too… so big and intimidating. This is Mike, I remind myself. *My Mike.*

I reach up and lay my hand on his cheek, running my fingers along his cheekbone and then his jawbone and stubble from the day's growth. He exhales heavily. I want to tell him how much I missed him. I want to tell him how much I still, and always will, love him, but the words stick in my throat. I swallow hard, fighting to keep my emotions in check. His extraordinary, whiskey-colored eyes blaze as he stares at me.

The silence is so loud.

We stay like this for a long moment, staring into each other's eyes. Speaking without actually saying anything. I slowly drop my bag on the floor then lift my hand to slide the bolt on the door. When it clicks, he leans in and takes my mouth. Hard.

Heat jolts through me like lightening. The feel of him is everything. Absolutely everything.

His hands land on my hips, and I slide my fingers through his short hair, gripping it, afraid of letting go… afraid he'll pull away.

Please don't pull away.

His lips lower to my neck as his hands move around to grip my ass. It feels so good. His touch, the burning of his hot tongue as he kisses his way down my neck. He tugs at my blouse with his teeth, popping the buttons until my lace bra is completely exposed.

I have never wanted anything more in my life. I can't remember the last time I felt this way. I can't remember the last time a man made me want him with something as simple as the look in his eyes.

When my blouse is unbuttoned, his warm hands lift to my bare back, skin on skin. The feel almost makes me gasp. Mike kisses me hard again and then stops to stare into my eyes.

"Rachel…" his voice is rougher than I remember, but I can still see the boy I fell in love with all those years ago. He's in there, inside this grown man. "Do you want this?" He lifts his hands to frame my face, pushing my hair back so he can see all of me. "I need you to tell me you want this as much as I do."

"Yes, I want this, God, I…" I'm fighting to keep my voice steady.

He uses his thumbs to lift my chin, tilting my head so he can kiss me. His tongue swipes inside my mouth before his teeth nip at my bottom lip. It's not much, but enough to have me squirming against him. I shrug off my jacket and blouse then quickly tug down the zipper of my skirt, before pushing it and my panties to the floor.

When I'm standing in only my bra, I grip the bottom of his t-shirt to pull it over his head, but before I have time, he grabs the neck and tugs it off for me. I try not to stare at his bare chest and the ink covering it, but I can't help it. He's sculpted like marble, and I'm struck dumb until I hear the rip of his zipper and then the sound of his jeans hitting the floor at the same time I hastily remove my bra.

Before I can react, Mike's hands grab my ass, and he lifts me off my feet as if I weigh nothing. A second later, he's lowering me down on his rock-hard erection. Then he's all the way inside me. It's tight—he's big, and it's the sweetest thing I've ever felt. It's everything I want in life. Him, inside me.

With my back against the wall, Mike slides into me over and over, and I'm trying so hard to be quiet, but I can't. I can't keep the cries at bay. This is my Michael. Our eyes are locked, and my hands are clamped on his shoulders; he feels so good. When my orgasm hits, I cling to him, my hands wrapping around him, trying to stay upright, but it's hard. When my body relaxes, he wraps an arm around me and says, "Hold on, baby."

His words and the endearment make me almost want to cry. It's all I've dreamed of for nearly fourteen years. I grip him tightly, praying he doesn't let go as he carries me into the bedroom of the suite.

He lays me down without pulling out, and within a second, he's pounding into me again, his eyes back to mine. It's so intimate and unexpected that watching him brings me to a peak again and before I can slow it down, before I can wait for him to come with me, I let go and lose myself in him again. Mike doesn't slow his progress, he grabs my hands and holds them above my head, tilted against me. My knees are up around his shoulders, and he's so deep, I feel like he's become a permanent part of me.

Within another minute, he lets go too. After a long groan and one more push, he drops on top of me.

CHAPTER SIXTEEN

Rachel

Dear Michael,

I'm sorry I haven't been writing lately. Life is busy, and our little girl is growing up. She'll be a teenager tomorrow, and I'm not sure how to digest that information. She's turned into such a beautiful person, and I'm afraid of what this life has in store for her. I'm fearful of the life lessons she still has to learn… some the hard way, but I'm hoping not all. I'm hoping things are easier on her than they've ever been on me.

The difference is, she's much smarter than I ever was. She's got a ton of common sense too. She's strong, and she's learning to protect herself. Life is full of bad people and horrible tragedies, and we can't always avoid them. I'm trying very hard to teach her how to prevent these tragedies and how not to be a victim of bad people.

We're both taking Taekwondo, and she's advanced very fast. I want her to be able to defend herself. I realize that, in her eyes, it's a sport, but in mine, it's a way to prepare her for whatever adversity she may face in her life. Whether that adversity is manmade or natural. She's learning self-respect, perseverance, discipline, and how to be strong in spirit and body.

I know you'd be proud of her. She's the very best of both of us combined.

Fun fact: Raegan is almost taller than me now. She definitely takes after you and not me. Thank God for that.

I think about you every day. I wonder what you're doing and how you are. I wonder what you'd think of our daughter… what you'd think of me. I regret so much of my life. I regret so much of what I've lost. I regret losing you. I think about looking for you… contacting you… telling you everything. Then I think about the years that have passed and I know… I know that mountain between us is too high to climb.

Sometimes I think I'm strong enough… and I begin the climb, but then something brings me crashing back down and reality hits… and I remember that I'm ridiculous and weak. And not having the nerve to reach out is proof of that.

I love you, and yes, I still miss you. I miss you so much. I ache with it. Every day.

Rachel

CHAPTER SEVENTEEN

Michael

There's a soft glow of light filtering in. It's enough to see her face clearly. She's been crying, and I get it. I want to cry too. Instead of crying though, I'm stricken with insecurity, wondering if she was crying because she didn't want me to find her or if she was crying because she's happy I'm here. This same insecurity—these same feelings—have me twisting away from her and sitting up. I shift and perch on the edge of the bed with my feet on the floor and my back to Rachel. I remember every moment I've spent with this woman and never once, in any of those moments, did I question how I felt about her or about being with her. Not even when we were inexperienced teenagers who didn't know what we were doing in bed. Jesus, I remember the very first time I watched her come. It was the most beautiful thing I've ever seen—and I gave her that, just like she was my first.

She's lying across my bed, and her eyes are on me. I want her so much, but I don't know how to ask for it. I also don't want to pressure her. It's not like we haven't done it. We have, but only once and I don't think she liked it.

I liked it, but she seemed to be in pain the entire time. Even though she said it was fine. I lean over and kiss her. She's still smiling when

I pull away, so I let my lips travel down her neck as I slide onto the bed next to her. I'm sure she can tell how turned on I am with my erection jammed against her.

When she lowers her hand to rub it through my jeans, I lift my eyes to look at hers.

"Is this okay?" she asks, and I almost want to laugh at the question.

"Of course it's okay." I lower my hand to rub between her legs, and as I do, her eyelids flutter closed. "Is this okay?"

She nods and spreads her legs for me. Her eyes are still closed, and I'm afraid that means I'm hurting her. "Rachel, can you open your eyes when I touch you?"

She grins seductively but shakes her head.

"Why?" I ask. "Do I look funny or something?"

"No, I'm just..." She shrugs. "I'm shy." When she says this, her eyes pop back open.

"Don't be shy, it's just me. You have no reason to be shy of me. You already know I love you."

"Yeah, but still."

"Still nothing. I'm going to touch you, and I want you to watch me. If I can see your eyes, I know I'm not hurting you."

"You've never hurt me, Michael."

I unbutton her jeans and slowly lower my hand under her panties, sliding my fingers between her folds; she's so wet and warm. As my two fingers enter her, her eyelids start to flutter closed again. "Does that hurt?"

"No," she moans. "It feels good." She lifts herself closer to my hand and with a breathy voice, she says, "Rub right there... that... that's perfect."

I do as she says, and then she starts moving with the motion of my fingers. Her mouth parts and her face flushes, but her eyes are still closed.

I stop moving, and her eyes pop open. "Why did you stop?"

"I'm afraid I'm hurting you..."

A gush of air escapes her mouth as she says, "You're not hurting me... just don't stop."

"Keep your eyes open. Look at me so I can see you."

"Okay, okay, just don't stop."

I start rubbing in the same spot as before and her legs spread further. Her hips are moving with the motion, but her eyes are locked on mine. Watching her makes my dick so hard, and I want to start rubbing myself, but I want her to feel good first. Her mouth opens further, and little cries are escaping like gasps. A moment later, her forehead creases and her eyes slam shut. At the same time, her entire body tenses and her head lifts off the bed.

Jesus! Watching her is so hot. I tug on the waistband of her jeans while trying to get mine off at the same time. Once both our pants are gone, I lean over her. Her beautiful eyes open, and she's smiling. "Do it," she says. "I want to feel you now."

Dammit. What am I doing here? How stupid and irresponsible of me to get tangled up with her without even having a conversation first. I don't know her, not anymore. All I know is that this girl left me without an explanation. She disappeared—deserted me after promising to follow me anywhere. She's hurt me more than any other person in my life... probably because I've loved her more than anyone else. Do I have abandonment issues because of it? Fuck yeah, I do.

"Fuck." I prop my elbows on my knees. I hate that my first reaction after having her is regret. I hate it. And it's such a contrast to every memory I have of being with her.

"Michael..." I feel her hand rest on my back. "I thought you wanted to talk?"

"Yep. That's what I wanted. To talk. This wasn't part of my plan. I sure fucking hope you're not married to some other guy."

"I wouldn't have done this with you if I were committed to someone else. You know I wouldn't."

"I don't know you at all. I thought I did once, but I came to find out you were a complete stranger."

"I'm the same person. I didn't leave you by choice, Michael. My mom sent me away. I didn't have any other option."

"You didn't have a choice to leave?" I shake my head and say, "What about a phone call, Rachel? You fucking gutted me."

"Do you think I wasn't gutted? Do you think that was easy for me?" Her voice cracks but she keeps going. "Jesus, I still have dreams about you. There's so much you don't know, but you must know that I never stopped loving you. Not one minute." She lifts up, and a second later, I feel her heat against my back. She clings to me, her arms and legs around me, her scent surrounding me, throwing me back in time—back to a time I thought I had shit figured out. To a time when I had everything I wanted... until I didn't. "Please turn around and face me. Hold me and have this conversation with me."

"I'm hurt, Rachel. I can't pretend I'm not."

"If you're still hurt, that means you also still have feelings for me."

I can't answer.

She hesitates for what feels like an eternity. Then her soft warm lips land on my shoulder and she says, "We have the same scars. We have the same hurt. I know you don't want to believe that, but it's true." She hesitates, allowing the room to grow quiet, but I can hear her breathing and feel the rise and fall of her chest as she rests against me. "My mother threatened to tell everyone you sexually assaulted me if I told you I was leaving. She said she'd contact the police if I talked to you... she'd call the press and ruin your future if I told you where I was."

"That's such bullshit. She couldn't prove I assaulted you, not unless you agreed to lie. She manipulated you, Rachel."

"I know that, but she made a lot of threats." Her arms tighten around me. "I was scared and backed into a corner. I had nowhere to go and no one to help me, not without hurting you." I can hear the waver in her voice as if she's trying not to cry and it makes me angrier.

I finally twist out of her embrace and turn to face her. "Your mother couldn't hurt me. Even if she made the accusation, she couldn't prove it. I'd never be convicted."

"You'd never be convicted in a court of law, but in the press, she'd ruin you. What school would offer you a spot on their team—offer you a football scholarship—with those kind of rumors hanging over your head? Don't forget my uncle is a reporter. She had the resources to hurt you if she wanted to."

Her eyes lower to her naked body and her cheeks pink in reaction, as if she's just remembered that she's naked. She stands and goes to grab a towel from the bathroom. I watch her, noting the changes to her body, things that weren't there when we were together years ago. A few very faint stretchmark scars low on her abdomen—and what looks like a surgery scar.

Rachel is so beautiful. Luscious in a way I don't remember. She's pinup-girl-hot with hips that want to be grabbed and breasts that bounce when she walks. Fuck, I want her again. Her raven hair swings as she wraps the towel around herself and her lips pout as she knots it together.

She props herself on the bed again and says, "Believe it or not, I'd planned to contact you in the next couple of days. I looked you up last week, and I was pretty surprised to find you here in Sacramento."

"I tried searching for you a couple of times, even when I was on the East Coast for a while. Do you know how common a name Rachel Williams is?"

"Yeah, about as common as Michael Murphy. You sort of disappeared after graduating U of O. You came up in a search this time because of the CrossFit gym you opened in town. But why the East Coast?"

"After you disappeared, your mom told me you moved to Boston for a private boarding school. Of course, I had to pound on her door every day for weeks before she even told me that much." I shift so we're facing each other. "I guess you were never in Boston."

"I've never been there." She reaches out and lays her hand over mine. "Can you tell me why you're not still playing football?"

"I got hurt. Broken leg and a nasty concussion." I shrug because it's not really the reason I'm not playing, it's just the reason I decided I didn't want to play. "I don't want to be one of those washed-up players who spend their later years in pain. That concussion affected me for a long time. After that, I decided it wasn't worth it. I loved the game, but I didn't really care about the fame and the money. I'd rather be healthy than rich."

"I'm sorry you were hurt, and I'm so sorry I wasn't there for you." Her brows draw together, and for a moment, I almost believe her.

"I don't understand. You promised to follow me anywhere."

"I know I did. When I made that promise, I meant it. A football player or a personal trainer, I don't care what you do, I just want you to be happy. I hope you know that."

I scoff at that. "Really? You want me to be happy?" I can't help my sarcasm. "That's interesting, considering how badly you hurt me. What happened, Rachel? Why would your mom go to such extremes—and why at that point?"

She lowers her eyes again, and within seconds, tears are spilling down her cheeks. "I'm so sorry. I hope you don't hate me when I tell you, but I guess you couldn't feel any worse about me than you already do."

"You owe me an explanation." I stand to pace and unlike her, I don't care if I'm naked. I just need to rid myself of the angry energy. "You'll never understand what it feels like when someone you love disappears and you're stuck wondering about them every day of your life."

I watch her for a long time: she's crying and I'm so confused.

"What happened, Rachel?"

Her bright blue eyes lift to mine and they're startling in color because of her crying. She gets to her feet and faces me, her head high and her shoulders back. "I got pregnant." Her words are breathy and from the way she's standing, it looks like she's prepared to physically defend herself, and that throws me off. "My mother figured it out when my period was late. She forced me to leave town because I was pregnant, Michael." Her watery eyes focus on mine and I clearly see the fear she's hiding with her fighting stance.

"What?" It's as if my brain stutters. I stare at her, connecting the dots. Her stretch marks, the surgery scar. Impossible. I narrow my eyes at her. "What the fuck are you talking about?"

"I… we… have a daughter. She recently turned thirteen."

"That's impossible." I pace in a circle, not sure what to think—what to do. "That can't be true. There's no way you'd do that to me. Please, *please* tell me you didn't do that."

But her expression tells me I'm wrong. She lifts her hands to her face, covering herself for a moment, then she mumbles, "I'm so sorry."

I walk out of the bedroom and snatch my clothes off the floor. It takes me seconds to get dressed, and then I'm pacing again. "You're sorry! I can't believe this." My heart is racing so fast it hurts. I rub my chest while trying to take a deep breath.

I have a child.

"I know you're hurt and disappointed in me, but—"

"Disappointed in you? Are you fucking kidding me?"

"You have to understand how cruel my mom was when she found out. She tried to force me into getting an abortion. When I refused, she made other threats. She started calling her lawyers and talking about private adoption. I was scared and I had to protect you—I had to protect our baby." Rachel approaches me, but I jerk away from her.

I can't believe it.

"You've stolen from me, Rachel. Your mother has stolen a life from me." This thought alone makes me rage. I lean down and get right in her face. "I had plans—plans I wanted to share with you. She stole that from me—you stole that from us when you disappeared."

"I know, babe. I—"

"*You* took that away when you didn't trust me enough to come to me."

"Come to you with what? Seriously, Mike, what could you and I have done alone? It's not like your parents were any more understanding than mine were."

I stare at her, and I know she's right. I can't argue with her on that. Their behavior toward my sister and niece are proof of that. I point between us and say, "We—you and I—could have made it work."

"How? By ruining your prospects? All while trying to fight a custody battle against my parents?" She steps closer, one eyebrow raised. "I understand *now*. Now, at my age, I understand that she didn't have any rights to my child—to my future with you and our baby—but back then, I didn't understand that. I was scared she would take everything from us."

"Rachel, she did take everything from *me*!" I'm shouting, but I can't help it. "Do you realize that in all your efforts to salvage things, in all your efforts to *protect us*, that *I* still lost everything?"

"But you didn't!" Her voice peaks and tears are streaming down her distraught face. It hurts to see her so upset, but I can't think about that now. "You didn't lose your dream of playing football." She points to my chest and says, "That might not mean anything now, but back then, it was everything to you."

"No!" I grasp her arms and bring her closer. "You were everything to me. *You*, Rachel, not football." I'm staring into her eyes as they plead for me to understand. Those astonishing blue eyes begging me to forgive her. After a moment she closes them and says, "I was scared she'd take my baby. I'm sorry." She turns out of my arms and says, "I had to make a choice, and I chose our baby."

I scrub my hands across my face, not sure I understand. I take a deep breath and fight to calm my heart and my mind. "Are you telling me she actually forced you to choose?"

She nods, causing a curtain of silky, dark hair to hang over her face, shielding her from me. Her shoulders are lifting and falling along with her sobbing and it's killing me to watch her. When I can't take it any longer, I close the distance between us and wrap my arms around her tightly. I hold her for a long time, breathing her in. She still smells exactly the same. All these years and she still smells like oranges.

When her breathing settles, I whisper, "I'm sorry."

She takes one more deep breath and draws back from me. She grabs a tissue from the box on the table and brushes it across her face. "When her threats against me didn't work, she threatened you, she threatened adoption, she... *scared me*. I didn't know what else to do so I made a deal with her. I promised I wouldn't contact you or tell anyone about my pregnancy if she left you alone and let me keep my baby. She agreed only if I agreed to leave town permanently." Rachel lowers herself down onto the couch and says, "I wasn't even allowed any time to think things through. She had me packed, and we were on an airplane within a couple of hours." She lifts her hand and lets it fall to her lap, defeat clear in her eyes, and seeing it there causes a spike of pain in my stomach. I should have been there for her, but how could I when I didn't know? She grows tearful again and says, "Mike, I was sixteen and pregnant and... and I had no one to confide in. Do you have any idea what that's like? Jesus, even my dad wouldn't stand up for me. He gave in to her every demand."

"I would have been there for you every step of the way, I'm sorry." I try to breathe through the anxiety I feel at the thought of not having any control over my life, the thought of what it must have been like for Rachel. Only now, knowing I have a child out there who doesn't know me, do I have some understanding of what that's like. But I can't tell her this… honestly, I don't know what to say. As much as I hate what happened to her, I'm having a hard time getting past the fact that I've had a child all these years and I didn't know it.

"I can't believe you did this. All these years, Rachel."

"I know… so much has happened… there's so much I need to tell you."

I shake my head in pure irritation. I can't do this with her now. I can't even think straight, much less have a reasonable conversation with her. I need some space so I can calm the fuck down. "I don't want to fight and scream at you. That's not how I want to do this, okay? I need a few days to think. I need to find a way to wrap my brain around… everything so we can talk. Really talk, okay?"

She nods, almost frantically. "Of course." Then she gets up and walks over to grab her clothes from the floor. "I understand." With her clothes wadded up in her hand, she grips the towel wrapped around her chest as if to hold it in place and, before I can say another word, she turns into the bathroom. I get a glimpse of her face as she quickly closes the door behind her. Her tears are streaming again, and she looks absolutely miserable.

I wait for a few minutes, but when I realize she's not coming out of the bathroom, I jot down my phone number so she can reach me, then I leave. I can't stick around any longer. I'm starting to feel like a caged animal and I really don't want to lose my shit in front of Rachel.

I storm out of the suite, and exit the building, trying to calm my racing heart… and trying to digest this new reality. *I have a daughter.*

This is real. There's a real-life little person that I'm responsible for—that I *should be* responsible for. Fuck. I can't even… I don't know what to think about this. As I tug the driver's side door open on my Tahoe, it hits me. Holy shit! I have a daughter… and she's been emailing me.

CHAPTER EIGHTEEN

Rachel

I spend half an hour in the bathroom of the suite, licking my wounds and waiting for him to leave. I can't hear anything outside, so I don't know if he's gone, but when I creep out, the room is empty. I quickly get my shoes on and reach for my purse, which is on the love seat... not where I left it near the door. Sitting on top of my purse is a quickly scribbled note on the hotel notepad.

Rachel, if you need me, here's my number. I didn't get yours, but I hope it's okay if I call the hotel when I want to talk to you. I apologize for my actions today. I didn't intend on taking advantage of you during a vulnerable moment. I hope you know that.

I groan as I read it. It's just like him. He's respectful almost to a fault. What a refreshing change from what I'm used to. And as if. As if he took advantage of me. Like I didn't want that as much as he did. I grab my phone and enter his number. Then I shoot off a text.

Me: *This is Rachel, and now you have my number too. I hope you know that I've never once felt taken advantage of by you. Today included. I... ugh. I have so much to say, but mostly, I'm sorry.*

It takes him a few minutes to respond, but finally, the bubble pops up, and a moment later, a text appears.

Michael: *Thank you for telling me that. I will be in touch. Just give me a few days to clear my head. I want to speak openly without saying something I'll regret, but it's too hard when I'm angry.*

Me: *I understand. I'll be waiting to hear from you.*

I sigh in relief and wonder how the hell I'm going to face Raegan when I pick her up. She's going to see it on my face as soon as I step inside the house. I take my purse into the bathroom and try to straighten my hair. When I realize it's a complete loss, I wrangle it into a ponytail. Then I wash my face and try to reapply some makeup so I don't look like the walking dead. There isn't much I can do about my puffy red eyes, though.

Once I'm finished, I stare at myself in the mirror, then plaster a smile on my face. Ugh. I look ridiculous trying to smile when I feel so utterly horrid. Crying has brightened my blue eyes, and they're practically glowing against the redness. What can I do? Absolutely nothing, so I turn, and head home.

On the road, I call Isla's office to give her an update. She left a couple of messages while I was with Mike.

"This is Isla, can I help you?"

"Isla, it's Rachel."

"Oh my God, thank you for calling. I've been worried about you. Did you make it home okay? How are you feeling?"

"I actually just left the hotel. Mike was in the lobby waiting for me earlier. I took him to suite 108, so we could talk."

"Wow… how did that go?"

I fight tears and try to find a way to tell her without losing it. "Um, well, let me start by saying I'd really appreciate it if you'd ask housekeeping to turnover suite 108."

She's quiet for a moment then she says, "That good, huh?"

"Not entirely. It started out well, but then it went south. He didn't take the news well. He's angry and hurt and... he asked for some time to clear his head."

"I don't think that's unreasonable, do you?"

"Not unreasonable. He was actually quite kind about it. He should hate me, and as rejected as I feel right now, I think he still cares about me." I hold my breath for a moment then try to say, "Can you care about someone you hate?"

"Rach, give him the time he asked for and give him a chance to accept the news. He'll come around. Until then, what are you going to tell Raegan?"

"I'm not telling her anything. Not until I hear back from him. I don't want to get her hopes up. He could still reject her."

"I don't think he's going to. He seemed like a great guy. I mean, think about it, what kind of guy accompanies his female best friend to meet with the wedding coordinator?"

"Um, a gay one...? But I *know* he's not gay."

Isla laughs a little too hard at that, but I guess if I were in a better mood, I'd find it funny too.

"Do you have time to chill before you pick up Raegan?"

"A little bit, but I'm heading over there anyway. I just need to get my head together and keep moving forward. It's what I've been doing since I found out I was pregnant with her."

"You're strong. Remember that."

"Thank you, I hope you know how much I appreciate you."

"I know." She chuckles again and says, "I'll have that suite cleaned. Call me if you need me."

I disconnect as I'm pulling into my uncle's driveway, the same driveway that used to be my father's. After my dad's death, Uncle Mitch moved into the house at my mom's request. He and Annie take care of the place, which is a relief for me because I'm not interested in living here.

I sit in the car for a full five minutes and find my thoughts turn to my parents. College sweethearts, they fell in love and married before they even finished their degrees. My dad always had ambitions to become a politician, and my mother always wanted to be a politician's wife. The problem was, they couldn't stand each other once they got what they wanted. Shortly after I was born, my father won his first election. By the time I was five, he'd won his second, and by then, my mom was done with him. She didn't divorce him though, because that would have ruined their image. Instead, we carried on the pretense of being a happy family. We lived like that for years.

When I was ten, my mom packed us up and she and I moved into her father's big, empty house in Portland. Her father had died years before, and so we simply moved away quietly while my parents continued with the façade of a happy marriage in public. When my dad had to campaign, we'd return to California and be right by his side. As soon as the election was over, Mom and I would head back up to Portland. It was a horrid cycle, and I hated it. It wasn't until high school that my dad stopped campaigning. He'd been elected to the State Assembly and finally felt he could make a difference there. After all, that was actually his goal. He wanted to do good things for the people of California, that part of his campaigning was genuine. My parents still didn't divorce—why should they? They were happy living apart but still pretending to be a happy couple. It was the perfect disguise for them both. All it took was a couple of trips to California every year to maintain the status quo, and my father continued to bend to her every desire until he died.

Most people knew my mother and I lived in Portland away from my father, which I always found a little strange. Now that I'm older, I realize it's not uncommon for politicians to live away from their families.

When I became pregnant and moved to California permanently, they didn't hide me, not from the public, just from Mike. It's not like I was stuffed in the basement and forced to give birth on an old mattress or anything like that. My dad didn't hide me from his friends and colleagues either, he just didn't advertise the fact that he had an unwed and pregnant teenage daughter.

Unlike my mother, my dad was more affectionate. He tried to help me with Raegan and he loved her so much. It was hard… excruciatingly hard to maintain a good relationship with him after what he and my mother had done, though. If he had attempted to stick up for me once, just once, things might have been different. My father was decent, unlike my mother. He had to have known he was wrong to let my mother bully me into keeping Raegan secret from her father.

I pop the handle and get out of my car, praying I can get in and get out without Mitch noticing my mood. I don't have it in me to lie about my day.

When I walk inside the house, Raegan is sitting on the couch with the TV on and a book in her lap. I fight for a smile, mostly because I know she's still pissed at me and that means she's not going to have a kind word to share.

"Hey, babe, how are you?"

"Fine," she says without looking up from her book. "Why are you so early?"

"Bad day, I had to get out of there early. Is Annie or Uncle Mitch here?"

"Annie had to go out, but Uncle Mitch is in his office." She finally looks up at me, and her eyes soften. "You okay, Mom?"

I really smile this time, so happy she cares. But then again, I know she cares about me, she's just angry, and she has every right to be. "I'm fine. Like I said, it was a rough day. You ready? I'm kind of in a hurry."

She nods and starts packing up her stuff as I walk down the hall toward my uncle's office. When he hears me, he holds up a finger as if to ask me to wait a minute so he can finish what he's typing.

"I'll see you tomorrow. I need to get going." I'm fighting to keep my voice normal, but I know it's not.

"Rachel?" He removes his reading glasses as he turns to give me a closer look. "Are you okay? Has something happened?"

I nod, pursing my lips, not sure how to get out of this conversation. I hardly ever challenged my parents. I was raised to show respect to my elders and taught that ladies don't raise their voices. I love my uncle. He's always been around when I needed him, but even he never tried to stand up for me with my mother. What is it about her that makes men stupid?

"Yep, totally fine," I say, this time averting my eyes. "I really need to go."

I turn, but he stops me with the one question I can't ignore. "Did you fight with your mother again?"

"Nope, we're not fighting."

Not yet.

"So, what is it then?"

I stop and turn back a couple of steps so that my voice doesn't project down the hall. "I ran into Raegan's father today. I told him the truth."

"Rachel, why the hell would you do that?"

"Excuse me!" I lift my arms in question and say, "Why wouldn't I do that? Jesus, Uncle Mitch, do you realize that Raegan asks about her dad? She'll barely speak to me because I haven't told her his name."

He brushes a hand in the direction of the living room as if it's nothing. "She's fine; she's a lot better off without him."

"How do you know?" I point to him and say, "You don't know her father. You don't even know his name. You don't know anything about him. You never even asked!"

"Why would I ask about the little punk who got my niece in trouble?"

"He wasn't a little punk, and he didn't get me in trouble. I had sex with him because I wanted to. I loved him, and it was my choice. That's my responsibility, and he would have stepped up for me, and for Raegan, if he'd been given the chance. But he wasn't given a chance. I was forced to keep her a secret and now that secret…" My voice cracks as I try to say the words I don't want to say, but I do. "That secret is affecting my daughter. She's missing something in her life because of it, and she's feeling incomplete; she's feeling lost and abandoned because of that secret." I point again as tears drip from my eyes. "Screw you if you really think she's better off."

I turn and storm out of the office. Just as I hit the end of the hall, he shouts, "Rachel! What has gotten into you?"

I start laughing, nearly hysterical with the anger I'm feeling, I think because that anger feels a bit like freedom. It's the strangest thing. I'm happy to be angry. I feel the need to tell Mitch and the rest of the world to kiss my ass, which is so unlike me… it's almost liberating.

"My voice! My voice has gotten into me. I'm going to start using it, finally!"

"What are you saying—what does that mean?"

Ignoring him, I turn and walk into the living room, where Raegan is sitting with her backpack, staring at me with wide, confused eyes.

"Let's go," I say, pointing to the door.

CHAPTER NINETEEN

Rachel

Dear Michael,

I'm so scared. I don't know if I can do this. I need you so much. The doctor admitted me into the hospital, and they're worried about the baby and me. I'm not due for three weeks, but my blood pressure is too high, and they won't even let me out of bed. They've scheduled a C-section for this evening, but now they're saying we shouldn't even wait that long. They're only delaying because my dad insists they wait for my mother. The doctor wants to do it now, but Dad's made such a fuss about it. I can hear them in the hall, arguing about it.

I'm not afraid for myself, but I can see the worry in the eyes of the nurse. She hasn't left my side in hours, and I'm so grateful to have a friendly hand to hold. My dad's been here too, but he's too angry to see what I'm going through. He's too worried about my mom getting here to be concerned about the baby and me.

I'm not sure I'm going to survive this, but if I don't, I've written you a letter of explanation and given it to the nurse, along with your phone number. Her name is Raegan Pope. She's promised to mail it out if something terrible happens. I don't trust my mother to not put our little girl up for adoption. I will not let her do that, not even in the event of my death.

Michael, if this is the end, and I don't get to see you again—if I never get to explain what happened to us, I hope you'll remember all the times I told you I loved you. I hope you understand how much I meant those words.

I have to go—the anesthesiologist is here to give me an epidural. Raegan said the doctor refuses to wait any longer.

I love you!

Rachel

CHAPTER TWENTY

Michael

I drive around for a while and my thoughts are focused solely on Rachel. The feel of her in my embrace. The citrusy scent I've missed so much and the silky texture of her raven hair. Jesus… the sweet sound of her cries when she comes. It almost makes me angry to remember it.

It pisses me off that I already want her again. I don't want to want her. Not right now. I want to rage at her for lying. For keeping secrets that have changed the course of my life. I want to rage at her for the child who's reached out to me with cryptic messages, trying to get my attention. Trying to connect with her missing father.

Now I'm questioning whether or not I should respond to those emails. It's been weeks since I've received them and that makes me wonder why they stopped… and why she didn't tell me who her mom was. But I don't know what she knows about me, about my relationship with Rachel, or how she found me.

"Jesus, Rachel," I mutter, knowing that no matter what, I can't hate her and I can't rage at her. That's not going to solve anything—which is why I ran out of there as fast as I could. All the years we've lost when we could have been—*should* have been—a family. Years I've lost with Rachel and the daughter I've never met. It's so unfair.

Of all the scenarios that played out in my mind after she left town, none of them included an accidental pregnancy. Rachel's question comes to mind again. *Do I have any idea what it's like to be pregnant at sixteen and not have someone in my corner to confide in?*

I don't.

I always had my brother and sister when things went crazy with my parents. When we lost Bradley, Diana and I became each other's constant supporters. We're still close, seven years after Bradley's death. Of course, our parents are still fucking crazy, so we sort of need each other.

I have to wonder which is harder, living the last fourteen years in a foolish ignorance, or having spent them with a secret hanging over my head, trying to raise a child on my own. No, I don't think what she did was right, but that doesn't mean I don't empathize with her and what she's been through.

When my phone rings, I'm surprised to see it's my sister. What timing. I hit the answer button and say, "I was just thinking about you."

Diana's voice booms over the car speakers, thanks to Bluetooth. "I just booked our flights! We're coming up for your grand opening."

My shoulders slump in relief instantly. "Thank God." I take a deep breath because I didn't realize how much I needed to talk to her until this very moment. "I'm so glad you're coming, I could really use the support right now."

"Why, honey, what's happened? Are you okay?" Her excitement from a moment ago now sounds like concern, and I feel bad for making her worry.

"You're not going to believe it when I tell you. I'm still not sure I believe it."

"What, Mikey? You're scaring me."

"I'm fine. There's nothing wrong, really. But… I found Rachel. She lives in Sacramento."

"What!"

"Yep. She's right here. She's been here all along. Her mom lied about Boston."

"That bitch!" She breathes into the phone. "I can't believe it."

"I wasn't even looking for her. I went to the hotel Kelley picked for her wedding, and Rachel's the hotel manager. We were both stunned."

"Was she happy to see you? Did she explain what happened? Jesus, this makes me want to come up there and kick her ass. I can't believe she left you the way she did and never even called to explain."

"I think she was happy to see me. I mean, things are different, and she explained what happened all those years ago. That's the part you're not going to believe."

"What! Tell me."

"She left because she was pregnant. Her mom packed her up and brought her down here to live with her dad. Made a bunch of threats against me and the baby if she told me."

The line is silent, and I'm not sure what to think about that.

"Crazy, right?" I say, hoping the call wasn't dropped.

"*Michael.* Are you telling me you have a kid? Wait—how old? That's impossible, it's been too long. Like fourteen or fifteen years since you've seen her. Jesus! A teenager?"

"It's true. I have a thirteen-year-old daughter."

I park my truck in front of Kelley and Mac's house. My heart's racing again and I wonder if telling Diana was a mistake.

"I *am* coming up there to kick that bitch's ass."

"No, you're not. It's a long story. Lots of things have happened. I don't even know everything yet. If you don't think you can be nice to her, don't come up here. As pissed as I am at her, she's still the mother of my kid, and you will treat her with respect."

"Why? How can you care about someone who's kept your child a secret? I don't understand."

"Listen, I'm pissed off too, but there's a lot you don't know about the situation. You need to stop, okay?" I close my eyes for a moment and say, "I could really use some family right now, but if you can't behave, don't come. This is important to me, and I don't need you coming up here and making trouble."

"Fine." Her voice is flat but after a moment she says, "I'm coming. I'll behave. I want to meet my niece, and I want to be there for you. I'll try to be understanding and give Rachel a chance."

"You two used to be friends," I remind her.

"And then she broke your heart. It's hard to forget how badly she screwed you up."

"I haven't forgotten either. I'm treading carefully, I promise."

"What's her name... your daughter?"

I start laughing because I know that should have been my first question. "Funny story. I didn't ask. I don't know what her name is. I literally found out less than an hour ago."

"Oh, God. Talk about timing." I hear her phone clunk around, and then she says, "I'll be there midday Friday—unless you need me sooner. I'm bringing Olivia with me. I'm renting a car so you don't have to worry about picking us up."

"I don't mind."

"Nope, I know you're super busy. It's not a problem and I'm sure I'll need a car while I'm in town anyway. Do you want me there sooner?"

"Thank you, but I'm fine. You don't have to change your plans."

"Okay. I love you, Mikey. I'll see you Friday."

"I love you too, sis. I can't wait to see you guys."

I disconnect the call and look up at Kelley and Mac's front door and wonder if it's a bad time.

I get out of my truck and slowly walk up the front steps and knock. I hear Luna barking and then Mac telling her to stop. He swings the door open, and he's smiling until he gets a good look at me, then the smile slips from his face.

He opens the door wider and says, "You look like shit, man."

When I step inside, Kelley is there waiting for me. "I guess things didn't go well."

I walk into their living room and drop down on their couch. A few seconds later, Luna lumbers over with a wagging tail and amused eyes. I rub under her ears until she's completely pressed up against my legs. "You're right. It didn't go so great."

Kelley and Mac sit across from me. I lean back against the cushions and say, "I have a kid."

"Wha—" Kelley's eyes are wide, and she turns to look at Mac, who's staring at me like I just confessed to being an alien. Then she looks back at me, confused. "A kid? Like, as in, you're a father?"

"Yep. She left town all those years ago because she was pregnant. I have a thirteen-year-old daughter."

"Shut the fuck up," Mac says. "Who keeps that kind of a secret for so long?"

Kelley's eyebrows lift in amazement, then she says, "That explains her reaction when she saw you."

"She said her mom made a bunch of threats against me and threatened to put the baby up for adoption, so Rachel agreed to keep the pregnancy a secret."

"That's total bullshit, Mike. Her mom couldn't put the baby up for adoption, not without her consent," Kelley says.

"Right. I know, and she knows that now, but she said she didn't understand that back then, and I can see how that could be. Her mom was always controlling and kept her pretty sheltered." I exhale heavily and say, "Her mom also threatened to have me arrested for sexual assault—and to tell the press that I took advantage of her daughter."

Kelley shakes her head and says, "What an evil bitch. That would have completely derailed your football career." She blows out a long exhalation and says, "Poor Rachel, I wouldn't want to be responsible for something like that either."

I blink several times, not sure I heard her correctly. "We're talking about a child, Kelley. That's more important than football."

She nods and says, "Yes, I know. But if you think about this from the perspective of a teenage girl, you have to see it a little differently. I'm sure her mother told her that by getting pregnant, she'd ruined her life. At that age everything is the end of the world. Life is full of always and never, black and white. There's no gray area when you're young." Her eyes lift to the ceiling, and she looks a little upset, then says, "It's horrible to say, but she probably thought it was stupid to ruin both of your lives. She probably thought it was better for her to carry this burden alone and save you from an uncertain future."

Mac whistles really low and says, "She's got a point, Mike. When you're in high school, your world is pretty small. It's hard to think about anything beyond the next weekend or exam."

"I had no problem thinking about the future," I say.

"I didn't either," Kelley says, "but I knew exactly what I wanted. I'd already been working in my chosen career. I was already a member of the dance company. You were playing football… people were already pegging you for the NFL draft."

"I was clueless," Mac said. "I didn't have a plan outside of going to college. I didn't even know what I wanted to major in until I was forced to pick something."

As I consider this, I know in my heart they're right. Rachel's only plan was to follow me to college. She didn't even care which college… she only wanted to be with me.

I sit there for a long moment, not sure what to say, but then Kelley finally asks, "How did you guys leave things? Are you going to meet her—your daughter?"

"I told her I needed time to think. I was angry, and I didn't want to say something I'd regret."

"That's smart," Mac says.

I get to my feet and say, "I should get going. I have three PT appointments tonight, and my sister called to tell me she's coming into town. She'll be here on Friday. That means I need to finish unpacking and prepare for house guests. Thanks for the talk, guys."

"I can't wait to see Diana and Olivia." Kelley reaches up and gives me a hug, and as she's holding me, she says, "Mike, just because I understand why Rachel didn't tell you about your kid, doesn't mean I think it's okay that she kept it from you all these years."

"I know, and that's what I'm having trouble with."

She smiles widely and shakes her head. "Wow… Mike. You have a daughter. That's so crazy. What's her name?"

I laugh at the question, knowing how insane it is that I didn't get my own daughter's name. Of course Diana and Kelley would both ask the one thing I couldn't answer, but should be able to answer. "I have no idea. I was too distracted with the news to ask."

Kelley lifts a brow and says, "Typical man. Call if you need anything, even just to talk."

"We're here for you if you need us," Mac says, reaching a hand out to shake mine.

"Thanks. Seriously. I'll keep you updated."

CHAPTER TWENTY-ONE

Raegan

I'm a little afraid of my mom right now—and a little impressed. She doesn't usually get mad… not like this. I mean, I've seen her angry, worried, annoyed—you name it, but I've never seen her shout at anyone, much less Uncle Mitch. She doesn't even curse, really. Once in a while, one will slip, and then she looks guilty and apologizes.

Now she's crying, and I don't know what to do, but I'm not so sure she should be driving in this condition. Good thing we don't live very far.

"Mom, what happened?"

She shakes her head and says, "Life, Raegan. Life happened, and somewhere in the middle, I got lost."

"I don't understand, but I'm sorry. Maybe you should stop and ask someone to pick us up. I can call Isla or Annie."

"I'm fine. I just…" She maneuvers the car into a parking lot and stops. Once the car is in park, she looks over at me with sad eyes. "I'm sorry. I didn't mean to scare you."

"I'm not scared… but I'm a little worried. I've never seen you like this. What did Uncle Mitch do?"

"You know, Rae, it doesn't even matter anymore." She shifts in her seat so that we're facing each other. "I'm sorry you had to hear me fight with him."

I almost laugh but then say, "Don't be sorry. I like seeing you stand up to him. I wish you did it more often."

Her brows draw together. "How much of our conversation did you hear?"

"None of it." I shrug and say, "I just heard you shouting at him that you were using your voice—and I think it's about time."

Her face softens. "I know… I'm way overdue, aren't I?"

"Yeah, Mom. Why do you let him act like you're some clueless twit?"

"I don't think he's that bad, but he does seem to believe that women are inferior to him, and I hate that." Her eyes drift around the car, then she says, "I'm enrolling you in the afterschool program next year. I don't want you going to Mitch's house every day after school any longer."

"Why?"

"Because he's *not* a good influence. He's not spending time with you, which is why we arranged for you to go there. He just sits on his computer all day muttering about politics and leaves it to Annie to take care of you. Not to mention his attitude toward women isn't healthy. I should have stopped taking you there years ago."

"But, Mom, I don't need anyone to take care of me at all."

With a deep breath, she says, "I'll look for some summer camps to keep you busy until school starts."

"No, I'm too old for summer camp, Mom. I'm too old for an afterschool program. I can stay home, though."

She rests her head back and says, "I don't know if that's a great idea either, but I'll think of something. Okay?"

"Yeah, sure, but don't arrange something without talking to me first. I should have a say too." I feel the need to point this out because she often treats me like I'm a kid who can't think for myself. As if I need a babysitter or something. "That's fair, right?"

She reaches in and hugs me. "Yes, babe. It's totally fair. I'm sorry if I haven't been giving you the respect you deserve. You're a brilliant young woman." She withdraws and lays a hand on my cheek. "You're a good girl with a good head on your shoulders, and I need to let you be more involved with what's happening in our family. I promise I will try harder to listen to you."

"Thank you, Mom." I'm trying really hard to fight the guilt I feel over my lies about Mike Murphy. I had to do something though, and I need to stand my ground about this summer camp thing, but I'm glad she's finally listening to me. "I'm sorry if I've been mean to you, but sometimes I feel like you don't see me as my own person."

"I know." Her voice comes out like a whine as she fights to keep from crying again. "God, I get it. My mom is the same with me, still. You'd think after all these years, she'd have some respect for me." She gives me a long look, then says, "Raegan, I want you to promise me that you'll always use your voice, okay? Don't let people force you to be silent. Speak out when something is wrong. Tell me if I do something I shouldn't. Being a girl doesn't mean your voice doesn't matter, okay? I want you to promise."

Her eyes are so sincere, and she really does look miserable. "I do already, Mom. At least I try."

"I wish I'd had your courage when I was young." Her brows draw together in a frown, and I feel so bad.

"Mom, you look so sad. What happened today? Just because I'm only thirteen doesn't mean you can't talk to me."

Her frown disappears, and she smiles at me, and it's a real, genuine smile. "I know, and I appreciate that. I'm not ready to talk yet, but when I am, you'll be the first person I come to."

She puts the car in gear and drives the rest of the way home. It's not until we're in the house and getting ready for dinner that I realize she could be upset over my dad. I wonder if she reached out yet. Maybe he rejected us, and that's why she's so upset, but what does that have to do with Uncle Mitch?

Just as Mom is about to start making dinner, the doorbell rings. She answers it to find a busboy from the restaurant at the hotel. He says something and hands her a bag, then he's gone.

"Who was that?"

She lifts the bag with a thankful smile on her face. "Isla asked Gerard to send us dinner so I wouldn't have to cook. Isn't that sweet?"

"Sweet is right. What did he make for us?"

She takes the first container out and lifts the lid. With a chuckle she hands it to me. "This must be yours."

I take it and revel in the smell of fresh, hot spaghetti. "Oh, God. I love his spaghetti with meatballs. Tell him thank you when you see him tomorrow."

Mom opens another container and laughs. "They know me well. How sweet…" She shows me a full-size cheesecake and I have to laugh too.

"You really did have a bad day."

With a nod, she opens the next and shows me her favorite butternut squash ravioli. "It's nice not to have to cook."

We eat in silence, mostly because I don't want to say anything to make her feel worse, but I have so many questions. I pull out my phone and check my email. Mike hasn't responded to my last email. I'm not sure why. At first, he sent back questions, but then he went silent. I know he's been busy with the opening, maybe that's why.

To: mmurphy@crossfitforlife.com
From: shouldbemurphy@email.com
Subject: A secret

Did you see my mom today? Did you get confirmation that you have a kid? I ask because she's really sad. I haven't seen her this upset in a long time. She won't tell me anything but that she had a really bad day at work. Please don't be mean to her, okay? She's never mean to anyone, and she needs you. Also, did she tell you my name?

Before I can change my mind, I hit send, then put my phone in my pocket and rub my sweaty palms on my jeans. I feel like things are changing and I'm not sure I'm ready for that. If my mom talked to Mike today, I hope he was nice to her. It's hard to imagine him being mean because he's been so nice to me every time I've met him. I'm going to feel really bad if I forced my mom to make contact with someone who mistreated her or wasn't good to her.

I didn't really think about that when I was asking about him. In the past, when she's talked about my father, she's only said positive things. Of course, I can count on one hand how many times she's mentioned him. Would she ever say anything bad? She's not the type to talk about people like that. She never even badmouths my grandma, and Grandma is horrible to her most of the time.

I quickly peek at my phone again, but there are no new alerts. I really hope Mike answers my message this time. I need to know what happened today and find out if he's the reason my mom is so unhappy.

CHAPTER TWENTY-TWO

Michael

As soon as I finish with my last personal training session for the evening, I sink down in my office chair and check my email. Oh, sure, no problem! There are only eighteen new messages since the last time I looked. I sort through the membership requests and file them so my new admin assistant can help with those tomorrow. Then I reply to emails from current members. Every new member has to complete a certain number of PT sessions before they can work out in the open gym or join the classes. I want to make sure everyone has a tailored experience. Also, I want each member's level of fitness assessed by a coach before they join classes—I don't want people to get hurt.

There's a new email from shouldbemurphy. Which is odd since it's been a couple of weeks. If this is my kid, I have to wonder if Rachel talked to her about me after what happened today and that's why she's reaching out again.

I hover over it before I click. What if this isn't my kid? She's thirteen… would she have an email yet? I don't know what level kids are on these days.

I click the email and read it.

Wow. This really is my daughter emailing me. Huh. What do you know? I read it again and feel really bad. I didn't mean to upset Rachel like that. I know I shouldn't feel guilty. I'm the one who was lied to; I haven't done anything wrong. She's the one who kept my child a secret. Of course, that doesn't make me feel any better about how upset she is, and the kid is right. She's never mean to anyone.

When we were young, I remember once calling her a doormat because people would take advantage of her, and she wouldn't do anything about it. She had an excuse ready for everyone and for every offense. She always saw the best in people.

I pick up my phone and text Rachel.

Me: *Are you okay? Should I be worried about you?*

It takes her a minute but then I get three messages in a row.

Rachel: *Fine.*

Rachel: *Why do you ask? Did I look that bad when you left today?*

Rachel: *Should I be worried about you? You're the one who got big news.*

Me: *Thought I'd check on you. I know it couldn't have been easy telling me that after all these years.*

Rachel: *Thanks for checking on me. It's actually a relief. Honestly, I'm struggling with what I've done. However, those two amazing orgasms you gave me earlier helped a great deal.*

I laugh out loud when I read this. My girl has lost some of her shyness—she never would have said the 'O' word when we were in high school. Warmth spreads through me as I remember that Rachel and I used to laugh together all the time.

Me: *It's always a good stress reliever, but I'm sure not enough to make this day easier. At least it wasn't for me.*

Rachel: *I know, I'm so sorry. If only I could go back in time—fix things.*

Me: *Honestly, Rachel, I'm not sure what to do… or think. I'm so upset with you for keeping this secret for so long. I'm not interested in holding a grudge, so if that's what you're worried about, you can stop, but I really don't know how to proceed right now.*

Rachel: *Grudge? No. I know you're not like that, at least you never used to be. I'm angry, too, at myself. I'm mad that I let this go on for so long. I've turned into a horrible person, and I'm not even sure how. I still have so much to tell you and I'd understand if you did hold a grudge. Just don't let your feelings for me keep you from having a relationship with your daughter.*

Mike: *I would never do that. I want to have a relationship with her, I just need a few days to get my bearings. That being said, you can stop being so hard on yourself.*
Rachel: *I'm HONEST with myself. What I've done is as bad as anything my mother did. I have so many regrets.*

This is Rachel to a tee. She beats herself up to the point of self-loathing. It pisses me off because it's hard to be mad at her when she's so damn hard on herself. I'd rather she fought with me. I'd rather she makes a bunch of excuses and tells me it's not her fault. It'd be so much easier to be mad at her if she didn't take full responsibility like she's doing. Fuck.

I glance at my watch and see that it's after ten p.m.

Mike: *Here's some advice from your personal trainer. Make a cup of hot, herbal tea, then get into bed and read a book. It's late, and you need some rest. The book will help you get your mind off things, and the tea will help you sleep.*

Mike: *If that doesn't work, download some porn from the internet and masturbate while thinking of me. That will always help you sleep. LOL*

Rachel: *I see you haven't lost your dirty mind. What makes you think I need porn if I'm thinking about you while I masturbate?*

"Nice," I say as I'm typing out my response.

Me: *Whatever works for you, babe.*

Rachel: *Thank you. I missed you, and even if you decide to hate me for the rest of our lives, I'll still have the memory of today.*

Me: *Goodnight, Rachel.*

Rachel: *Goodnight.*

As if I could ever hate her. Yeah, I'm pissed she didn't tell me I have a kid, but I can't let that get in the way of having a relationship with my daughter. And I can't do that if I'm harboring hate for her mother. Rachel was always the kindest person—she was so honest in school, it annoyed me sometimes. She never wanted to break the rules.

Is our daughter like Rachel was when she was young? Is she naive and trusting? Does she make excuses for people who wrong her? Hopefully, she's too young to have been wronged. Has Rachel tried to give her any street smarts at all, or has she sheltered her too much? Or is she more like me? More leery of people and less likely to trust? This thought almost makes me laugh. I've only gotten less likely to trust because of Rachel. She's made me jaded in my adult life. I don't want to be hurt again. I don't know if she'll ever understand what she's done to me, and that's outside of the lie about our kid.

I'm still so shocked. I have a daughter, and it burns me up to know that I've missed so much already. I don't know anything about this girl. She doesn't know anything about me… at least I don't think so. But she did find me, and she's obviously fiercely protective of her mother. That makes me smile. Rachel's done that much right. What is this girl going to think of me? I look down at myself, at the tattoos. Will I scare her? What kind of crowd does Rachel spend time with? What are her friends like?

The more I think about having a daughter, the more I want to know. But I also don't want to screw it up. As mad as I am at Rachel, I don't want to screw that up either… which is why I asked for time.

The anger will pass, I know that. All I can do is get through this, get on with what I need to do and right now, that's getting this gym open—and preparing for my sister to visit. With that thought, I know I need to get home and get some work done on my apartment.

CHAPTER TWENTY-THREE

Rachel

Dear Mike,

I've just arrived home from the hospital. My dad isn't doing well. The doctor says he'll only survive for a few more days. I needed a break, and some time alone. I've been there every day for weeks. I don't know how much more I can take. Watching him wither away—fighting to hang on. And for what? To be in pain? I don't understand. I told him to let go—I've begged him to let go and end his pain, but he insists he needs to be here for me. FOR ME? Jesus Christ! I'm so upset and angry at the same time. How dare he say he's hanging on for me? He's never been here for me, not really. Not without an ulterior motive and certainly not without following through with whatever cruel plan my mother had. All either of them has ever done is criticize me and tell me what a disappointment I've been.

I don't know how much more of this I can take. I'm trying to be the bigger person. I'm trying to let go of my own anger, but it's so hard!

Michael, I miss you so much. I'm not sure how to navigate this. I don't know if I want this life without you. I've tried to be a good daughter. I've tried to be a good mother. But has it ever been good enough? You and Raegan are the two most important people in my life, and I've hurt you both without even trying.

I made a mistake. I got pregnant—but I'm not sorry! I could never regret Raegan. Never! But I never meant to leave you, and I know you hate me. Why do I live in a world so cruel that I had to choose between you and our child? I hope you can forgive me someday. I hope before I'm lying on my deathbed full of regret that we meet again and you choose to forgive me.

There is nothing fun about my life right now, but I want you to know your daughter and what she's like, so here's a fun fact for you: Raegan is a straight-A student. She's smart without even trying. She must get that from you. Every day she resembles you more and more. Lately, I see your sister when I look at her. She's got long dark hair like Diana, and as she matures, she becomes softer, more girl-like. Don't worry, though, she loves sports. She's very active… like you.

I love you always!
Rachel

PS. After a three-year-long battle, my dad died this evening at ten-fourteen p.m. When I finished this letter to you, I realized what Dad needed for him to let go… and so I forgave him. With a lighter heart, I told him that I loved him and that I forgave him for everything that happened in our past. He smiled at me and told me he loved me… and that he was proud of me. Then he let go. It was one of the most precious moments of my life and one of the hardest. I can't stop crying, but I'm relieved he's out of pain.

PPS. On the bright side, my mother will now be returning to Portland. She doesn't like living in Sacramento.

CHAPTER TWENTY-FOUR

Michael

After spending my entire Friday morning processing new members and scheduling personal training sessions, I get out of my chair and go for a run. I don't go far, but I need the fresh air and sunshine. I need to stretch my legs. I'm not used to sitting at a desk for that long. When I get back, I do some more stretching and clean up from my sessions. As I'm walking back toward the office, the door opens and in comes my sister Diana. My face splits into a grin, and I hold my arms out as she approaches me. "Oh, my God, am I happy to see you!"

She jumps into my arms with her little mini-me daughter, Olivia, wrapping herself around our waists. I'm so happy she's here, I could cry. I hold on for a long time, squeezing her small frame. As my older sister, there was a time she towered over me, but since high school, I've continued to get bigger, and she somehow stopped.

"Me too," she says, slapping my back. Then she tilts away, getting a good long look of my face.

"I'm okay," I say, trying to reassure her. "Healthy, strong, I'm eating good and spending some time in the sun. Don't worry."

"It's not your physical health I'm worried about. How's your heart?" She drops back on her heels while I lift Olivia off her feet and embrace her.

"You have grown so much! What are you feeding this child?"

Olivia squeals as I squeeze her. "Ah! Uncle Miiiiike!" I set her back down and hug her again as I kiss the top of her head. I didn't realize how lonely I was until they stepped through that door.

Diana takes a long look around. "It's so nice!"

I walk over and flip all the lights on so she can see everything.

"It's bigger than Oakland, isn't it? More square footage?"

"Yes, and more outdoor area."

"I love it! I love the green!" She glances down at her daughter and says, "What do you think, Olivia?"

Olivia nods approvingly. "I like it."

I give them the full tour, hoping to keep Diana from asking me about Rachel. I know the talk is coming, but I'm still not sure how I feel about it, and so I'm avoiding the topic for now.

After the tour, Diana convinces Olivia to sit down in the kids' area and color for a while. We head to the office so I can finish up what I need to get done. The open house is next Saturday and with a full week to get everything ready, I'm a little nervous about it. I still have to confirm the caterer, the bouncy house for the kids, and the coaches' meeting I'm planning for the morning before.

Once we're out of earshot of Olivia, Diana immediately brings up the subject I was trying to avoid. "So, have you seen her yet?"

"Seen who?"

"Don't play dumb. Have you seen your daughter yet?"

I shake my head, my eyes drifting to my computer screen. "No. Not yet."

"Jesus, Michael, you found out on Monday. It's been nearly a week. What are you waiting for? Surely it's not Rachel keeping you away? She wouldn't do that after finally telling you about her."

"No, it's not Rachel. I'm just trying to process it all. I'm not sure how I feel about it."

"You're not sure how you feel about being a dad?" She rests her hand on my arm so that I'll look at her instead of working.

"What on earth are you unsure about? She's your child. Your flesh and blood, Mike."

"I know that, but just because I have a kid doesn't mean I know how to be a dad. I can't jump in with both feet. I… I'm not sure about it all yet."

"I hate to say this, but the first hard lesson in being a parent is to learn that it's no longer about you. It's about your kid. She doesn't care if you know how to be a dad. She doesn't care that you're pissed at her mother. She's gone a damn long time without you; every minute you take trying to figure out your feelings is a wasted moment you don't get to spend with her. More wasted moments, Michael." She gestures to where Olivia is playing. "Take it from a sister… a daughter, and a mother: tomorrow isn't promised so don't waste today."

I close my eyes and take a deep breath. "I know that, Diana. I'm not avoiding the issue, just giving myself time to get used to the idea."

"What are you going to do about Rachel?"

"Fuck if I know. Seriously. I don't know."

"How do you feel about her? What happened when you first saw her on Monday? What went through your head?"

"Ha! I'm not sure you want to know that." I grin widely, I can't help it. "She's incredible."

"Don't tell me you've already slept with her."

"No! Don't be stupid." *Deny, deny, deny…* it's all I can do even if my face gives it away.

"Oh my God, you did! How did that even happen?"

I laugh at her reaction even though it's not funny. The woman is like a drug, and I'm addicted. "Don't ask me if you don't want to know."

"Michael!"

I laugh again and say, "If it makes you feel any better, we did it before she told me about the kid."

She wags her finger at me and says, "I bet that news shriveled your dick right up."

"You better believe it!" I snicker and say, "Man, am I thankful she waited until after to tell me."

Diana laughs and says, "Typical guy."

"I still have some things to do today." I glance at my laptop and say, "How about I pack it up and bring it home with me? I can work later tonight, let's go get some dinner."

She nods in agreement. "And a drink… because there's something I need to tell you."

"Shit, now what?" I say, not ready for any more surprises.

She sucks air through her teeth. "Mom and Dad are coming down next week."

"You're kidding!" I stare at her, shocked. "They're coming here?"

"Mom said they wanted to be here for the grand opening… and for you."

I'm so torn about this. "That's good, I guess. I mean, yeah, that's good."

"Mom said you guys have been talking. She said you were getting along."

"We are, but they've never volunteered to visit me."

"Consider this an olive branch. And it's about time. I'm tired of fighting. I'm tired of grieving. We have so much to celebrate and be thankful for, including your daughter and the gym."

"You know Kelley's going to be here for the grand opening? Mac's bringing a crew from the station and doing a live broadcast."

"That's great press. Do you think Kelley will be okay seeing them?"

"I don't know. I hope so. I don't need any family drama on such a big day."

"I'll contact Kelley and see if I can get them all talking—get shit out in the open," she says.

"Yep—we're both going to need a drink. Let's do it." I pack up my laptop, grab the paperwork I need, then walk over to the mail slot to get today's mail. I pull everything out and among the mail is a heavy package wrapped in brown paper.

"What the hell is this?" I flip it over and read the return address. "It's from Rachel," I say as I carry it back to the office.

I sit at my desk and rip it open to find two journals… pretty old ones, too. One has a Post-it that says, *read this one first*. I flip through the pages and my mouth hangs open. I hear Diana behind me say, "Oh my God. Are those all handwritten letters?"

"Yeah, it looks like years and years' worth." I sit there in a state of shock for a long time. Then I shake my head and wrap them back up before throwing them in my messenger bag. I'm not sure what to do… I'm not sure what to think about it. It's been several days since I found her, but I'm still not sure I'm ready to face it.

CHAPTER TWENTY-FIVE

Rachel

Dear Mike,

I wish you were here. I need you. Raegan is sick, and I'm exhausted. Who knew a five-year-old could throw up so much, especially when she won't eat. I've finally gotten her to sleep, and I wanted to write you a quick note to tell you that I miss you. Of course, in times like this, I wish I had your help, but I miss you during the normal everyday stuff too.

Raegan asked me yesterday why she didn't have a daddy, and I cried. What else could I do? How do you explain this to a five-year-old? What do I say? The truth? Gee, sweetheart, I never told him about you, so he doesn't know you exist. God, Mike! I'd give anything to have you here right now, and the really shitty part is, I don't have any idea where you are. I've done a couple of searches, and I can't find any sign of you. What happened to playing football? I thought by now, you'd have a football career… be an NFL player. That's why I've done this. That's what I was protecting. I don't understand. What happened to your dream?

Fun fact: Raegan starts school in a couple of weeks. Kindergarten! Can you believe it? Also, I graduated from Sacramento State a couple of months ago. The entire day I kept wishing you were there with me.

I love you,
Rachel

CHAPTER TWENTY-SIX

Michael

I'm absolutely floored. I've read several of her letters, and each of them feels like a knife to the heart. I can see why she mailed the journals to me instead of giving them to me personally.

Every letter bleeds her pain and loneliness. Knowing Rachel like I do, it's hard to imagine her being so deceptive, but reading the letters puts it in perspective for me. I don't think sending them to me was a ploy to gain my pity. That's not the type of person Rachel is. Not the one I remember...

When Diana and Olivia come out of the bedroom, Diana gestures toward the journal in my hand. "How's it going?"

"It's not light reading, that's for sure." I hand her the first journal. When she starts reading, I feel a little weird about it. She sits down next to me and as much as I think she shouldn't be reading Rachel's personal thoughts, I need someone to talk to about this. I don't know how to process it, and her understanding might help. She's a few pages in before tears start streaming down her face.

Diana's eyes lift from the page and I can see the questions stirring there, but I also recognize sympathy. "Why didn't she try to find you earlier, Mike? I get why she didn't in the beginning, I can see why she made the choices she did, but it's been years. She's an independent person, and surely her mother's threats don't still work on her. Why did she wait so long?"

"It sounds like she tried for a while, but she was busy… She finished college, her dad retired and then got sick. She was raising a daughter on her own… it seems like she finally gave up."

Diana practically snorts. "I can relate to being busy." We both look over to where Olivia is perched in front of the TV. "I'm constantly on the go. Between all the school stuff, appointments, and work, I barely get any time to myself. Time goes fast, and it seems to speed up when you're watching your kid grow."

"I get it. I swear Olivia was three years old last week." I look back at Diana. "She was scared of what she'd find. She was afraid I'd reject her and our daughter. I'm sure she's been treading through life, trying not to think about it because she didn't want to face things."

Diana starts reading again and so do I. Every few minutes she mutters a fact that stands out. "Emergency C-section. Wow… and her mom is a complete psycho bitch."

Every single letter ends with *I love you*. In every letter, she tells me she misses me. She needs me.

"Her father died of cancer," I whisper as I read about it.

"Her name is Raegan," Diana says, glancing up at me.

I pause mid-sentence and let that sink in. Her name is Raegan… I'd read that several times, but for some reason it didn't click until I heard it said out loud. I rest back in my seat and stare at Diana. "Jesus, Diana. Raegan is my daughter." When she gives me a confused look, I say, "Shit. I've already met her. At least, I think I have. There's a young girl who's been hanging out at the gym called Raegan."

"What? That's insane."

"It's completely insane. I know! I need to go see Rachel, tell her. I'm sure she doesn't know." I rub my hand up and down my leg, feeling uneasy. "I'm not happy Raegan lied to me. I don't want to start a relationship with her on that type of foundation."

"You need to give the kid a break, Mikey. If she worked out who you were, how could she stay away?"

I pick up the first journal and continue reading where I left off before Diana joined me. I force myself to read every entry. Diana reads too, and every once in a while, I hear her sniffle. Every word is heart-wrenching, especially when I have to read about her dating some other guy… yet being too in love with me to really be able to have a relationship. It's exactly what I've been going through all these years—I've never been able to let her go.

Before I realize it, it's pitch-black outside, and Olivia is asleep on the couch. Diana gets up and carries her to bed, then returns to my side and says, "I shouldn't be reading these. Now I feel bad for invading her privacy."

I lift my tired eyes and say, "I don't know what to do now. It's hard to be mad at her, knowing what she's been through."

"Then don't. There's no rule of thumb here, Mikey. Follow your heart."

"My heart can't be trusted, Diana. My heart knows no boundaries and I'm sure I need them with Rachel. Besides that, I wasn't very nice to her when we first talked… she's gonna be totally skittish of me now."

"Read this," she says, turning the second journal toward me. "If she's skittish, this is probably why."

I grab it and glance at the date. It was written over four years ago, and it's written in a very shaky hand.

Dear Michael,

I thought I was moving on. I thought I was learning to love someone else. I thought I had you out of my system. I thought I could move on and maybe even be happy… but I can't. I'm such a fool. I'm not even sure what made me think anyone could be like you. I'm sorry. I'm sorry for making comparisons.

He'll never be you, and I'll never forgive myself for believing it was possible.

I've been seeing someone for a few months. Raegan didn't know, I didn't want her to meet him until I was sure he was a good guy. I thought I was being smart. I'm glad she's never met him, but I realize how stupid and naive I really am.

Tonight I found out who he really is and it's not the kind man I thought. He's nothing like you. He showed up at my house drunk, and I'm so glad Raegan didn't wake up—I'm so glad she didn't see! I've never felt so betrayed—so wrong about someone in my life. I can't bear to tell you – but if he ever comes near me again or my daughter, I'll kill him.

Michael, I wish so much that you were here. I need you. I miss you every day.

I love you,
Rachel

The last line, where she tells me she needs me, is so shaky I can barely read it. As I stare at the page my heart rate is rising, and my breathing hitches. Still holding the journal, I physically come out of my chair. I close my eyes and fight for calm.

"Jesus Christ. What the hell do you think he did to her?"

"I don't know, but it couldn't have been good. There's also a long gap between this one and the next letter."

I flip the page and look at the date of the next letter. It was over two years later. "When I said skittish, I didn't mean in this way. She wasn't physically shy of me. Hopefully, that means she wasn't raped."

"Or it means she trusts you even when she hasn't seen you in years."

"I need to see her." I can't fucking pretend this isn't agonizing for me—I can't pretend my feelings for Rachel are only about our daughter. "Fuck, Diana, what should I do?"

Diana tilts back in her chair and says, "Go find her and make her talk to you. She owes you that."

"She owes me time with my daughter, she doesn't owe me anything else."

"Mikey, if you still have feelings for her, you need to work through that—and you need to let her know. She's not going to make the first move, not after what she's done. She has to assume you don't want a romantic relationship with her."

I run my hands through my hair and say, "I'm not totally sure what I want with her… I know I love her but… I love the girl I knew in school, not the woman who's hidden my daughter from me for all this time."

"They're the same person." She takes the journal from me and says, "You need to reconcile that in your head before you do anything else. You can't love her and hold a grudge."

"I don't want to hold a grudge at all. Love or not."

"Mike, go see her. Make her talk to you. Really talk. You've put it off for too long. Haven't you lost enough time with her and Raegan?"

It's true. I've not only missed all these years with my daughter, but I've also missed all these years with the woman I once loved more than anything else in life. Even though I was a kid, she was my world. She hasn't been a part of my world for a long time but that doesn't mean I stopped loving her. Knowing we have a child together has only increased that love. I rub at my chest, trying to ease my aching heart. I want her, and I'm not even sure why I told Diana that I didn't know what I want. I do know. I want Rachel to want me too.

Diana crosses her arms over her chest and says, "Maybe she's scared. I can't blame her. After reading some of these letters, I don't think it'd be a reach to say it's probably been a while since she's experienced any kind of functional adult relationship. Maybe she doesn't have much experience with men."

My stomach turns just thinking about her with another man. I stare at Diana, not sure how to ask what I want to ask, but finally, I blurt it out. "Am I stupid for still having feelings for her? Is this toxic?"

"Maybe. But we can't help who we fall in love with. Right?"

I press my lips together and nod my head. "I feel like an idiot for wanting this after what she's done, but I can't help how I feel."

"That's your answer. You can't help how you feel. I'd like to give you shit and tell you you're a pansy—tell you you're a sucker for wanting her after she hurt you so badly, but I can't. I think it takes courage to move past what you've both been through."

"You think?"

"Absolutely. I think it takes a hell of a lot of backbone to put yourself in the line of fire when you've already taken a hit." She shrugs and says, "That being said, I'm not sure how much courage *she* has. You might have to do all of the fighting on your own." She taps the journal and says, "This girl is exhausted. I don't know if she has any fight left in her."

"I need her to show me she wants this too. I can't be the only one putting it all out there."

"You're missing a very fundamental fact about her—and this is never going to work if you don't try to understand it."

"Understand what, Diana?" I lift my arms in a sarcastic shrug. "If you're so smart, tell me what I'm missing."

"Essentially, Rachel is a long-term abuse victim. Think about it, Mike," she says, ticking marks off with her fingers. "She's overloaded with guilt, she's lonely, she's withdrawn, and she's afraid. She's a victim. She's forgotten how to fight. Her spirit was broken a long time ago, I'm not sure she'll ever be who she was before she got pregnant. Jesus, she probably doesn't even think she's worthy of love—much less love from you."

I think of the strong, beautiful woman I saw at the hotel, a single mother in a position of real responsibility, and that image doesn't jive with what Diana is saying. Even as upset as Rachel was on Monday, she still held her ground. She still told me what she needed to tell me and then she stood ready to defend herself if she needed to.

"She doesn't seem mentally unstable. You're making this sound really bad."

"No, it's just..." She drops her head back on her shoulders. "So hard to explain to a man."

"I'm not dense, you know. I can understand complex problems."

She laughs and says, "That's not what I mean. Women regularly deal with shit like this. We're constantly dodging abuse in one form or another. We're fucking experts at walking through life seemingly untouched by our environment. We smile through the pain and keep moving forward even when things seem impossible. Whether our bosses are trying to grab our asses or our fathers are treating us like we're idiots because we're *just girls*, or whether we're pretty enough—but not so pretty that we become targets for assault." As Diana talks, she grows more agitated and her voice is raising. "Rachel's become an expert at it, especially since her mother raised her to believe she is *just a girl*. Telling her shit like 'don't get fat because you'll never find a husband' instead of teaching her to be an independent woman who doesn't need a man to be happy."

"Did you feel that way... about Dad? Have I ever made you feel like that?"

She shakes her head. "No, you haven't, but Mom and Dad have. Why do you think they were so pissed when I got pregnant? *How was I ever going to find a man as a single mom?* As if I couldn't possibly handle having a child on my own without the support of a man."

"You're great at it though... even as unplanned as it was."

She smiles and whispers, "Thank you. It's good to hear that once in a while."

"I mean it. I'm not saying that to make you feel better." I glance at my watch and say, "Would you get pissed if I left you here alone for a while?"

She grins and says, "You do realize it's after midnight? She's probably in bed."

"I don't mind waking her up."

She waves toward the door. "I'm going to bed, so, by all means, go work out your shit, and do it quickly. I want to meet Raegan."

It's late, but I want to see them—even if it means getting them out of bed in the middle of the night. I give my sister a big hug and thank her for the talk, then I rush out the door with absolutely no plan.

CHAPTER TWENTY-SEVEN

Rachel

"What the hell is that?" I grumble, throwing my robe on. I trip in the dark and stumble around for a second before clicking my bedside lamp on. Then I hear the doorbell again. I glance at the clock as I head toward the door. Jesus! My thoughts immediately go to Raegan—something must have happened.

When I get to the door, I see the porch is lit up because of the motion sensor light. I peek out the peephole and see Mike standing out there, his eyes on the door. As if he knows I'm looking at him, he says, "It's just me. Open up."

I punch in the code to turn the alarm off then swing the door open. "What's wrong? Has something happened?"

"No, everything's fine, but I want to talk," he says as he steps inside.

He rushes past me before I've registered what he said. Not only am I half asleep, but I'm struck dumb by how beautiful he is. Dressed in all black, his hair styled into a neat faux hawk, he's the most glorious thing I've ever seen… and he's standing in my living room.

I'm trying to wake up. Get my damn wits about me. "I'm sorry?" I say, still a little stunned by his presence in my home, and my heart is still racing from waking so abruptly.

"I'm sorry for barging in but we need to talk. Is Raegan in bed?"

"She's not here. She's spending the night with her friend Maisie. How did you find me?"

"You sent me the journals and your return address was on the package."

I shake my head. "Right, sorry, I'm still half asleep."

"Are you awake enough to talk? There're so many things we need to clear the air about—and it's probably a good thing that Raegan isn't here." He's looking around, his eyes drifting from one thing to another, trying to make things out in the dark. I reach over and click the lamp on, making him squint. Even as distracted as he is, he keeps talking as if he knows exactly what he's doing. "Because, after a long talk with my sister, I've decided clearing the air is definitely something we need to do." He points to a photo on the mantle and says, "Where was this taken?"

I peek around him to see which photo he's talking about. "That was taken on a hike with Rae. We were in the Santa Cruz Mountains." I quickly scan the room to make sure it's tidy enough. I wasn't exactly expecting company. Thankfully, everything's in its place. "I'm sorry, but what do you want to talk about in the middle of the night?"

He glances at me over his shoulder. "Rae? Is that what you call her?"

"Yeah, sometimes."

He points to the photo again. "I used to live there," he says, ignoring my question. He moves onto the next photo. "Give me a tour. I want to see your space."

"Um, okay. This is the living room." I lift my arms to indicate the room we're standing in. "You used to live in the Santa Cruz Mountains?"

He wanders over to the bookcase and examines the rows of books and then the photos propped on top, spending time on each one. "No, Santa Cruz. That's where I trained to be a CrossFit coach."

"Oh, okay." I follow him as he heads into the dining room and I realize I'm not so much giving him a tour but following him around. "Dining room," I say, clicking the light on. "Not much to see here."

"Do you ever sit in here?"

The question almost makes me laugh. The dining room table seats six, and as I answer his question, I realize the entire room is a little ridiculous for a family of two. "No, never. We eat in the kitchen." As I say this, Mike turns to look at me. I'm not sure what prompted it, maybe my chuckle at his question, but he looks me up and down. That's when I realize I'm wearing a very thin nightdress and my short robe is thrown over it haphazardly. I glance down at myself and close the robe before tying it tightly. His gaze lingers for a long moment, then he heads into the kitchen.

"Wow, great space. I bet it gets great light. You've recently had it remodeled?"

"Yeah, last year."

He stops and looks over the photos on the fridge. "It's funny... when I met Raegan, I didn't see the resemblance, but now it's hard to miss. She actually looks a lot like Olivia."

"When you met Raegan...? But you haven't met her."

"I have. I didn't realize who she was until I started reading your letters. She's been visiting the gym. I even received a few emails from her. Last week, she brought me a consent form to join the gym. Who's Mitchell Crawford?"

Now fully awake, I try to take in what he's telling me and I'm so stunned my heart is lodged in my throat. "Mitchell is my uncle."

As if sensing my confusion, he says, "Raegan wanted to join the gym. Rachel, she's been coming around for a couple of weeks. She hangs out, even helped me and my partner Gavin paint one day."

"Join the gym? How was she going to do that without telling me?"

"For starters, she got the form signed by your uncle. She also told me she didn't think her mom would pay the dues, but I wasn't worried about that. I told her if she helped me out with some things, I'd waive the fee."

"You said she's emailed you?" I clear my throat, and feel the blood drain from my face at the thought of Raegan doing this without telling me. "How? I mean, what has she said?"

Mike takes out his phone and brings up an email. "I thought it was a joke. I thought one of my friends was playing a prank on me. I didn't make the connection until after I left the hotel on Monday." He scrolls over the email chain and says, "Looking at it now, I can see that she stopped emailing me when she started coming to the gym... at least until Monday." He stops on the last email in the chain. "Look at the last email. She's the reason I texted on Monday night to check on you."

I read it and instantly choke up. "She's been worried about me since I came home upset. Considering she's barely spoken to me in the last two weeks, I was happy to get the attention."

"Why wasn't she speaking to you?"

"One day, out of the blue, she asked about you." I lower my eyes, now ashamed of my reaction to Raegan on that day. "I told her to leave it alone. It'd been so long... I tried before to find you with no luck. I didn't think trying to find you again was a good idea. I was afraid you'd reject her, and I didn't want her to get hurt."

"Why would you think that?" He steps toward me, eyes blazing. "Why would I reject her?"

"Mike, I didn't know. When she brought it up, I wasn't prepared to answer questions about you. I didn't know where you were, I didn't know if you were single or married, I didn't know if you had other children, I didn't know how you felt about me after the way I left. I had no idea, and I was trying to—I don't know—be realistic about your reaction... and I needed to buy time. I needed to prepare myself for the search and for facing you."

"And when did you start looking for me?"

"The evening Raegan confronted me about you, I told her I would find you and see if you were ready to meet her, but I didn't give her your name. That same night I did a search online, and it led me to the news about the new CrossFit gym... and you."

"I guess she took it upon herself to find me before that. How on earth did she do that on her own? Jesus, Rachel, I met her over three weeks ago, she must have already known when she asked you about me."

"She's a smart girl... I'm not sure how she could have gotten your name, unless she's been snooping through my stuff." I laugh sardonically. "I'm so stupid for underestimating her. I wish she'd have told me."

Mike rests back against the counter and crosses his arms over his chest. God, he looks amazing. His toned and tanned arms flex as he considers what I've said. "I think we need to confront her about this together."

My eyes drift to the ceiling in an effort not to stare. I sigh and think about what Raegan's done and how I drove her to it. It kills me to think about everything I've done to protect her—only to force her to make choices like this. It scares the crap out of me that she made contact with a strange man without mentioning anything to me. "I'm supposed to pick her up tomorrow after work. She'll be at her friend's until then. Do you want to come over after we're home? We can have dinner together."

"Tomorrow is Saturday. You're working?"

"Yeah, we've got a big wedding booked. I need to be there to help Isla."

Mike watches me for a long time, as if trying to decide how to proceed. "Yeah, let's do that. I'll bring dinner. We need to talk about this. I understand why she did what she did, but I don't like how she went about it. She should have been open and honest with you at least."

After we agree, he starts looking around the kitchen again. I'm not sure how to act with him there. Now that we've worked that out, he's gone quiet and so have I. I try to break the silence by asking about his sister. "You mentioned Diana. Does she live in town?"

"No, she lives in San Diego, she's here with her daughter for the opening of the gym."

"I guess her daughter is Olivia?"

"Yeah, didn't I say that?"

"No, you just said Rae looks like Olivia." When he doesn't respond, I say, "Won't Diana be upset you took off on her? I'm sure she wants to spend time with you."

"No, hell, she's in bed." He goes back to examining the items on the fridge again and says, "Are you trying to get rid of me?"

"No! God, no, I… I'm sure she's angry with me, knowing what's happened between us."

"Diana? She's not angry with you." He points to Raegan's most recent report card. "She gets good grades."

"Always. She's very smart, and she works hard."

He nods at that and then gestures around the kitchen and says, "Do you cook?"

"I do. I enjoy cooking. Are you hungry?"

He grins, and his eyes crease, making my heart skip a beat. "No, but thank you." He points to the kitchen nook and says, "This is where you guys eat?"

The bottle of wine I emptied when I got home is sitting there next to a single glass. "Yes. We probably spend most of our time here."

"Wine drinker, huh?"

"Yeah, well, we all medicate in our own way, right?"

This makes him chuckle, and his entire face brightens with it. "Very true. Do you have another bottle?"

"You want a drink?" I ask with raised eyebrows. "I have some whiskey too if you'd prefer that."

"Whiskey?" Approval washes over his expression.

"Bulleit Bourbon okay with you?"

"Sounds good." He turns to inspect more of the kitchen. "I run."

I lift the bottle from the cabinet and grab a couple of glasses, and then realize my robe has slid open again. I pour us each a short glass then tie it back into place with a glance at Mike. He's watching me, his eyes traveling the length of me. It makes me feel as if I'm wearing nothing at all. The heat in his eyes when they lift to mine is hard to ignore. "You run? What do you mean?" I ask, handing him a glass, trying to break the tension.

"That's how I medicate. I started after you left. It was the only way to clear my head."

Ouch. The smile slips from my face. As happy as I am that we're talking, sometimes his words cut. But at least we're not fighting. I'm not sure why I expect everything to be a fight with him. When did I turn him into a combative person in my mind? His anger is more than understandable. I take a sip of the whiskey and let the heat of it slide down my throat. Then another sip in the hope that it will calm my nerves a little.

Mike looks over his glass at me. "What next? Can I see Raegan's room?"

"Of course," I say, leading the way. "Just don't tell her we were in there."

He follows me into the hall, and I creak open her bedroom door. I hit the light switch, and I'm relieved to see it's not too messy. It looks lived-in, but not terribly bad. Her room is painted blue and trimmed in white with white plantation shutters covering her window. She's got a mix of motivational posters, Marvel Comics posters, and some printed nerdy memes from the internet.

Her laptop is still sitting on her bed where she left it, and the shelves above her desk display the few trophies she's earned in soccer. She's also got a couple of swimming medals and a spelling bee trophy from a regional win a few years ago. Hanging next to the shelves is a framed photo of her with the Sacramento Kings basketball team and a rack holding all the belts she's earned in Taekwondo.

He points to the trophies. "She likes sports?"

"She does. She played soccer for years, and she loves basketball and baseball too."

"Any boyfriends yet?"

"Don't even say that—Jesus, the universe might hear you!"

He laughs and says, "You were thirteen when I met you."

The sound of his laughter makes me smile. "Yeah, I know, but we were friends first."

He steps closer. "Best friends. Right?"

"Yes, we got close very quickly. I always felt a connection, even at that age."

"That's what hurt… when you left. I lost my best friend." He says it quietly but I have no trouble hearing him.

"I know, I'm sorry. I… ah… lost a lot too, but I know it doesn't compare."

"It does…" he says. "With the exception of Raegan, it does compare. You don't have to pretend it wasn't hard. You don't have to hide your hurt and your regret because you think it's less than mine."

I meet his eyes and say, "Thank you, but you don't have to say that."

"I'm saying it because I mean it." He gestures around the room and says, "Show me more."

I nod and turn out of Raegan's room. I move toward the hall and point to rooms. "Bathroom, closet. This is my guestroom and office combined."

He pokes his head in and says, "How often do you have guests?"

"Um… not very often, actually."

"What next?" he asks. "Show me your room."

I nod and lead him further down the hall. My door is open, so I step inside. It's obvious I was in bed when he knocked. The blankets are thrown back haphazardly and the small lamp on my bedside table is on. Mike walks inside and looks around, as if trying to get familiar with everything. I'm suddenly very self-conscious to have him there, and that makes me start talking randomly.

"I didn't tell Rae about last Monday, but she must have figured it out when I came home upset." I smile and say, "I can't believe she told you not to be mean to me."

"She loves you, and she cares. It's hard to see people you love in pain." He meets my eyes and says, "I'm sorry you've gone through so much and that you had to do it alone."

"Michael, you're apologizing? It's my fault. I did this to you, not the other way around."

"I know it's easy for you to take the blame. You're that kind of person. You've always wanted to carry the burden for everyone, and as much as I want to rage at you, I know you never would have kept this from me by choice—not without a good reason. I believe that."

"I wanted you to read those letters so you could get to know your daughter, not to gain your pity or to obtain forgiveness I'm not entitled to. You have every right to hate me."

"Rachel, you have to know, I could never hate you."

I purse my lips and say, "Right, I know that. Hate might be harsh for you. I understand."

"What do you want from me, Rachel?" He stares for a moment and I stare back at him. The tattoos, black jeans and his dark t-shirt make him look brooding, almost menacing, but it's a complete contrast to who he really is. I know this man's soul. He's sweet, caring, and full of light. "What do *you* want?"

It takes me a moment to comprehend what he's asking. When I do, my answer is easy—immediate. "I want my daughter to have a father. I took that away from her a long time ago, and I need to right that wrong. I want you to get to know your daughter. I owe you that."

"And for yourself? What do you want for yourself?"

"I... ah, want..." My gaze drifts and I'm quiet for a long time, not sure what to say. What I want is so far out of reach. It's not something I've even thought about, not in years. Isn't that what all moms do... give up their own desires to satisfy their child's? "I just want everything out in the open."

"That's all, huh?"

"I want you and Raegan to have each other, and I want you both to be happy. What's wrong with that?"

"Why do you insist on being a martyr?"

"I'm not a martyr, Mike. Do you think I'm faking this for your pity? I'm not trying to burn on a cross here. I want to right a wrong." I shift my weight, trying not to be uncomfortable with the fact that we're having this conversation in my bedroom in the middle of the night—me in my nightdress, him fully dressed. I've never had a man in here, but Mike's not just any man. "I honestly don't know what you want me to say."

He lifts his hand then lets it fall, and I can see he's a little frustrated now. He walks around for a moment, looking at things, giving me the chance to take in every little nuance of his body and the way he moves. He's like a wild animal stalking inside a cage. Every inch of him is covered in taut muscles, all of them flexing slightly when he moves. I watch as he tucks his hands in the pockets of well-fitting jeans. I'm watching him so closely, I'm surprised when he asks, "Have you always lived alone with Raegan?"

"Yes... well, I lived in my dad's guest house through school, and once I got my full-time job at The Sutter, I moved into an apartment. After a couple of years, I was able to buy this place. It's been perfect for the two of us."

"No live-in boyfriends?"

"No!" I say, almost defensive. I think about the question for a long moment, and that's when I realize what he's really asking.

"I've had a couple of relationships. I was with someone in college for about a year, but when we graduated, he moved away."

"Who else?"

"I dated someone a few years ago… it didn't work out."

"Why?"

"What do you mean? Why what? Do you really want to talk about the guys I've dated?" I'm a little irritated by the twenty questions, and now I feel like I need to be on defense. "It just didn't. He wasn't right for Raegan and me."

"How long did it last?"

I think about that before answering, and I'm wondering how many of my letters he had time to read, and how much I actually wrote about. "A few months, not very long. But, again, why do you want to know this?"

He shrugs and says, "I guess I want to make sure you're okay. That you've been okay…"

"I've been fine." As I say this, I can't stop my gaze from lowering to the floor, easily giving away my lie. He's veering into territory I'm not ready to talk about and I wish he'd stop.

He walks over and looks between the slats in the blinds to see the backyard. "Nice pool. I could picture Raegan out there swimming."

My irritation immediately fades into relief. "She's had many backyard birthday parties and playdates out there."

Mike nods, then he turns to face me. "I've missed a lot, you know that… But what you don't seem to understand is how much I missed *you*."

I keep my eyes locked on his, mostly because his honesty takes me by surprise, but I won't shy away from him, not now, not when I see such heart-rending tenderness in his gaze. A tenderness that strips me of all my defenses.

"I carried you with me every day," I whisper. "You're a permanent part of me. It's hard to get involved with someone else when you know where you're supposed to be." I take a deep breath, fighting the emotions that want to surface. "I *knew* you were the only man I'd ever love." Even as I say this, my body feels like a live wire being near him. I've never gotten a sexual buzz from anyone else like I do from Mike. I've never felt any sense of belonging with anyone but him. "For years, I've felt like the world kept turning around me while I stood still."

He approaches me, getting close. "You were never far from my mind, Rachel. Sometimes I was mad, other times, I just missed you."

"I'm sorry…"

"I'm not trying to make you feel bad, I want to make sure you understand how I feel, and I want to know everything I've missed over the years."

"I want you to know too, that's why I wrote the letters. I'll answer any questions you have."

"The second guy? Did he hurt you?"

I go rigid at the question. Did he do that on purpose? Tell me all that to get me to drop my guard? Now my pulse is jumping erratically. "Mike, I meant I'd answer any questions about Raegan."

"But not about you?"

I close my eyes for a long time, trying to focus on my breathing. I try to center myself, get my wits and prepare to face him with the truth, but I'm not ready. When I open my eyes, he's closer.

"Do you have any idea how beautiful you are?" He's so close, I'm almost afraid to respond. I'm not sure my words would be coherent. "Do you have any idea what kind of effect you have on me?" he asks.

This almost makes me laugh. I huff out a little breath and say, "Do you have any idea what kind of effect you have on me?" I whisper.

"No, why don't you tell me."

"It's been a long time." I close my eyes again because I want to be honest, but I'm so afraid. "I'd given up… given up on

relationships, on men, on the idea of ever being touched again…
but then you were there. Right there in that hotel suite, making
me feel things I thought I'd never feel again."

"I know we need to talk, and I want to finish this, but right
now, I want *you*, Rachel, and I'm not sure how much longer I can
keep my hands off you."

I meet his eyes and he's so close, I can feel the heat from his
body and it's as if he's slowly waking mine up. I'm tingling from
head to toe, my breath is quivering, and my heart is pounding.
I'm so unsure of my own voice that all I can do is nod.

When I do, he lifts his hand and slowly swipes my hair from
my shoulder. A moment later, I feel his gentle touch along my
collarbone. "I want to feel the rush I've only ever felt with you…
I want to experience you again and remember why I've never felt
this with anyone else." Then his finger grazes my throat before
traveling along my bottom lip. "And I want to strip you naked and
remind you why you've never felt like this with anyone else too."

His words send an instant jolt of heat through me. His eyes are
smoldering, burning into me as he tucks a strand of hair behind
my ear. "Is that okay?"

I wet my lips and say, "Yes." The word gets lost when he kisses
me, his hand cupping the back of my head and bringing me closer.
He tastes like the whiskey, his mouth hot and demanding. Oh,
God, it's all I've ever wanted.

"Rachel," he moans as his lips slide across my jawbone. "I never
stopped wanting you, not for a minute."

"You can have me, Michael. You already own every inch of me,
all you need to do is take it."

He unties my robe, then pushes it off my shoulders, roaming
deliberately, teasingly over my nightdress. He slides his hands up
my body, then cups my face as he kisses me, his movements gentle
yet torturous. When he lifts the straps of my nightdress away, his
lips land on the curve of my neck, then my collarbone. The heat

of his tongue, then the graze of his teeth torments me ruthlessly. A moment later, his hands are under the fabric and slowly gliding up my back.

Every inch of me is sensitive to him, my nerves exposed as he explores. When he lifts my nightdress and tugs it over my head, goosebumps rise on my skin from the contrast of his hot mouth traveling down my shoulder. I lean back and grip the dresser behind me, holding on for dear life. My knees want to buckle, and it's all I can do to keep from sinking to the floor.

He touches my breasts, palming them, pressing hard, but not hard enough to satisfy. I remember how much Mike loved my breasts. They're larger than average, and that fascinated him when we were teenagers. Going through my pregnancy and having Raegan has only made them fuller and, from the glow in his eyes, he doesn't mind.

"Fuck… your body is incredible, Rachel."

I almost want to laugh at that. I've only gotten wider since we were in school. Hearing something like that from someone with a perfect body like his is crazy. Mike's hands slide down and over my hips, gripping them and holding me tightly against him. His erection is hard, pressing into my stomach, and I want it. I want it in my hand, my mouth, my body.

I push on his hips slightly so I can unbutton his jeans, and as I reach my hand between us, I hear another moan. Mike's mouth is locked on my right breast, and I can feel the nip of his teeth. When my hand wraps around his cock, he bites down, causing a squeak from me.

"Sorry," he mumbles, licking away the pain, but as I rub up and down his length, he sucks harder, then he switches. It feels so good, even when he's rough. Having his hands on me is a dream come true. It's every fantasy I've had for fourteen years finally coming true.

I tug my hand free and push on his jeans—I need them out of the way, I need all of the clothes out of the way. As if sensing my urgency, Mike removes his shirt then kicks his jeans the rest of the way off.

Staring at him, I can't help but lick my lips. He's so cut, with the perfect V leading to his very large, erect cock. He cups my face again, and then he whispers, "What do you want, baby?"

I look up into his eyes, and they're nearly black with desire. "Michael, I want you. You're all I've ever wanted." The words come out on a moan, and it's all I can do to keep the tears at bay. It's true. Having him in my bedroom is all I've ever wanted.

He runs his hands through my hair and fists a handful, kissing me hard. I wrap myself around him and explore the feel of his skin. He's warm to the touch and solid rock, but soft, smooth. I run my hands down and around the curve of his ass, and it's perfect. Then I slide around and grip his length.

Mike pulls his mouth from mine, and our eyes meet. I lower myself to the floor in front of him and with his hands still fisted in my hair, I lick the tip of his cock and draw it into my mouth. I've only ever done this with him, and I remember the first time like yesterday.

I remember how powerful I felt, bringing him to climax with just my mouth. It's one of my favorite memories. Having gone through so much of my life feeling helpless and out of control, that little act gave me more of a confidence boost than anything else ever could.

As I slide my tongue up and down, then bring him into my mouth, his grip on my hair tightens. He tastes deliciously manly, and clean. And as I grip the base of his cock and move him in and out of my mouth, I feel him tense up. Then he slides from my mouth, panting as he lifts me to my feet. "You have to stop. Jesus, you have to stop before I lose it."

"That was part of my plan," I mumble, bringing my lips to his chest. I suck on his nipple and graze it with my teeth like he did mine. Exploring the hills and valleys of his body, I find every inch is firm yet smooth. The planks of his chest and abs are so defined, I can feel the bulge of every muscle.

"But it's not part of *my* plan," he says, lifting me off my feet so that I can wrap my legs around his hips. When he sets me down on the bed, I scoot back to make room for him, but he doesn't lay next to me, he hovers over me, and he's big. So much bigger than I remember. I run my hands over his chest and with the light of the small bedside lamp, I can see the ink and the definition of every inch of him. "You're so beautiful, Michael."

Our eyes are locked again, and it's as if I can see the intense feelings swimming around his mind as he watches me. "*You* are so beautiful… I can't believe I'm here with you," he whispers. "It's been so long. I'd given up on ever having this with you again."

I know exactly how he feels. My mind is reeling too. "I don't want to screw this up again."

"Would making love to you right now screw it up?" he asks in a husky voice.

"No!" I say, a little louder than I meant to. "*Not* making love to me might do some damage, though."

I love the way his eyes crinkle when he smiles. I bring my hand to his face and run my finger over all the edges. "You're older and larger than I remember, but you're still you… You're still the boy I fell in love with all those years ago. You're still the boy who gave me my greatest gift."

"You've changed too. More amazing and more beautiful." He grips my hip and says, "You're sexy as fuck too. More womanly and softer. Incredible, Rachel."

"Fatter."

"No." He reaches up and pushes the hair off my face and says, "And don't say that. You're perfect… with perfect curves that I can't wait to explore." As he says this, he lowers his mouth to mine, then kisses his way down, his hands roaming every inch of my body, getting reacquainted with every nuance. His movements are slow and methodical, almost torturous as they roam my breasts, then my hips before gliding down my thighs. I try to close my eyes and enjoy the sensation, but I'm afraid if I take my eyes off him, he'll disappear. When his lips land on my hip, a quiet moan escapes.

When his hands slide under my ass, he lifts me slightly closer so that his lips hover over my C-section scar. He caresses the scar with a gentle finger as he follows it along my lower abs. "I'm sorry I wasn't there for you. I'm sorry you had to go through it without me."

I'm about to protest his apology when his hot tongue swipes inside me. His words fade, and the only thing left is the feel of him. Now I have to close my eyes, I can't help it. I lift my hips higher, enjoying the sensation. Enjoying the feel of his hand braced on my stomach as his tongue enters me again. My hips jerk hard, involuntarily, and that urges him on.

Heat rises inside me, and I feel the all-over body blush as it does. Sweat builds along my forehead and between my breasts. I'm teetering on an edge, and as Mike's tongue moves inside me, my core tightens. He's got one arm curved under my thigh with a hand clamped on my hip, and the other hand splayed on my stomach. I'm surprised by his strength. He holds me in place, not allowing my hips to move with him, and that's all it takes for me to completely lose control.

"Michael!" I fight not to scream, but in spite of that, I'm much louder than I wanted to be. His hand lowers down my abdomen, and with the perfect amount of pressure, his thumb presses my clit. At the same time, his tongue moves inside me again. His expert manipulation sets me on fire and I let that fire burn until I'm dust.

CHAPTER TWENTY-EIGHT

Michael

All I want is to drive inside her before she finishes, but I'm trying to take it slowly. I'm trying to enjoy her, not *wham bam thank you* like before in that hotel suite. I shouldn't have done that, and not at her work, but it was impossible to keep my hands off her.

This time, I want to experience every little inch of this luscious body, and I want her crying my name, like she just did, only I want to hear it repeatedly. When she's settled and the writhing stops, I lift up and watch her eyes flutter open, waiting for her to get her bearings. Fuck, she's sexy. When our eyes meet, her sated look kills me. She smiles like the cat that got the cream, and I wonder what she's thinking.

As if pulling the thoughts from my head, she says, "I was planning to blow your mind, not the other way around."

"You are about to blow my mind, babe. Sinking into you has been a constant need for the last fourteen years. I'm not going to delay for another second." I line my cock with her opening and slide inside her, and as I do, her eyes flutter in complete bliss. I feel it too, the absolute satisfaction I've been searching for. The feeling only she can give me. I'm struck with a strong desire to put another baby inside her and watch her grow with life—something I missed before. And *fuck, where did that thought come from?*

I lift then sink again, and Rachel lifts too, meeting me thrust for thrust. Her eyes drift open again, and I stare into them, the blue so bright after her orgasm. I lean in and kiss those perfect swollen lips and feel my balls tighten. I'm not ready. I'm not done getting my fill so I hold off. The longer I'm inside her, the longer I want to be there.

I sit back on my knees and lift her ass so she's in my lap, then I bend her knees. This puts me deeper, tighter inside her, and I can see it in her wide eyes. Her huge breasts are bouncing and watching them sway pushes me further. Rachel's close, I can see it in her stormy expression, and as I drive inside her, with our eyes locked, I know I can't hold off much longer.

I grab her thighs and pound more feverishly. When her hands seek me out, I release her legs and lean forward until she's wrapped around me, her nails digging in as she clamps down. Her cries are so fucking hot, I can't wait another second. I'm losing control and thrusting every ounce of strength I have inside her.

"Rachel, oh God, baby, oh God!"

After one last thrust, my entire body tenses, then relaxes as I collapse on top of her. Empty... yet full. My heart wants to pump out of my chest and a solid lump forms in my throat. *What the fuck is wrong with me?* I shift to my side, bringing her with me. Holding on for dear life. Holding on to my life. The life that was stolen from me all those years ago. The family that was stolen from me.

I knock on her front door, but there's no answer. The drapes are closed, and Mrs. Williams never leaves the drapes closed unless they're in bed or out of town. I glance down at my watch. Rachel wasn't at school today, and none of her other friends have heard from her either.

I asked Carly to call the house and ask for her. I know Mrs. Williams would be less weird about a girl calling than she would with me. For some reason, she doesn't like Rachel and I seeing each other. Not that I give a shit that she doesn't like me, but she's always giving Rachel a hard time about it.

Where the hell could they be? I stare at my watch. Four o'clock… Could she have gone out of town without telling me? Not likely. Even if her mother was being a complete bitch, Rachel would have found a way to contact me. She always did.

I walk back to my car and wait. I'm parked on the street about thirty yards away. I can watch from here. When I see them come home, I'll feel better. I can't help this ache I have in my chest. Like something's wrong. Even if I can't spend any time with her today, at least I'll know she's home and all right.

Hours later and they're still not home. It's nearly midnight, and I already know my mom's going to flip the fuck out when I get home. Jesus, Rachel, where are you?

I start the car and head home, fear gripping my insides like a vice.

When my heart stops hammering, I release my grip slightly and lean back to see her face. I have so many feelings rushing through me as I stare at her. Her eyes are swimming with emotions too, the blue looking like the dark sea.

"Rachel, I love you. Do you know that?"

She nods, causing a tear to slip out. "I love you, too—I never stopped."

"I need you to know… fuck." I stop for a moment and rest my forehead against hers. "I need you to know that if you hurt me again, it's going to destroy me."

"I will never hurt you," her voice cracks as she says this. "What I did, leaving like that, it nearly destroyed me too, Michael. Nothing was ever the same no matter how hard I tried to get past it, get past you, I just couldn't."

I lay a long hard kiss on her lips and say, "Good." I withdraw and meet her eyes again. "I'm sorry you were hurt, but Christ, I'm so happy I'm not some shmuck who's been pining for a girl who never gave him a second thought after leaving town."

"Oh God, no! I've thought about you every single day. I've watched our daughter grow to be more like you and it's been so rewarding, yet so heartbreaking at the same time."

"Rachel, there's something else I need to ask."

"I told you to ask me anything."

"I'm sure this is the last thing you want to talk about, but there's something I need to know."

Her nose crinkles, and she looks confused. "What is it?"

"Something happened. Someone did something to you... I want to know what he did and who he is."

It takes a moment, and then recognition flashes in her eyes. She shakes free of my grip and lifts up. "What are you asking me—and why now?"

"I want to know everything I missed."

Her face has gone hard, and her eyes frosty. Maybe I should have waited, but it's nagging me, and I need to know what she's been through. She crawls under the blankets and brings them up to cover herself. "No... Jesus... did I really write about that to you?"

"Yes. It was vague, but you wrote a letter about it."

"I shouldn't have done that. I don't remember doing it."

"Tell me what happened."

"No, I—no. I'm not talking about that, and you shouldn't want to either."

"Rachel, you shared so much of your life with me in those letters. Please don't hold back now. I told you I'm going to want to hear every story. The last fourteen years are a puzzle to me. I need all the pieces if I'm going to understand why it took you so long to find me and tell me about Raegan." I pull the blankets away so she'll look at me.

She shakes her head and closes her eyes. After a long moment, she says, "That's not fair."

"Nothing about this situation is fair."

"This isn't something I want to share with you."

"Okay, can I ask why you don't want to share this with me? What about this is different to anything else you've written in those journals?"

She ducks her head forward and lifts the blankets up over her face again. A moment later, I feel her shudder, and I know she's crying. "Babe, why is this different?" I drag the blankets back down and with my finger under her chin, I force her to look at me. Her watery eyes are so sad, and I can barely stand to look into them, but I need to know.

"I don't want you to see me differently. If I tell you this, things won't be the same."

"Rach, there isn't anything you can tell me that would change how I feel. Jesus Christ, you kept my daughter a secret, what could be worse than that?"

She looks stricken after I say this, and that makes me instantly regret it. "I'm sorry. Look, I'm not trying to use Raegan as a weapon, but—"

"But you are!"

I cup her face, wishing like hell I'd thought this through before bringing it up. "I'm sorry, babe. I just want to understand what you've been through." When her eyes focus on me again, I say, "In your letter, you said he showed up at your house drunk and that you were glad Raegan didn't hear… then it was two full years before you wrote another letter. What did he do to you?"

She shakes free of my grip and sits back up. Then she wipes her face clean of her tears. "I don't want to talk about this. Not now, not here… not like this."

"Why does here and now make a difference? Because we're in bed? Or because you don't want to think about it when you're with me?" She tries to get out of bed, but I hold onto her. "Please, Rach... if you trust me, you'll confide in me." I reach out to touch her face and say, "I'm struggling with the fact that I wasn't here to protect you... please tell me what happened."

"You really want to know?"

"I really want to know."

She looks me dead in the eye and says, "He raped me." Her voice is hard, and she lifts her chin as she says it. That's when I realize what's happening inside her head. She's ashamed, even though she knows she shouldn't be. I think about everything Diana said. Having to muscle through life with a smile pretending things are good, even when they're not good. Fighting through the pain. That's what's happening here. She knows she's not responsible in her head, but in her heart, she feels like she deserved it.

"I'm sorry..." I don't know what else to say. I want to kill someone, but I don't want her to see a severe reaction. I told her I wouldn't see her differently—and I'll do whatever is necessary to avoid that. "I'm sorry that happened, and I'm sorry I wasn't here to protect you."

Tears start falling from her eyes again and as she looks away from me, she says, "I'm fine. I got through it."

"How?"

"Therapy... lots and lots of therapy."

"Is he in jail?"

Her head whips around to look at me. "Why are you asking that?"

"Because if he isn't, I want to look the guy up. Pay him a visit."

"No... and no. I didn't report it."

"Rachel, that asshole is still walking the streets."

"Don't do that. Don't act like it's my duty to turn him in—you don't know, Mike." Her voice pitches and she tries again to get some distance from me. This time I move away. I don't want her to feel trapped. "Don't lay that guilt at my feet. You'll never know what that was like for me. I had a security system installed on my house, and I learned how to defend myself. I made sure Raegan knows how to defend herself, too. I have to be accountable to myself and Raegan… I don't have to be accountable to the rest of the world."

"Does anyone know? Your parents? Raegan?"

When I ask this, she shakes her head vehemently. "No. Nobody knows." She nudges a hand at me. "You know… my therapist knows. That's it."

"You had to go through that alone? What about your friends?"

"I've never told anyone outside of therapy, just you."

"It wasn't your fault… you understand that, right?"

"I should have fought harder, but I couldn't do anything," she says. "I couldn't do anything to stop him… he was so strong… and I couldn't wake Raegan." She wraps her arms tightly around herself and says, "I hate that. It's pathetic, and it makes me sick… and for a very long time, I couldn't even look in the mirror."

"Still wasn't your fault, Rachel."

She nods, causing more tears. "I know that now." It comes out in a small whisper, and I feel bad for making her tell me, but I'm also so glad she shared it with me.

"You're so strong, do you know that? God, Rachel, you're raising this amazing kid on your own and running that beautiful hotel… you've been rocking life without me."

Her eyes cut to me when I say this, then she shakes her head. "No. I'm a mess, Michael. I never wanted any of this without you." Her beautiful lips turn into a frown, and she says, "After that day, I gave up any thought of finding you. That's why I stopped searching. I knew I'd never be the same person you fell in love with. I knew I'd never have the courage to share this with you. I felt you'd lose all respect for me when you found out. I…" Her lips quiver and it takes her a moment, but then she says, "…let it happen… that I let that happen a room away from our sleeping child."

"Rachel, my God. Baby, you've been carrying this around with you for all this time?"

She nods, more tears dropping from her lids. "I've been on antidepressants for four years… if it wasn't for Raegan, I'd…"

"You'd what?" I say, afraid of the answer.

"I don't know," she says. "I'm not sure I would've survived it without her, and she doesn't even know what happened."

I draw her against me and hold her close for a long time. I'm not sure how to even digest what she's told me. "I'm so sorry you went through that, but, babe, you have to stop. You have to let it go. I'd never, ever blame you for such a thing. Jesus Christ, if you'd have fought harder, tried to get away, he could have really hurt you *and* Raegan."

"I know that… I do." She buries her face in my chest and says, "You're the first person to touch me since then."

"Why did you allow me to touch you, Rachel? Didn't I scare you… in that dark hotel suite?" *Jesus, I want to kick myself for being so rough with her. What an ass.*

She squeezes me tighter. "Of course not. I've never been afraid of you. I never thought you'd hurt me. Honestly, it never crossed my mind to pull away from you. I never once thought about what happened to me when I was with you. I went by instinct and followed my heart."

"I'm so glad." I kiss the top of her head and say, "I don't want to let you go tonight. Do you mind if I stay?"

"You didn't think I was going to let you leave, did you?"

This breaks some of the tension and makes me laugh.

"I'm so glad you're here," she says. "I feel like I can breathe for the first time in forever."

"I know… me too. We both have scars. Right? But we're going to get through this together."

CHAPTER TWENTY-NINE

Rachel

Dear Mike,

I had a dream about you last night. It happens a lot. Several times a year, actually. This time, we were sitting inside your bedroom, talking about having children. You were smiling as if it was exactly what you wanted. I know we never actually talked about kids when we were together, but in my dreams, you're happy about being a dad, and that always makes me feel uncertain about my life.

Something happened to me some time ago, and it's really damaged me. I'm uncertain about everything now. My decisions. My ability to be a good parent. My ability to do my job. My ability to interact with people in general. The only thing I'm certain about is that I want to protect our daughter. I've thought a lot about you over the last couple of years, not that I didn't before. The difference is, I've stopped looking for you. There are a few reasons for this, and a lot of questions.

What if I find you and call you, but you don't want anything to do with her?

What happens if I find you and you're happily married to someone else with other kids?

What happens if I find you and you tell me you love me… and I have to tell you how damaged I really am?

Raegan is eleven, and she needs a father. But does her father want a child? These thoughts keep me up more often than I want to admit. I know one day I will see you again. Hopefully, on that day, I'll be certain about something. Anything.

Right now, I know that I love you and miss you.

I know that I'm no longer worthy of you... if I ever was.

I know that my subconscious doesn't want me to forget you.

I know that Raegan will love you and I want you to love her back more than anything else in the world... I want you to love me back just as much, but you shouldn't because I'm a complete mess.

What is this life... seriously? Why am I here? Some days Raegan is the only thing that keeps me going.

Here's a fun fact: Raegan loves computers—already! She's going to be a handful. One summer camp program and now she wants to be a hacker. A HACKER! I'm afraid of how smart this girl is.

I love you,
Rachel

CHAPTER THIRTY

Michael

We hold each other for a long time, bodies entwined and arms locked around each other until I feel her relax, then I hear a strong sigh. A sigh that says a lot. The more I learn about her and Raegan's life, the more I want to be there for them. I want to take Rachel's worries from her. Not that she needs to be rescued. She doesn't, I know that, but she needs a partner. Someone to share the burden of these worries with… someone who loves her and will be there for her without putting her under pressure by trying to control everything in her life. Like her mother.

"Why are you worried?" I ask before I can stop myself. I place my hand on her face and lift it toward me, so we're eye to eye.

Her shoulder inches up in a slight shrug.

"I can sense the stress you're feeling. Share it with me."

"I'm worried about Raegan. I don't know how this is going to affect her."

When she says this, I realize I have a lot to learn about parenting and a lot to learn about being there for my family. "You think our relationship is going to have an effect on her?"

"Yeah, I have to assume it's going to. I'm just not sure how she's going to react. I think we need to move slowly. Give her time to get used to the idea."

"I'd like to officially meet her before we spring anything else on her. My sister's chomping at the bit to meet her too… and my parents will be here next week."

Rachel stiffens and then her eyes close. "Oh… crap."

"Don't worry about them. I'll handle it. But I'm not sure what to do with Raegan. It's so weird that she already knows about me, but she's pretending she doesn't."

"I know. I'm pissed at her for lying. What if you weren't her father? What if she'd gotten it wrong?" she says.

"And how in the hell did she figure it out? That's insane to me."

She laughs, and I feel it move her body up and down. "You cannot underestimate that girl. She must have gone through my stuff to get your name."

"Do you think she read those journals?"

"No, those were locked up, but I have some boxes in my uncle's garage. Wait!" She sits up quickly and slides off the bed, grabbing her robe from the floor. "She's not here, I can snoop through her room."

"No, Rachel, you can't do that."

"The hell I can't," she says as she rushes from the room. "I'm her mother, not her friend. I'll do whatever's needed to protect her—even if I have to protect her from herself. The first rule of parenting, Michael. Sometimes you have to fight dirty."

I stand and look down at my nakedness. I can't wander around her house like this. I walk into the bathroom and grab a towel and wrap it around my waist then head toward Raegan's room. Rachel is opening and closing drawers.

"There must be something…"

I glance around and see a backpack sitting in the bottom of her closet. "She's out of school for the summer, right?"

"Yeah. Why?"

I point and say, "What about that backpack?"

"Oh, smart!" She rushes over and unzips it. "That sneaky little girl!" She takes out what looks like our high school yearbook and a zipper pouch, then a large t-shirt. She lifts the shirt and unfolds it.

"Holy shit, that's my shirt." I reach out and take it, pointing to the few little paint spots. "I gave her this when she helped us paint. I didn't want her to get paint on her clothes… I completely forgot about it."

Rachel takes it back and holds it to her face and closes her eyes. "She kept it… wow." After a moment, she walks over and sits on Raegan's bed. She's upset, but I'm not sure why.

"You okay?"

She nods and quickly wipes her face with the t-shirt. "She's missed you as much as I have… I'm such a fool, Michael. Look what I've done to her. Forced her to seek you out and keep you a secret." She bows her head and takes another moment. "She wants her dad, and I've put her off because of my own stupid fears and insecurities."

I squat down next to her and brace a hand on her knee. "Listen, Rach, we can't fix the past. Right?" She nods, and her eyes look so heavy it's hard not to take her in my arms and love the worry away for her, but I know she needs more than that. "We can only move forward, but we need to do that together. We can't let anything else prevent us from fixing this."

"I promise you, Michael, I will never let anything come between us again."

"I don't want you to continue to beat yourself up over this either. We'll talk tomorrow, and you can say whatever you need to say to Raegan to make amends, but after that, I don't want you walking around with all this guilt. That won't help anything."

"Okay… I'll let it go. Hopefully, she can too."

"She's going to follow our lead, so we need to lead her in the right direction."

"You're right. Thank you."

I hand her the other stuff from the backpack, and her eyes brighten. "Wait until you see this." She unzips the pouch and shows me what's inside.

"Oh, wow, notes. I bet there's some good stuff in there. Are those all from me?"

She nods. "I only kept yours. I threw the others away. I had these in storage at my uncle's house."

She carries the pouch and the yearbook into her room and tosses them on the bed. As she does, several photos slip out from between the yearbook pages. There are three or four, and they're all of me. I pick one up: it's worn, and the corners are bent. Rachel snatches it and flips it over.

"That little thief. This was in my desk drawer."

"You kept my picture in your desk drawer?"

"Of course." She glances down and picks up a few more. "She must have gotten these from storage. Well, now we know how she got your name. It's written on the back with the date. It's from the summer before she was born."

We both climb onto the bed as she unzips and dumps the folded notes I gave her in high school into a pile. We both start unfolding them and reading.

"Man, I was a dork."

"No, you weren't. You were the coolest guy in school."

I come across a note about one of our former teachers. "Do you remember Mr. Gardner?"

She snorts out a sarcastic laugh. "How could I forget? My mom ruined his life."

When her sad eyes lift to mine, I realize how important that memory is for her... and now me. I remember all the news stations camped out in front of our school. "Do you really think she did that?"

"I have no doubt it was her."

"Do you think she was lying about the girl?"

"Do you think Mr. Gardner would make out with a young girl in his car?"

"I always thought Mr. Gardner was gay."

"So did I."

"That's why you left me, isn't it? You knew she really could hurt me if she wanted to."

She nods, and I can see the heartbreak all over her face. "I'd already seen her do it. I had no doubt, and I wouldn't let her do that to you."

"I'm sorry she put you in that position. That was a terrible thing for her to do… I wish I knew why she hated me so much."

"I wish I knew too. I mean, she always acted like you weren't good enough, but it's not like you were some drugged-out hoodrat. You were an honor student and captain of the football team… you came from a great family."

"Yes, but I did get you pregnant." I fold up the note I just finished reading and say, "That's a really great reason for her to hate me."

"It takes two, Michael."

"I know, but still—Christ, Rachel, you were a mother at seventeen."

"How frightening is that thought with a teenager?" She scoffs and says, "Of course, the difference is, I've taught my daughter to talk to me. She's not sheltered, and she's nowhere near as naive as I was."

"I hate to break it to you, but, Rach, she didn't talk to you. Not when she figured out who I was."

Her face grows sad, and her eyes lower. "I know, but that's my fault. When it came to you, I always shut her down. I couldn't deal with it." She refolds the note she was reading and says, "Even after I promised to find you, I still put it off. Even now, I haven't told her anything. I was trying to give you the time you needed, and I didn't want to get her hopes up."

"We're getting this all out in the open tomorrow—are you ready for that?" I reach for her hand and haul her to me. "Why the hesitation? What are you afraid of?"

She links her fingers with mine and says, "I should feel relieved. I should be celebrating, like a war is ending, but instead I can't get past the sense of dread. Like everything I've been fighting with for all these years is about to be lost."

"Not lost. Found." I push the hair from her face and say, "Get your mother's voice out of your head. Stop with the emotional beat down. Listen to me, not her. *Everything is going to be okay.* You are a wonderful mother and a wonderful person. We, together, created that child and she wasn't a mistake. Your parents' interference in our lives and our decisions was the mistake. Okay?"

She meets my eyes, and I see the shimmer of tears lingering.

"I'm not saying this isn't going to be a tough adjustment, and I realize teenagers are volatile creatures, and I realize she may be angry and difficult at first, but it will work out because this is what we all want."

"And what is that, Michael?"

I smile at her because I know she's scared too, just like Raegan's going to be, but I refuse to be anything but optimistic. "A family... *our* family."

When her mouth spreads into a smile, I tug her closer and devour it. I'm not sure I'll ever get enough of her now that she's back in my life. I'm not sure I'll ever not want to be buried balls-deep inside her. That thought alone has me pushing the notes and yearbook off her bed and pinning her down. But as soon as I brace her hands over her head, I hesitate. I don't want to scare her, and as this thought enters my head, I understand why she didn't want to tell me about the rape.

Fucking Christ. She's right. I do want to treat her differently now. I feel the need to be gentle, and that's not what she wants.

"I want you to ride me, Rachel," I say, trying to save face. This is something I need to get past, not something she needs to focus on... and I will get past it. I'll have her every day if I have to.

I slide my hand around her waist and flip us over so that I'm on my back and she's on top of me. She shrugs the robe off, and I'm faced with her perfect double D's. Fuck, she's gorgeous. Every fucking inch of her is sweet perfection. I reach up and pull her down so I can kiss her.

"Ride me, baby, I want to watch you."

She grinds against me and says, "My pleasure." Then she lifts her ass and lines herself up on my erect cock but stops there.

"You're killing me. Do it." I lift my hands to her hips and try to pull her down.

"No, you don't. I'm doing the riding, remember."

"Yes, baby, yes, I want you to... go now."

She smiles and then slides the rest of the way down. Once she's fully seated, the smile slips from her face, and instead she's wearing the expression of someone completely enthralled. Her head tilts back, and her mouth is open. She sits there for a moment, and I'm about to beg her to move when she leans forward and grips my chest.

Her hips lift and slide back down. It's the most beautiful thing I've ever felt.

"You are so incredible, baby. Please don't stop."

She lifts again and then finds her rhythm. With each thrust, she groans and her boobs bounce inches from my face. I lift one hand to grip her breast and the other clamps down on her hip, pushing her to keep the steady pace. When I lift my mouth to suck her nipple between my teeth, she groans again, and it's loud.

God forbid we ever do this with other people in the house because I'm not sure she's capable of being quiet. Honestly, I'm okay with that. Listening to her cries is one of my favorite things, and it spurs me forward. I start lifting my hips to meet her thrust for thrust, and the sound is so erotic. She's so sexy. It's amazing to see her so uninhibited and free. I love her like this. Confident and happy.

When I feel her tighten around my cock, I lift hard, grunting as I fight off my release. Rachel's panting, but then she sits upright on her knees and starts lifting then lowering herself down in a position that feels completely different. It must feel different to her too because the look on her face is one of complete pleasure.

I reach down and place my thumb over her clit and move in a circular motion. This causes her eyes to pop open and meet mine.

"Let go, babe, I've got you, I promise."

She lifts then lowers a few more times, but she's having a hard time staying upright, so I link my fingers with hers to give her some leverage. She shifts, grinds and the sensation is fucking amazing. Then she does it again, and her head falls back.

"Oh, God, Mike. Oh, God." One, two, three more times, and she's a goner. Her eyes slam shut, her head tilts forward, and it takes everything I have to hold her up as she comes. When she rests on top of me, I grab her and flip her onto her back. Then I drop into a plank and pound her over and over until she's doing it again. Fuck, yeah, that's what I want. Her screaming my name. "Rachel, sweet Jesus. Rachel, come for me again, babe."

I take her mouth with mine, and I feel her tighten again, her nails biting into my skin as she does, and once I'm sure she's finished, I let go too, releasing every ounce of energy I have.

CHAPTER THIRTY-ONE

Rachel

Waking up with Mike's warm body wrapped around me is the absolute best thing in life. I'm so content and happy, I momentarily forget what we have to do today. I don't move because I don't want him to pull away. He's spooning me, and his large arm is draped over my hip. It's bliss. Everything about this morning is pure bliss.

As if he senses I'm thinking about him, he draws me closer until I'm flush against him. A moment later, a quiet moan sounds against my neck then he says, "Good morning." It comes out in a deep baritone, and the sound sends a jolt of heat down my center.

"Good morning," I whisper, trying to hide the smile in my voice.

Warm lips land on the back of my neck, and then he says, "What time do you have to be at work?"

"I should be there by nine. It's going to be crazy soon after that. It's a big wedding and we're at capacity. How about you?"

"I have a PT session at nine and then an appointment with the electrician at ten. I'll probably have lunch with my sister and then two more PT sessions this afternoon."

"You have a full day scheduled, are you sure you can be here this evening?"

"Are you seriously asking me that?" His voice is clear now, no more sleepiness.

"Um, yeah… I know you're busy with your grand opening."

"First of all, you and Raegan are more important than that. You're my new priority. Second, I already have everything under control. This evening isn't a problem at all. I'll have all night. Diana can't even complain because she wants everything worked out with Raegan as much as I do."

Hearing all of this brings a huge smile to my face. It's been so long since I've been anyone's priority. Everything about this morning is precious. Hearing about his day is mundane yet so exquisite at the same time. Should I be afraid that maybe it's too perfect?

I think about the last week and how things have developed, the few things I've learned about him, about the discipline it takes to run a business like CrossFit. As I think about the man he's become, I realize I can't wait to see him as Raegan's dad.

I slowly roll over to face him, and as I do, he keeps me close. Not that he has to worry. I have no intention of leaving this bed yet. I rest my hand on his face, and this forces his dark eyes to open and focus on mine. He's so lovely and I so regret the time lost. The things he's gone through that I wasn't there for. The things Raegan and I have been through that he wasn't here for. This is when I remember he lost his brother.

"Michael…?"

His eyes twinkle as he stares at me. Then he says, "What, baby?"

"I'm sorry… I read about Brad last week. I'm sorry you lost him. That must have been hard."

The light in his eyes dims a little. "It was a really rough time. He was on the verge of having everything, and he threw it all away."

"I read that it was a drunk-driving accident and that he was engaged to his partner."

"Yeah, he was engaged to Kelley. They were planning to get married the following October. Instead, he got himself killed and really screwed up her future at the same time."

"You sound like you're still angry with him."

"I guess I am. I'm angry for Kelley's sake, not to mention having to watch my parents stumble through their grief. It's been a mess, but I still miss him. We were close, but he was also so reckless most of the time."

"The opposite of you. I don't remember you ever being reckless."

"No, because I always had to follow him around and keep his ass out of trouble."

"And it's not in your nature to be like that. You're a thoughtful person. You always have been."

"You act like you know me or something," he quips. "Maybe I've changed over the last several years. I'm a big scary man now, you know, full of brooding darkness."

I can't help but laugh at that. "Ha! Yeah, okay. The big scary guy who gives free gym memberships to neighborhood teenagers—not to mention still worrying about his dead brother's fiancée years after his death."

"Shh," he hisses, "don't tell anyone, I don't want to ruin my reputation." I laugh at that but then he says, "You know who she is, don't you? Kelley?"

"I vaguely remember Brad's dance partner, but I couldn't point her out if I met her on the street. Why? Should I remember her?"

"She's the reason I was at The Sutter on Monday. She's the friend whose wedding I'm helping with. Kelley's husband is Mac Thomas, the radio DJ."

"Oh, wow! That's her? It sounds like she's doing better now."

"Yes, she's finally happy and moving on. She bought her own dance studio, and she's teaching kids. She's doing well now."

I smile at him. "And you're standing up for her at the wedding? That's so sweet."

"We're close friends. She's important to me. One of my ride-or-die people. You know what I mean?"

I nod, but it makes me sad because I don't have any ride-or-die people—I'm not that close to anyone, except my daughter.

"What about you? Any friends you couldn't survive without? People you've known since you moved here?"

"No… Well, Isla is my best friend, but she's really all I have." I shrug it off and say, "I guess I'm not good at getting close to people. I had a hard time making friends in college because I was the mom of a small child. I couldn't go out and have a good time. I couldn't drop everything and take off to Tahoe for weekends, and I couldn't go to parties… things like that."

"I imagine you have trouble trusting people too, after what's happened."

"Yeah… I think my expectations of how men should act, and how they actually do act, are very different."

"What do you mean?"

"I mean… well, most men aren't very gentlemanly. You know? These days it's all about the quick hook-up. I'm a single mom. I don't have time for that nonsense." I think about the way Adam acted last week and feel that familiar sense of dread. "For the most part, men don't approach me. And when they do, they're not usually worth the trouble."

"Don't take this the wrong way, but good." He grins and I like it. "I'd rather they all stayed away from you."

"Since I know my day is going to be crazy, I'll give you the spare key and an alarm code in case you beat me here this evening." When my phone starts vibrating from the nightstand, I lean over to see the display. "Crap. It's my mother."

"Ignore it."

"Pff! Yeah, I'm certainly not answering it." When it stops, I push out a big, heavy sigh. "Okay… I guess I'd better get up. She's going to be calling the hotel looking for me and I don't want her abusing my employees."

*

When I get to work, I'm still smiling like a loon. Isla's going to know something's up as soon as she sees me. Once I'm inside my office and booting up my computer, my phone pings. I pick it up to see a text from Raegan.

Raegan: *Good morning.*

Me: *Morning, babe. How are you? Did you have fun with Maisie last night?*

Raegan: *Yeah, it was okay. What time are you picking me up?*

Me: *About six. Why? Everything okay?*

Raegan: *Yeah, fine. But I have something I need to talk to you about.*

I wonder if she plans to tell me about Mike tonight. I hope so. I'd love to get home and tell him that she came clean before we had to confront her.

Me: *Okay. You know you can tell me anything. Can we talk tonight?*

Raegan: *Yeah. I love you, Mom.*

Me: *I love you too, see you when I get there.*

As I place my phone on the desk, Isla steps into my office carrying a steaming cup of coffee. She sets it down and says, "Howard is at it again, spoiling us with his mad coffee-making skills."

"Oh, that man! His wife is a lucky woman." I pick up the mug and say, "Thank you so much! How are you this morning?"

She gives me a good long look. "Not quite as well as you, I see."

I grin and say, "I don't know what you mean."

"Sure you don't," she says with a hint of sarcasm.

"Do I look as tired as I feel?"

"Miss some hours of sleep last night, did you?" She hums for a moment, then says, "Who's to blame for that?"

"Someone showed up at my door after midnight last night, wanting to talk."

"Rachel, oh my gosh, that's so great! I guess things went well."

"Raegan was at a friend's house, so he stayed the night. It was amazing, Isla. I'm so happy. We're talking to Raegan this evening and telling her everything."

She lifts a brow. "Everything?"

I bob my head and say, "Okay, not everything. We're going to take our relationship slow until we think she's ready for it. For now, we're focusing on getting her familiar with her dad."

"That's probably a good idea."

"I'm not going to lie if she asks, but we're just going to move slowly."

When I hear a tap, I glance over to find Howard hovering near the door. "Everything, okay, Howard?"

"Yes, everything's fine, but I thought I'd let you know that we received a call from your mother this morning. She's coming into town later this week and wanted a reservation."

My heart nearly jumps out of my chest. I completely forgot she called me. "Please, please, Howard, please tell me you told her we're fully booked."

"Oh, yeah, I told her. She wasn't happy and wanted to speak to you, but after telling her you weren't in yet, I convinced her that we don't have any availability because of a week-long wedding fair. I thought I'd let you know in case she calls you. I didn't want you to be blindsided by it."

"Howard, you're a life-saver! Thank you so much."

"You're welcome, but I'm just following your instructions."

"Yes, I know, and I appreciate you lying for me like that. I know you're uncomfortable with it."

He tips his hat and says, "I don't mind for you, boss." He flashes me a huge grin then he's gone.

Once he's out of earshot, I look up at Isla and fight not to scream. "Holy crap, Isla! She couldn't be coming at a worst time."

"She won't stay with you, will she?"

"No, she'll go to Uncle Mitch's house." Out of agitation, I stand up and pace around my office. "Jesus! Do you think she knows Mike's here?"

Isla arches a brow at me, her eyes following me around the room. "You need to get a grip, girl. Just stop."

I lean forward and take several deep breaths. She's right. Jesus. What the hell is wrong with me?

"Even if she knows, it doesn't matter. You're grown-ass woman, if she doesn't like how you live your life, you need to tell her to fuck off."

"Yes, yes, yes. I know. You're right." I straighten up and try to focus. "You're right. I need to tell her to get the hell out of my business—my life."

"Do not let her come here and push you around. Okay?"

I nod decisively at her. "No, I won't."

"As a matter of fact, I'd make a point of telling her you reconciled with Mike and that Raegan is excited about meeting her dad."

"Yeah, but I'm definitely going to wait until after tonight. I don't want anything to interfere with that." I take a deep, steadying breath and say, "I'm not even going to call her. I won't even acknowledge that I know she's coming to town. She can call me to let me know she's coming."

"That's my girl." Isla smiles at me and says, "Don't let her bully you anymore."

"I'm not." And I won't. She's right. I'm much too old and independent to be afraid of my mother.

I take a few calming breaths and try to get it out of my head and get on with my work day. I will not let her lead me to distraction. Barbara Crawford Williams' reign of terror has come to an end. I've taken my life back.

I think about Mike and how good I feel about our future.

I've taken my love back.

CHAPTER THIRTY-TWO

Michael

Two personal training sessions down and after a six-mile run, I feel good. Things feel on track. I spent an hour before my run making calls and confirming vendors. I dealt with the electrician and I've scheduled three classes for the opening. I thought that'd be a great way for people to see our coaches in action.

Honestly, I'm praying I get more than just my family here. But I guess that's always the fear, right? That no one will be interested. I know it's unfounded; I have several new members who I know will be here with their families, but that doesn't mean I don't worry about it being a flop.

Fear is good for the soul, though. It promotes courage, and well… knowing what I'm facing tonight with Raegan requires all the courage I can muster. I'd like to say it's going to be easy since we've already met, but I'm nervous as fuck. What if she decides she hates me? What happens when I try to parent her and she laughs at me? I have no clue what I'm doing.

I take several deep cleansing breaths and wonder if I should go for another run. But no. I have too much shit to do still, including lunch with my sister. Then I need to figure out what I'm going to do about my parents coming to visit.

*

I meet Diana and Olivia at a deli near the gym. As I sit down at the table, I feel the weight of exhaustion dragging me down. That's what I get for staying up all night making love to Rachel. Regrets? Not one. I'd do it all over again if I could. But of course, I'm not likely to get the chance anytime soon since Raegan will be home and I don't think it's a good idea for me to stay there until everyone is comfortable with our relationship. I don't want to make Raegan think I'm taking over. I want her to grow comfortable with our relationship at her own pace. If that means I need to move slowly. I'll do it.

We order our sandwiches and after a few quiet moments, Diana says, "So, what's the plan, Mikey?"

I grin at her because I know how badly she wants to ask me a hundred questions, but she's holding back because Olivia is with us. "Rach and I are going to talk to Raegan this evening. That's still the only plan. I can't think beyond that yet."

"What are you going to tell Mom and Dad when they get here? What are we telling them?"

"We can tell them about Raegan, although I'm not sure if she's going to be ready to meet them. Same for you." I set my sandwich down and say, "Speaking of Mom and Dad, do you know if they've made hotel reservations?"

"Oh, I don't know, but there really isn't enough space at your place. I don't know if they have a plan, but I could ask."

"I was thinking of asking Rachel if she has a room available at her hotel."

"That's not a bad idea. It's close enough, and it's a nice place. They'd probably dig that."

"I thought so too. I'll ask her about it later."

"So, I know we're taking this whole Raegan thing slowly, but I was thinking of planning a family dinner when they're here. Even if it's only the three of us with Mom and Dad." She waves a hand at me to keep me from interrupting. "Look, I know you want to work things out with Rachel and Raegan, but I think it's also important for you to spend some time with our parents. I know they've been complete…" She glances down at Olivia, who's quickly devouring her apple slices. "…assholes," she mouths silently. "But we need to move on from the weirdness, and I think now is the perfect time for the four of us to do that, and especially because of Raegan. We don't want to introduce her to a completely dysfunctional family."

She's right. I know that, and I want things back to normal too. "Listen, I'm fine with all that, but they need to work things out with Kelley. I'm not going to be completely comfortable with them until they apologize to her for the crap they put her through."

Diana purses her lips and agrees. "You're right, they need to. Maybe I'll take them over to see her when they get here."

"That would be a great thing, Diana."

"Okay, so once that's out of the way, what do you think about the dinner idea?"

"I'm sure we can do it. Let's make it Saturday after the opening. I'm facing a hellish week, let me get through it without Mom and Dad obligations."

"Yep, okay, family dinner tentatively planned for Saturday night after your grand opening. We can celebrate with the whole family—hopefully."

After lunch, I head over to The Sutter to talk to Rachel. I realize it's only been about six hours since the last time I saw her, but that doesn't mean I don't already miss her. When I walk inside, I smile and greet Howard. He's extremely polite, and when I ask him if Rachel is there, he only hesitates for a moment before calling her.

"She'll be right out," he says after hanging up the phone.

A few minutes later, she steps into the lobby and waves me in her direction. I follow her into her office. It's larger than I was expecting and clean and modern, considering the age of the building. You can tell the entire office space used to be a drawing room or some other sort of large room of the Victorian mansion.

The office walls are glass and look temporary, but neat with clean lines. She closes the door behind me, but that doesn't mean the space is private. Now I realize why she brought me to a suite on Monday instead of her office.

"Hey, beautiful." I lean in and wrap an arm around her waist and pull her to me, not really caring if people see us.

"Hey, yourself," she says, smiling widely. "What have I done to deserve this surprise visit?"

"I'm sorry, I know you're busy with the wedding. I hope this isn't—"

She waves off my apology. "No, I'm due for a break and Isla has things handled."

"I was hoping you could help me out with something." I release her and have a seat in one of the chairs facing her desk. "My parents are coming into town on Thursday, and I don't have enough space in my apartment. Do you have a room I could reserve for them here?"

"Oh." She looks surprised but pleased. "I could absolutely make a reservation for them. Do you want a suite or a king room?"

"What's the price difference?"

"I could give them a suite for the price of a king room. We have two weddings happening next weekend, but they're both local couples with guest lists under twenty-five people. Hardly any guest rooms have been reserved, so there's plenty of availability."

"That would be awesome. Thank you."

She turns in her chair to face her computer, and I watch her for a moment, fighting the hard-on I get as she works. Sometimes it's the simplest things. Rachel, in proximity to me, is all it takes today. She's so fucking hot without even trying. I glance around at the glass walls and realize I need to stop and pretend I can behave myself. Then I face her again and say, "So, my sister is trying to plan a family dinner for my parents and us on Saturday after the opening. I told her I couldn't make any promises because of what's happening with Raegan, but if things go well, what do you think about my family meeting her then?"

"Have you told your parents yet?" she asks, looking a little hesitant.

"No, but I'll tell them everything when they arrive."

"Um… hum." She turns her chair back around and says, "The reservations are made for Edward and Sharon Murphy, so they're all set." Then she taps her fingers against the glass surface of her desk. "Raegan's been wanting this so I can't think of a reason for her to react badly when we talk to her tonight. I was hoping to take the rest slowly, but since they're coming, we can talk to her about meeting them and see how she feels about it."

"Thank you, Rachel. I realize this is an adjustment for you too."

"Don't give it a second thought. Really. I want this too, Michael. I will adjust faster than you think." She looks tired, and it's a reminder that I kept her up late last night. "Thank you for coming over last night. I think the first step to making this work with Raegan is you and I being on the same page."

"Babe, I want us on more than the same page." I give her a long look, and as I do, I see pink brighten her cheeks. "I hope that's what you want too. If it's not, then maybe we have a lot more to talk about."

"I've always only wanted you." She leans forward and rests her elbows on her desk. "I've never been more excited about the future than I am right now… at least not since before I found out I was pregnant with Raegan… and that's the truth. I want you in my life. I want you in Raegan's life. The sooner we get her used to the idea of you and me together, the better. Is that okay with you?"

It's so weird… I'm not used to getting butterflies, but when Rachel talks frankly about what she wants—and when what she wants is exactly what I want— I get butterflies. I lean across her desk now too, so that we're nose to nose. "I love you, Rachel Rose Williams."

Her lashes flutter, and her cheeks pink up again. "That's the best thing I've heard all year," she whispers. "I love you too, Michael Edward Murphy."

I wince hearing my middle name but then smile. "You're the only person allowed to use my full name. I hope you understand that."

She throws her hand back in a laugh, and I have to fight not to drag her closer so I can bite the beautiful smooth skin of her neck. "Well, thank you for allowing me the privilege."

I lean in and plant a quick kiss on her lips, then stand. "I have some things to get finished before dinner so I'll get going."

"Okay." She stands too and takes a slip of paper from the printer. "Here's the confirmation for your parents' room. I made the reservation for three nights. If they need longer, they can let Howard know when they check in."

"Thank you very much." I wave goodbye as I step out of her office, feeling pretty fucking fantastic about life.

CHAPTER THIRTY-THREE

Rachel

Dear Michael,

Today is a big day in the life of Rachel Williams. I've been promoted. That's right, I'm officially hotel manager. It's odd really because it wasn't something I was striving for. I loved planning the weddings. It's been the best job, and usually a lot of fun... even when it made me sad.

When my manager announced his retirement a month ago, I thought long and hard about asking for the promotion. It turns out, I didn't have to ask; they made me an offer before I had the chance. They want me to take over. It's a huge job, but I know I can do it. The extra money will be a good boost for me and Raegan and it'll be nice to work less weekends.

I think the change will be good for me. It's not always easy to watch happy people join their lives when I know I'm nowhere close to such happiness with someone. I've barely even dated in years. Between my dad being sick, raising Raegan on my own, and this full-time job, I don't have time for dating. Even since losing my dad, I haven't had time... but that's okay. It gives me more time to devote to Raegan and to this new opportunity.

Raegan is doing really well. She plays soccer and really loves it. Yes, that means I'm a soccer mom. She has perfect attendance at school this year and she's won several school awards, including student of the month, a good citizenship award, and she's on the principal's honor roll list. Recently, she won a spelling bee. It was amazing! I really wish you'd been there. My mother was here for it, although she spent the entire time criticizing everything she could think of.

She's only gotten worse with Dad gone. I think it's boredom. Maybe she gets a kick out of making me feel bad about myself. Fortunately, she doesn't include Raegan in her rants about what a screw-up I am. And to answer your question before you even ask it, no, she's not impressed about my promotion. She doesn't care. As a matter of fact, she rolled her eyes when I told her. Then she said, "Really, Rachel, can't you find something better? Don't you get tired of being the help? Who would have imagined you'd enjoy a job serving people."

I hope you're well. I hope you're doing something you love and I hope your life is everything you dreamed it would be. I miss you so much… every day.

I love you,
Rachel

CHAPTER THIRTY-FOUR

Raegan

It's been a long day. Maisie is starting to get on my nerves, and I want to go home. I want my mom. I'm going to tell her I love her and that I'm sorry. I want to tell her about Mike Murphy. Especially now that I'm sure I was mistaken about him being my dad. I know this is what I need to do. Besides, if Mike really was my dad, he would have responded to my last email. I'm sure I'd have been *talked to* by my mom by now if he was the guy.

When she shows up a little early I'm surprised but so glad. She looks super tired, and I wonder if she slept at all last night. I feel so bad for putting her through this—for making her do this for me. I wish I could take it back. I wish I'd never asked her about my father.

We climb into her car, and I get the usual questions. *How are you? Did you have fun with Maisie? Did you sleep well?*

"Did *you* sleep well, Mom? You look really tired."

She gives me a soft smile and says, "I didn't get a lot of sleep, but the few hours I got were very restful. Thank you for asking."

"So… Mom, I have something to tell you."

"Okay, babe, shoot."

"I changed my mind. I don't think you should look for my dad." As I say this, she's coming to a stop sign, and she hits the brakes really hard, causing us both to lurch forward. I throw my hand out and grip the dashboard. "Gosh, Mom!"

"Sorry. Crap, sorry, Rae." She pulls to the side of the road and puts the car in park. "Did you say you don't want me to find your father?"

"Yeah, I changed my mind. It's okay if I don't have a dad. I have you, and that's all I need."

The expression on her face turns very sad, but then she looks away as if trying not to cry. "Why have you changed your mind?"

I'm not sure what to say at first, so I think about it for a moment. Looking out at the road in front of us, I consider what I'm doing. It's all I've thought about all week, and I know it's what I need to do… and I'm really okay with it. "Did you see my dad on Monday? Is that why you came home so upset?"

It's as if I can see the thoughts as they shuffle through her head. I can tell she wants to lie about it, but that she also doesn't want to lie. "I did see your dad on Monday. I was planning to talk to you about it tonight. What does that have to do with you changing your mind?"

Avoiding her eyes, I stutter for a minute, trying to find a way to say this without sounding dumb. "Um… I just… don't really care who my dad is. You're my mom, and you're enough for me. I want you to know that." I look up into her eyes real quick then say, "I'm sorry if you had to go grovel to some jerk who was mean to you because of me. He must have been mean, right? That's why you were so upset. Honestly, I'd rather not have a dad."

"Raegan… that is…" She covers her face with her hands and starts crying. Now I feel really bad. Hopefully, I'm not telling her this too late. She scrubs her face clean of tears and beams at me. "God, Rae, I love you so much. You are so sweet and…" She laughs through her tears, and I'm not sure what that means. Is she happy or sad? Before I realize what's happening, she's reaching across the seat and hugging me really hard. "Thank you. I'm truly touched by that." She withdraws, her eyes meeting mine. "Your dad… he… he wasn't mean to me on Monday. He was understandably hurt and upset."

She shifts back in her seat and starts driving without saying anything else. I'm watching her, waiting for her to say more, but she doesn't. She's still crying, but she's not talking.

"Mom, I don't understand. Then why were you so upset on Monday?"

"Because it's been a very long time and I had to tell him about this secret I've been keeping for so long. It wasn't easy. You can understand that, right? I feel bad about what I've done to both of you." She's frowning now, and tears are streaming down her cheeks.

"I'm so confused. What's his name?" I ask, wondering if I was right about Mike… but if Mike is my dad, why didn't he reply to my email? Why did they wait all week to tell me?

She grins and says, "Let's get home. I don't think this is a good conversation for the car, okay?" Not that it matters because she's turning down our street as she says this.

After parking, she quickly hops out of the car and comes to my door to grab my bag. Once I'm out of the car, she hugs me again. "I love you, Raegan. No matter what, okay? You are the most important person in my life." Then she withdraws from me and stares into my eyes for a moment. "Even if I had to put up with someone who didn't like me. Even if he hated me, I'd do it for you. This is about you, and should have always been about you. Okay?"

I feel like crying now too, but I hold it back. "Okay, Mom."

She turns and faces the house, then walks to the door looking a little apprehensive. Which is weird, but she's upset, so I guess it's understandable.

I follow her into the house and freeze when I see him. I take a step back and stare at the two of them. Mike's very straight-faced, and that makes me nervous. I don't know what that means, but I'm a little afraid right now. I glance up at my mom and say, "Mom?"

"Raegan, this is Michael Murphy, which you already know. He's your dad." Her voice cracks as she says this, and I watch as Mike's eyes leave mine and focus on her.

I stay rooted to the spot, not sure what to do. Not sure how I feel about him or about her reaction to him.

"Mom, what's happening?" I ask.

"We're talking," Mike says. "That's what's happening." He waves me in, as if I don't live here—like this is his house. "Come inside, put your stuff away. We're going to have dinner and talk about things."

I take my bag to my room and then come back to find them in the kitchen, chatting quietly. I enter slowly and approach the table. When my mom looks up, she's saying, "I just... I'm glad this is finally happening." She smiles at me and says, "Have a seat."

I slowly lower myself into a chair and keep my eyes on my mom. She's watching me too, but I can't tell what she's feeling. Between her swollen eyes and faint smile, it's hard to judge.

"Raegan, Mike told me about the emails, and about you visiting him at the gym."

"Yeah, sorry," I say to her, "I was going to tell you tonight. I actually thought I had it wrong." I look around the table and see the stuff I took from my mom: the photos of Mike, the letters, my mom's school yearbook. "You went through my stuff!"

"Excuse me," she says. "You went through *my stuff*, Rae. And what if you had been wrong about Mike? Do you know how dangerous that could have been?"

I'm not totally sure what to think about this. I'm relieved and happy it's Mike, but I'm pissed she went through my room and I'm getting a vibe that he's not happy. I've been waiting for this for so long, but now I feel off balance about the entire thing. "I'm confused." I finally look up at him. "If you guys knew about this on Monday, why did it take you so long to tell me? And how did you get into the house?"

Mike presses his lips together and his eyes seem to search my face for a moment, then he says, "That's my fault. I asked your mother to give me a few days. I didn't tell her we'd already met until last night when I put two and two together. I know it's a surprise, and I'm sorry it took me so long, but I needed to think things through before… this." Then he gestures toward Mom and says, "As for how I got into the house, Rachel gave me a spare key. We thought me being here was worth the shock factor."

"Oh, I'm shocked all right!"

This makes them both laugh, and that relaxes me a little. I glance around the kitchen table again, and it's… weird. Usually, it's just Mom and me. I think I like it, though.

"I brought dinner with me," Mike says. "If it's okay with you, I'm going to make our plates while your mom tells you a story. I heard you like Italian so I picked up a lasagne from this great place near my house."

I nod and look at my mom. She's crying again, and that makes me feel bad.

"Raegan, your dad"—she gestures toward Mike—"didn't know I was pregnant with you. He didn't know you existed until Monday. He and I have had several long talks this week, and I've caught him up on most of your life, but now I want to catch you up on us." She hesitates for a moment as if she's not sure where to begin. Then she says, "Remember the story I told you about the pool… how he helped me when I got a cramp swimming?"

I start to answer her when Mike says, "When she was faking a cramp to get my attention—that's what she really means."

Mom smiles, and her entire face lights up with it. I've never seen her smile like that. Ever. I stare at her, not sure what to think. Her face is still swollen from crying, but she actually looks almost happy.

She rolls her eyes at his teasing and says, "Right, I was faking, but that's not the point. The point is, I fell in love very young. We were very close for a long time. Our relationship became physical when we were too—"

"Ew, God, Mom! I don't want to actually know how I was made. Jeez!"

This makes Mike bark out a laugh.

Mom lifts a placating hand and says, "My point is, I got pregnant at sixteen, which you know. What you don't know is that I left town as soon as I found out and I never told Mike I was pregnant."

My mom continues to tell me about her pregnancy and moving to Sacramento to live with Grandpa while we eat our dinner. As she's talking, I feel like she's purposely leaving stuff out. First of all, I don't understand why she left. I don't understand why she kept me a secret... and when I ask, she avoids the question.

By the time dinner is finished, my head is spinning, but of all the things she's told me, one thing is very clear. She's relieved the secret is out. Another thing that's very clear is that Mike—my dad—is fixated on her. I'm not sure if it's affection or something else. He's very attentive and careful about what he says, and he's careful around her. Every time he comes close to touching her, she draws away slightly, but I can see it in his eyes. Could they possibly be a couple again? I'm not sure how I feel about that. I guess if it makes my mom happy, it's a good thing, but I still feel like I'm not getting the entire story and I don't like that. I thought my mom was going to be more open with me now. I thought she understood that I'm no longer a child.

After the dinner dishes are cleaned up, we're talking again, but I see Mike look at his watch. "I think I should get going. It's getting late, and I know you're tired."

"Wait... already?" I say, standing quickly. I don't want him to leave. Not yet. "We have a guest room. You can stay the night. Mom, tell Mike he can spend the night."

"Oh, Rae, his sister Diana is in town—"

"Sister? You have a sister?"

"I do, yeah, she's here with my niece for the opening."

"Wait, I have a cousin? I've never had a cousin before." I stare at him, not sure what to think about that. "What's she like?"

"Her name is Olivia, and she's seven."

"Does she know how to swim? Maybe they can come over and swim with us. We have a pool. Do you like to swim?" Mike smiles, and it's not his normal smile. This one is different. He's staring at me, and it almost makes me shy. "Sorry… I didn't mean to bombard you with all my dumb questions."

"No!" he says, "I'm excited about this too. I'm excited for you to meet my family. I'm so glad you want me here… asking me to stay the night, that's really cool, Raegan." He glances over at my mom, and I do too, just to find her watching me like I'm about to turn into an alien or something.

She shakes her head and says, "I'm sorry… I… how about…?" She stops and looks around for a moment. "How about we have your family dinner here next Saturday, Mike? Do you think your parents would mind? I know you want them to meet Raegan and the girls can swim. We can all swim. I can cook… we can celebrate the opening… it'll be fun."

"Yeah, and Mom can pretend to get a cramp again—then you can save her." I laugh at my own joke, but they do too, so that makes me feel a little less stupid.

Mike's laughing, but then he nods and says, "I think that would be cool. I can ask my parents since they'll be in town. I'm sure Diana would love to bring Olivia, and she's dying to meet you, Raegan."

"Oh my God, I can't wait." I jump up and down and then hug him really tight. About halfway through the hug, I realize what I'm doing, and I realize how hard he's holding me. I'm so happy I hold on and let him do it. I inhale his scent and realize this is what dads smell like. I remember my grandpa always smelled good too. Even Uncle Mitch has a smell, and he's not even a dad.

Thinking about it makes me want to cry, but I don't want to make him uncomfortable, so I try really hard to hold it in.

When Mike lets me go, he lowers himself so that we're eye to eye. He stares at me for a long time, then he says, "Listen. I want you to know that I'm really happy. It's important to me that you understand that if I had known about you, I would have been here. I would have been here for you and your mom."

This does make me cry, but when I feel my mom's arms wrap around me from behind, I feel a little stronger.

"Raegan, I also want you to know that while I'm glad you found me, it could have been dangerous. Please don't keep big secrets like this from your mom. We..." He points between us. "Are living proof that big secrets only hurt people. This one worked out, but usually, they don't. Okay?"

"I know." I lay my hand over my mom's arm around my shoulders and say, "I'm sorry for lying to both of you, but I really was going to tell Mom tonight."

He nods and smiles at me, then his eyes light up. "Hey, do you want to hang out with me at the gym this week? You're out of school, right?" His eyes lift to Mom. "Is that okay with you?"

I feel her nod against my head and in a nasally voice, she says, "I think that's a great idea. But, Raegan, he has a big event this weekend, so you have to let him get his work done."

I hold up my hand and say, "I will, I promise."

CHAPTER THIRTY-FIVE

Rachel

I've decided to take half a day off work today to prepare for the party with Mike's family tomorrow night. I've felt light as air all week, and I'm glad it's the weekend so I have time with Mike and Raegan. I know it's his big opening weekend, but that's something to be excited about. It's something I get to be there for. I've missed so much with him, and he's missed so much with Raegan and me, that we have a lot of catching up to do.

Raegan has spent nearly every day this week with Mike at the gym and she's having a blast. I, on the other hand, have been avoiding him. It's hard to be close and not touch him or show my feelings openly. I don't think Raegan is ready to learn about our relationship yet. I want her to get to know him on her own first.

Mike texts and calls me regularly and, when Raegan isn't nearby, we're all over each other, but that's not often. She even spent some time with his sister and Olivia this week too, and that gave me and him a little time to hang out. She met Diana at the gym on Monday and they came over Monday night so the girls could spend time together and swim. It was a little intense at first. Mike wasn't there so I had to face Diana alone, for the most part, but with the girls swimming, we had a chance to talk. It was good, and I felt a great deal of relief after.

Diana actually apologized for reading the journals, but it wasn't necessary. I'd rather she read about the last fourteen years than try to explain them. Now, I have to face his parents. That's not something I'm looking forward to.

When someone approaches my door, I don't look up at first. I'm signing off my computer and about to leave, but then I hear Isla, and the tone in her voice when she says my name draws my eyes up. That's when I see my mother standing behind her. Isla's wide-eyed and says, "Your mother is here, Rachel. What a surprise."

I jolt out of my chair. "Mom! Yes! What a surprise."

"Yes, so I gathered," she says, not trying to hide her sarcasm. This is why I make my staff tell her we're booked when she calls. She's rude and inconsiderate, and I don't want her here abusing them. "It's funny how you're the manager here yet you can't manage to get your own mother a suite when she's coming to visit."

I walk around my desk to give her a kiss on the cheek, fighting against the nervous tension that attacks me at the sight of her. I wish like hell she'd just go away. I don't need this complication right now, not when everything is going so well with Raegan and Mike. After the quick embrace, I clamp my hands together so she doesn't see the slight tremor I'm having trouble hiding.

She's impeccably dressed in white slacks and a silk blouse. My mother is the complete opposite of me. She's very fair-skinned with hair so blonde it's almost platinum. She's angular and willowy, with no curves to speak of, which is probably why she likes to call me fat. Her hair is trimmed into a short pixie cut, and it's now nearly pure white, which I'm sure was done in a salon. She's only fifty-six, and that's much too young for white hair. As I take a step back from her, I get a whiff of Chanel N°5, her signature scent, and it actually makes me a little nauseous... and that pushes my usual sense of guilt to the surface. I love my mother, I really do, but I don't like her very much most of the time.

"Don't you want to stay with Uncle Mitch? I know he likes having you there."

"No, Rachel, I'd like to be close to you. I do actually come here to visit you and Raegan."

"I'm sorry. I wish I'd known you were coming, I would have had the chance to make arrangements."

"Darling, maybe it's time to sell that dinky little place you're living in and buy something larger. Then I could stay with you when I'm in town. It's not like you can't afford it. Uncle Mitch tells me your trust fund is still sitting untouched."

"No, I like my place, and I do have a guest room you could stay in."

"That's not a guest room, it's a…" She waves her hand as if looking for the word. "It's a workspace," she says as she looks around my office. It's like she's inspecting it. Looking for something wrong. "And where is Raegan today? I expected her to be at Mitch's. Doesn't she spend her off days there?"

I glance through the glass door to see Isla watching us hesitantly. *Now what?* She lifts her hands as if to show me bear claws, and her face scrunches into a growl. I'm not sure what that means, but it almost makes me laugh. I have to look away from her to keep my composure.

"Actually, I'm glad you asked about Raegan. She's… she's um…" Crap. I'm really not in the mood for this fight, and I really didn't want to have this conversation at work. "She's with her father."

My mother's head turns in my direction but slowly, which makes me suspect this news isn't a surprise. At least now I know she's here because of my last conversation with Uncle Mitch. "Raegan doesn't have a father, Rachel, so I'm not sure what you mean." Her entire body shifts in my direction, and once she's fully facing me, she crosses her arms over her chest.

"She does have a father. She might not have known him until recently, but she has always had a father. She's also very happy to have him in her life, as he is happy to have her in his."

"Are you telling me you went against what we agreed and reconnected with Michael Murphy? Really, Rachel, I thought you'd grown out of your high school fantasies. I'm actually shocked at how pathetic you must have felt to search out an old boyfriend *from high school* of all places."

I'm shocked that she remembers his name so well and, as horrible as she is, it almost makes me smile. I'm afraid of the amount of pleasure I'm going to get out of telling her this.

"Actually, Mother, Raegan found him herself."

"Rachel, that's ridiculous. Why can't you just admit that you've gone against our deal? What a disappointment it is to see you blame your daughter for this. Is it really that hard to find someone new at your age?"

"Excuse me!" My back straightens. "I'm not making this up. Raegan went through my stuff in storage in Mitch's garage. She found Mike's name, and she looked him up. He happens to live in Sacramento." I mirror her and cross my arms over my chest, my nervousness turning into anger. "Also, I'd like to say what a disappointment *you* are. After all these years, can't you be happy that Raegan is happy? Why is it, exactly, Mother, that you hate Michael so much? He was always perfectly respectful to you. Kind, even though you were never nice to him. Jesus, Mother, I remember him bringing you flowers on Mother's Day."

"He can't bring Raegan happiness. He'll only screw it up." She points her finger at me and lifts it, then lowers it to my feet. "Look what he did to you. Getting you pregnant... and you were just a girl."

Here we go... now, this. As if she didn't hate him before I got pregnant. I love how she breezes right over that fact.

"Get him away from Raegan before he screws up her life too. It's really the only thing the men in his family can do, destroy the lives of the women they love."

"What the hell does that mean? You've never met any of the men in his family. You wouldn't even take the time to meet his parents when we were in school."

She lifts her perfectly arched brow at my curse, but I don't care.

"I will not keep him away from Raegan. However, if you can't show Raegan's father some respect, I will keep *you* away from her."

"And what have I done wrong?" She lays her hand on her chest lightly as she feigns offense.

"You know exactly what you've done. You said yourself I went back on our deal. A deal you bullied me into making. A deal I haven't told Raegan about because, for some reason, I felt the need to keep the full truth from her… to protect *you*."

"Rachel, do not threaten me. Everything I've done was to protect you and Raegan. Surely you can see that? All of the decisions I've made have been in your best interest."

"What is it about Michael that makes you think he's not the best for me? I love him. I've always loved him. Do you not see the difference in me today versus the way I've been feeling for the last several years?" I take a step closer. "Look at me, Mother. Don't you see a difference?"

"I don't know what you're trying to say."

"Do you realize that I spent years in a suicidal depression? You pay close enough attention to me that you can criticize every aspect of my life, but you didn't recognize the signs of distress when they were right in front of your face. Honestly, Mother, are you purposely obtuse, or do you just not care?"

She rolls her eyes at this. "Now you really are being ridiculous. That's a complete exaggeration. You'd never harm yourself. You just wouldn't do that."

"Four years ago, I was raped. I know you don't know that… but telling you now feels like the only way to make you understand. After being raped, I was so distraught, I could hardly function." I fist then flex my hands when I say this and I realize it's not only out of frustration but a way to symbolize letting go. I'm letting it go—I need to.

"I'm sorry to hear that, but I'm not sure what this has to do with Michael Murphy."

"A lot of the reasoning behind those suicidal thoughts was knowing I could never face Mike after being violated in that way. I knew I couldn't tell him what had happened—I knew I'd never be able to explain why I didn't fight harder to stop it. Why I wasn't brave enough to report it. Why I'd never want another man to ever touch me again."

"I don't believe something like that could happen and you wouldn't share it with me. Does Uncle Mitch know?"

"No, I didn't tell anyone for a very long time. I've told my therapist… we've talked about it, and that got me through my depression—that and medication. I told Mike when we reconnected. It wasn't easy to share it with him, but a funny thing happened after telling him. Having him there, telling him everything about Raegan and sharing this with him, and having his forgiveness has given me a great deal of freedom—a liberation really."

She's staring at me, but she doesn't speak and more than anything I wish I could read her thoughts. I feel exhausted with this conversation, but I know I need to say these things to her. I need to get this out of my system and let her know what a huge part she had in this. "You see, Mother, I had to come to terms with the fact that I've allowed myself to be a victim of so, so many people, including you. I've spent my life not fighting back. I've spent my life allowing people to bully me and victimize me, including the man who raped me."

"I don't understand what any of this has to do with me. What have I done to victimize you? I suppose it's a good thing you're taking medication. You sound a little raving."

"You see, right there is a perfect example. You're a textbook narcissist. You constantly belittle me and put me down to make yourself feel superior."

"That isn't true. You act like I don't love you at all. You act like what you're saying doesn't affect me." She takes a step back and sits in one of my guest chairs and it surprises me. She's usually so on guard. Sitting during a fight is one of the biggest signs of weakness I've ever seen from her. "Have I been that horrible a mother to you? So bad that you blame me for not reacting to something I didn't know about?"

"You're missing the point. You taught me to be quiet. To not talk back to anyone. To not protect myself. You've taught me that because I'm a girl, I have no power." I tap my chest and say, "But I'm finally realizing that I do have power. That I have a voice and it's with this voice that I have to tell you… Mike, Raegan, and I are going to be a family. You can either embrace it, or you can hate it, but it's happening, and you *will not* interfere." I walk back around my desk and take my purse from the drawer, getting ready to leave.

"Rachel, stop," she says, and I'm tempted to keep going, but I don't. "Don't spew hate at me and then leave. That's no way to communicate."

I turn back to face her. "If you're truly willing to have this conversation with me, I will sit down and talk to you. But if you're going to criticize me or act like my feelings aren't valid, then I don't have anything else to talk about."

Her eyelashes bat for a moment and I can tell I've taken her by surprise. "I would like to talk," she finally says. When I sit down across from her, she links her fingers in her lap and says, "I am truly sorry you were hurt. I never wanted that. I've only ever wanted to protect you. When you were young, I was afraid Michael would eventually hurt you. I was trying to prevent that."

I stare at her for a moment, not sure what to say. She's never apologized for anything, not really. Sure, I've gotten some passive-aggressive apologies when she was only trying to shut me up, but never anything heartfelt. It almost makes me not want to believe her.

"What you need to understand is that losing Mike is my biggest hurt. Nothing ever could or ever will hurt me like losing him, and that's not to mention what it's been like for Raegan to not have a father."

She purses her lips and I can tell this is really hard for her. She picks off the tiniest bit of lint from her white slacks and says, "I'm starting to see that… I guess I didn't realize how important he was to you. But…" Her eyes lift to me and I see something I've never seen before. She's always been cold, even to me, her own daughter. But now, I can see emotions, regret, hurt… even heartache in her eyes. "No, that's not true. Honestly, I recognized how strong your feelings were. It's the reason I did what I did."

"You purposely did this because you knew how much I loved him?" I'm so confused by this conversation, and I'm starting to lose my patience.

"Rachel, I once loved someone like that, and it hurt me to my core. I felt that by taking you away, I was saving you from the same fate."

I'm absolutely floored. I don't know what to say. My mother has never, ever told me anything personal about herself. She's essentially been a stranger to me most of my life.

Sensing my confusion, she says, "My senior year of high school I fell madly in love with a boy who I thought loved me just as much. It was… we were…" She hesitates at first but then says, "Very passionate… I saw this with you when you were with Michael. It scared me."

"Mother… I'm sorry. I didn't know. Why didn't you ever tell me about him?"

She looks down at her hands and shrugs. Then her shoulders go back and she looks up at me. "Why would I tell you about someone I loved before your father?"

This, of course, makes me question if she ever did love my father. "It might have helped me understand why your feelings against Mike were so strong."

"Yes, well… it was never about Michael, and it wasn't easy to talk about." She clears her throat and says, "I was hurt badly and it's the kind of hurt you don't forget. I wanted to save you from it… but it seems my efforts were in vain."

"May I ask… what happened with him? Why didn't it work out?"

Her bright blue eyes lock on mine and for a moment I think she's not going to tell me, but then she says, "He met someone else. Someone completely different from me, which hurt even more, and confused me. We decided on the same college, and most of our first year was wonderful. I thought he loved me. But as summer approached, it became clear he had fallen for her… and betrayed me. They both betrayed me."

"So, you knew her? Were you friends?"

She nods. "She was my roommate. We shared a dorm room."

"Oh, wow. I'm so sorry. That's terrible."

She waves a dismissive hand and says, "In the end, it didn't matter. By fall, I'd transferred to UCLA and met your father. He was very good for me. We had the same ambitions and, well, it wasn't a fairytale, but fairytales are just make-believe, aren't they?"

I reach out for her hand and grasp it. "Thank you for talking to me. I wish you'd done it sooner."

"I guess I should have." She smiles and says, "If you want to work things out with Michael, I won't interfere. I would, however, like to have the chance to talk about this more, and make things right."

I pull my hand from hers and say, "Unfortunately, Raegan and I have plans for most of the weekend, but why don't we have Sunday brunch here at the hotel? I'll have the staff reserve a table for us."

"Oh. Okay. Bunch on Sunday sounds lovely." She gets to her feet and says, "Maybe I could spend a little time with Raegan. What about a couple of hours this afternoon? I can bring her home after."

I think about that for a moment and then finally say, "I'm sure Mike can spare her. He has a lot of work to do… and they have plenty of time to catch up. I'll give them a call."

"No, no, you were on your way out when I got here. I'll call her and set it up." She leans in and gives me a quick embrace and says, "Thank you, darling. I'll see you Sunday."

Then she's gone.

I watch her go, then give Isla a quick recap of what happened.

"That's crazy. All this time and you didn't know?" Isla asks.

"I had no idea." I glance at my watch and say, "I really need to get out of here or I won't have time to get my shopping done. I'll let you know how the weekend went with Mike's parents."

"Okay, see you," she says with a big wave and I rush out of the hotel and to my car.

Once in my car, I rest my head back and give myself a few minutes to calm my mind. What a day. After a few deep breaths, I start my car, but my phone pings before I can leave.

Raegan: *Mom, I worked out with Mike today, and he took me on a run. Look what we did.*

She's sent a video of the two of them tossing a medicine ball back and forth, and she's smiling so widely. They both are. I can hear him giving her instructions and making her laugh and I wish I was there too.

Me: *It looks like you guys are having a good time. By the way, Grandma wants to spend some time with you today.*

Raegan: *I know. She's picking me up, and I'm hanging out with her for a few hours.*

Me: *Can you try to be home by six? I'd like to get the house cleaned up a little for tomorrow and I need to clean the pool.*

Raegan: *Okay, Mom. I'll see you at six.*

Me: *Okay. I love you.*

I switch to Mike's contact on my phone and text him.

Me: *I'm sorry if my mom ruined your afternoon. She surprised me at work today. I just had a really long talk with her.*

It takes him a minute to respond to my text, and I'm a little afraid of what he's going to say. He has every right to be angry about my mother.

Mike: *It's okay. Raegan and I had a good morning. I have a ton to do still and I'll probably be here for most of the night. Thankfully, Gavin is here to help out. Honestly, I'm a little worried about Raegan spending time with her though. I'm sorry but I don't trust her.*

Me: *I know, but we had a long talk and she said she wouldn't interfere. I'll tell you about it when I see you. Thank you for being so understanding. How about we barbeque tomorrow?*

Mike: *Perfect! Whatever you choose will be perfect. I'll bring drinks and dessert.*

Me: *I can't wait. I have a lot to tell you about today.*

Mike: *I'll call you later when I get a break.*

Me: *Can't wait. Talk later.*

When I finish the text, I put the car in drive and head to the grocery store. I still don't know what we're eating, but I'll figure it out while I'm shopping.

CHAPTER THIRTY-SIX

Raegan

It's really weird that my grandmother called me and asked me to spend the afternoon with her. It's not like I've never spent time with her, it's just she's not usually so nice about it. It's as if her chipper, friendly attitude on the phone was put on, but I don't know why she would fake that. It's unlike her. Although true to her ways, she wouldn't take no for an answer. And now I feel bad for not spending the rest of the day with Mike like I told him I would. Thankfully, he wasn't upset about it, and I know he has a lot of stuff to do. I also know we have every day after today. It's not like he's going to disappear.

Mike follows me outside to wait for Grandma. He seems uncomfortable, almost angry, but I can tell he's trying not to show it. It makes me wonder if there's something about Grandma he doesn't like. Of course, it wouldn't surprise me if they didn't get along; he did get my mom pregnant at sixteen. But it's been a long time. Hopefully, they can get past it. Either way, I don't want to get in the middle of it, so when my grandma drives into the parking lot, I rush to the car. I give Mike a big wave and then hop in, hoping to avoid him having to speak to her.

Grandma doesn't give him a second glance. She drives off as if he wasn't even there. I guess that means she doesn't care either way. She's always been the type to ignore people she doesn't really care about, so I'm not surprised. Once we're on the road she glances over at me and the big smile she wore when she arrived is gone, and again I have to wonder what she's up to.

"How are you, Raegan?" Grandma asks, in a tone that's oddly soft. "Your mom told me that Michael was in your life now. I'm a bit surprised… how do you feel about it?"

"I'm happy about it, and I'm so glad to see my mom happy."

"Oh, did she say that? That's also surprising." She flashes a sad smile and then says, "I'm glad she's capable of putting on a strong face for you."

I stare at her for a moment, not sure I understand what she said. Then I think back to last Saturday and the look on my mom's face. She was happy, right? Wasn't she? I know Mike was. And I know my mom did a lot of crying. But they were happy tears.

"Why do you say that, Grandma?" I ask. "Why would she need to put on a good face? I don't understand?"

"Oh, well, if she didn't tell you, I probably shouldn't mention it either."

"Tell me what?"

"Have you had lunch yet, Raegan? Should we stop at the club?"

"No, thank you. I already ate lunch. But can you tell me what you meant?"

I look up to see that she's entering Uncle Mitch's driveway. She parks her car and then shifts in her seat to face me.

"Raegan, darling, if your mother didn't mention it, I don't think I should. I don't want to cause a problem between you and your parents. Although, I am a little concerned about you spending time with him. I hope she doesn't agree to that because she's afraid of him."

"Afraid of him?" I think back to Monday and the feeling I had that he'd hurt her.

"I really don't want to interfere with your parents' plans now that they've reconnected." She rests her very pale hand on top of mine and gives a slight squeeze. "I will ask you to be careful when you're with him. Especially when you're alone with him."

"Why?" I slide my hand out from under hers and place it in my lap. I'm not sure how I feel about her acting as if there's something wrong with Mike. He's been very nice to me, and I know he's glad to have me in his life. And he really seems to care about my mom. "Why would I need to be careful when I'm alone with him?"

"Raegan…"

"No, please tell me. It doesn't matter what my mom said and what my mom didn't say. You obviously have something to tell me, so please say it."

She gives me a long look then she touches her throat and makes a little clearing sound. Before she starts talking, she glances around to see if anybody's watching. It's all very weird.

"Did your mother tell you why she left town when she found out she was pregnant with you?" she asks.

"No, she didn't."

"Have you asked yourself why she would do that? Why she kept you a secret from him?"

"I asked her, but she avoided the question. I figured she'd tell me when she was ready."

"Or she won't tell you at all because she doesn't want you to know. That's why I'm reluctant to say anything now." She lifts her hand and then lowers it to her lap. "I'm just so surprised to hear she went looking for him."

"But she went looking for him because I pushed her to. It wasn't Mom's idea. I actually found him first."

"Oh, I see." Her face looks almost stricken, like she's received very bad news. "I guess that explains it. She did it for you, even though she might've been afraid. That's like her, isn't it?"

That makes my heart race. When I first asked her to look for him, she said she was scared. Then, on Saturday, when I told her she could give up looking for him, it was too late. She'd already found him. She said it was okay, that she wanted to see him, but did she say that just for me? Because it was too late? He was already in our house, it wasn't like she could abandon the plans with him at that point.

Have I put my mom in a dangerous situation, with someone who hurt her? Again, I try to remember how they both acted on Saturday night. Mike's behavior. It was a little controlling. The way my mom pulled away when he got too close to her. The expression on his face whenever he looked at her. Was it admiration or obsession? And she's kind of been avoiding him all week. I thought she was giving us time together but maybe it's more than that.

"You must know, right?" I ask. "Can't you tell me why she kept me a secret?"

She hesitates for a long time, and I can tell she's thinking about it. "It's just that… He wasn't very nice to her when they were together. She seemed genuinely afraid of him, and while I didn't want to believe it, I fear he was a bit abusive."

My stomach bottoms out when I hear this. I feel terrible. What have I done?

"To be honest, Raegan, I suspect he might have even raped her. She probably said no when he made advances toward her. She wasn't that type of girl, and he's always been very strong. Much bigger than your mother." She scoffs then brushes a hand toward the direction of the gym. "You see how burly he is. It's easy to see why she'd be afraid."

"I didn't know." I feel sick to my stomach, and I want to throw up. What am I gonna do now? Poor Mom. I have to apologize… I have to find a way to get her out of this situation.

"Of course you didn't know, Raegan. Your mother wouldn't want you to know that. I probably shouldn't tell you this, but when she got pregnant with you… she agonized over her decision whether or not to have an abortion. In the end, she already loved to you so much, despite what she'd been through with Michael Murphy."

"Wow... I wish she had told me."

"Darling, there isn't anything you can do. Just support her." She nods toward the house and says, "Let's go inside and get out of this heat."

I get out of the car and walk into Uncle Mitch's house, and as I do, I pull my phone out of my pocket. I bring up my mom's contact and type out a text.

Me: *Mom, were you raped?*

Then I backspace and delete the entire thing. It's too personal a question for a text message and I don't want to make her feel bad. What I need is a new plan. A plan to get Michael Murphy out of her life. She deserves better. I won't let her give up her happiness and freedom so I can have a dad. He may be nice to her now, but he'll go back to his old ways soon. A leopard never changes his spots. That's what Uncle Mitch always says.

My mom will stick it out too, she'd do it for me. She'd resign herself to the fact that her rapist is going to be a permanent part of her life. She is the type to do that. She always puts others' needs before her own. She always goes out of her way to make everyone else comfortable without any consideration for herself. I think that's why she's so successful working in the hospitality industry.

I hate that I've done this to her. I hate that I've put her in this position.

CHAPTER THIRTY-SEVEN

Rachel

Dear Michael,

I've never felt so torn in my entire life… including the day my mom shipped me to California after I found out I was pregnant with Raegan. It's nearly eight in the evening, and I've only now started to process the fact that I've seen you today for the first time in almost fourteen years. As much as I want to feel bad about how angry you are with me, I can't. After I've been given a chance to touch you again, to feel you against me, to have you touch me, I can't be upset. Seeing you, telling you the truth, lightens a huge load off my shoulders.

Believe it or not, even if you never forgive me, if you choose to hate me for the rest of our lives, if you never want to see me again, that's okay because I have the memory of today and that can never be taken away from me. I have the memory of your touch and the image of your eyes, so full of longing and desire, burned in my mind—and nobody can take that from me.

Whatever you feel about me, please know that I'm not Raegan and she is not me. She's done nothing to you. She has no knowledge of what's happened between us. She doesn't know that I didn't tell you about her years ago, but she suspects I never told you. She doesn't know what my parents did, but that doesn't matter. I'll take the blame. I'll take her wrath if you promise not to punish her for what's happened. She deserves a father. She deserves you as her ally in life and as her confidant. She deserves to have you and all your special gifts—all of your love and all of your affection. She deserves to have a large family like yours, and she wants it. Please let her have that no matter what your feelings are for me. She is worthy of all of that.

That being said, Michael, if you choose to forgive me, I can promise to give you the life and love we were always meant to have. I know that's a stretch for you, especially after finding out that you have a daughter after all these years. I know it's hard to trust me. I know you want to run, and I know that's what I deserve. But I promise you, I will never run from you. I will never betray you. I will never, not for one single day, stop loving you. You have always owned this ragged and damaged heart (for what it's worth), and that will never change.

Fun fact: Raegan has been the one true shining light in my life, and I hope you are lucky enough to see her shine too.

I love you,
Rachel

CHAPTER THIRTY-EIGHT

Michael

It's not without effort that I let Raegan leave with Rachel's mother. After everything that woman has done, I'd rather she never see Raegan again. Of course, I'm new to this parenting thing… I'm trying not to make waves. I don't want to drive a wedge between Rachel and her mother, even though her mother drove a huge wedge between my family and me.

I watch them drive away and take a deep breath. If I didn't have so much to do, I'd go on another run. As this thought enters my head, I hear Gavin come up behind me. "Where'd she go?"

"She's spending the rest of her day with Rachel's mom."

He gives me a strange look. "The same woman who caused this mess?"

"The very same." Before I can say more, my sister pulls into the parking lot with my parents. "Okay… well, it looks like I'm not getting any work done today."

Gavin slaps me on the back and says, "No worries, Mike. That's why I'm here to help out."

I glance at him and I'm so grateful. "I'm sorry for all the distractions."

"Just get your family situation sorted and don't worry about things here. That's why we went into this business together, to back each other up."

"Thanks, Gavin. Now get the hell out of here before I hug you and cry on your shoulder."

"Fuck you," he says with a chuckle, before stepping back inside the gym.

As soon as my mom is out of the car, she wraps me into a huge hug. I hold her for a long time because I've actually missed her. I miss the old mom. The mom she was before Bradley died. The mom who always smiled and laughed and was always welcoming and friendly to everyone she came in contact with. I squeeze her a little tighter and send up a little prayer that the old mom is the person I'm hugging and not the bitter, grieving woman I saw the last time I hugged her.

When I withdraw, she *is* smiling. She places a warm hand on my cheek and says, "You look good, son."

I grin at her and say, "You look good too. Happy, even."

She releases me so I can hug my dad. He embraces me like the bear that he is, even lifting me off my feet. That's not something that happens every day. When he sets me down, he slaps my back and laughs. "You're heavier, that's for sure."

"Hey, Dad," I mutter when he releases me. I glance at Diana, and she's smiling, then I see her mouth: *I told you.* I send her an acknowledging nod and say, "Welcome to Sacramento. How's the hotel?"

"Oh, it's a nice place," my mom says. "Be sure to thank Rachel for us."

"You'll get to thank her yourself soon." I wave a hand at the gym, "Let's step into the air conditioning."

I introduce them to Gavin and Brianna before giving them a full tour. During the tour, my parents are full of questions and encouraging comments. It's so weird… as if I'd stepped back in time. Their attitudes are a complete turnaround from even a year ago. When I've shown them everything, we leave Olivia playing in the kids' area and head into my office. It's going to be a little crowded, but I know they want to talk about Raegan. I told them over the phone a few nights ago and they were pretty surprised.

Once we're all tucked inside my small office, my mom surprises me when she says, "Guess who we saw today?"

I glance at my sister, but when she sees my confusion, she says, "We had lunch with Kelley and Mac."

"Oh, shit… okay. Did you…? Did they…? Wow."

"I called her last night and set it up. We didn't just show up on her doorstep," Diana says.

"Oh, good!" Feeling relieved, I take a seat and ask, "So, how did that go?"

My mom pipes in and says, "It was a bit tense at first, but we expected that." She gives me a surprised look and says, "She looks good. I'm so glad she's found someone, and she's happy."

I'm not sure if she's trying to put off telling me what happened or if she's genuinely surprised that Kelley's happy. "Mac's a great guy, and he loves her."

"Yeah," Diana scoffs. "He's super hot too. Why didn't you tell me that?"

I give her a *don't go there* look and say, "How'd it go?"

"Oh, fine," my mom says. "After we broke the ice and apologized, things were very civil. Honestly, at first, Mac did most of the talking. I think he was giving Kelley time to adjust to being around us."

"You can't really blame her for being uncomfortable," I say, honestly. "You guys really screwed her."

Shame clouds my mom's face, and I feel bad, but I don't take it back. They need to understand. "We know that, Mikey, and we're trying to make things right. We're sure it's going to take time, but that first step has been made, and now we need to move forward."

"We apologized to her and tried not to make a bunch of dumb excuses," Dad says, "We also wrote her a letter she can read later when she's alone."

"Thanks, guys. I'm glad you're trying to make it right. Kelley deserved better, and it sounds like things are moving in the right direction."

"Mikey, we also want to apologize to you... we're sorry for being so distant with you and Diana. We were lost for several years, and it's taken a long time to move on." My mom leans over and places her hand over mine. "We know we've hurt this family, but we're trying to... well... we're trying to be better, and we want things back to the way they were before. Losing a child..." She moves her hand to her chest and says, "It's like losing a piece of yourself. You must understand that now... well, I know it's a new thing, but I'm sure your feelings for your daughter are very strong already."

I'm immediately affected by what she says, and it takes some effort to find my voice. She's right, I do understand better than I did a few weeks ago. How that happened so fast, I don't know. It's the strangest thing. Clearing my throat, I say, "Thank you... I've missed you guys." I get to my feet and hug my mom again, so glad to have them here to meet Raegan and get to know Rachel again.

When Mom withdraws from the hug, she quickly wipes tears from her face and leans back against my dad. His eyes are glassy too, so I reach over her and give him another embrace. Once everyone is smiling again, I say, "So, I know you have questions about Raegan and Rachel. I'd like to talk it out before you meet her. I don't want there to be any tension when you see her."

"Mikey, we don't understand how this has been a secret for so long." She rocks forward in her chair and says, "Did you know she was pregnant when she left?"

"I didn't know. Rachel's mom forced her to move and wouldn't allow her to tell me. She made threats against the baby and against me, so Rachel left. She did it to protect me."

"That's insane." Dad takes a seat in the nearest chair and looks up at me, amazed. "That's... crazy. What the hell could she have threatened you with? Are you sure Rachel's not using that as an excuse for not telling you?"

"I believe her, Dad. I know it sounds sketchy, but I've had a few long talks with Rachel, and I believe what she's telling me. Her mother never liked me, not from the first time we went out. She did whatever she could to keep Rachel away from me."

"Rachel wrote letters to Mikey," Diana said. "From the day she left town until last week, she wrote him letters in a journal with updates about Raegan's life. She also wrote a lot about herself and about what she was going through. Once you read some of what she wrote, you have to believe her."

"Oh my gosh, Mikey…" My mom turns to look at my dad. "I can't wait to meet Raegan. Have you been spending time with her?"

I can't help the grin that spreads across my face. "I have. Diana and Olivia have got to know her this week too. She was actually here most of the day, but Rachel's mom is in town and wanted to see her."

"What?" Diana spurts. "What the hell is she spending time with that shrew for?"

I hold out a placating hand and say, "I don't like it either, but I'm new to this, and I can't come in making demands and telling Raegan she can't see her grandmother. But, I will talk to Rachel about it later. I just haven't had a chance. Personally, I don't trust her." I clap my hands together, hoping to change the tone of the conversation. "But, you guys get to meet Raegan tomorrow. We're having a family dinner at Rachel and Raegan's house."

"How exciting! I can't wait," Mom says.

"I'll text you the address so you can meet me there after the opening. We're going to barbeque. Rachel said around six, and there's a pool too if you want to swim."

"So… Michael… what is happening with Rachel now? Why a family dinner at her house?" My dad rubs a hand up and down his bearded chin and says, "Maybe you should talk to a lawyer about joint custody or at least visitation before this goes downhill."

"No, I'm not doing that. Nothing is going downhill between Rachel and me. She wants me to be a part of Raegan's life, and so does Raegan. I want to be a part of their lives... and not just Raegan's... I want to work things out with Rachel too."

"Are you sure that's a good idea? She's lied to you all this time. How do you know you can trust her?"

"Dad, I understand your reservations, but I know what I'm doing. I love Rachel, and I believe her—and I know what's kept her from contacting me over the years." I glance from him to my mom's worried face, to Diana, who nods at me as if to tell me she has my back. "You're going to have to trust that I know what I'm doing. And I don't want any tension or animosity toward her this weekend. Raegan's a smart girl, she'll pick up on it if you're not comfortable—and she's fiercely protective of her mother."

My mom and dad look at each other and then to me. "All right... if you're sure, I'll keep my mouth shut," Dad agrees.

"Thank you... and just watch... wait and see. It's going to be great, I promise." I wave my hands toward the door and say, "And I love you guys, but I really have to get back to work. I'll try to stop by the hotel tonight to see you before I head home. That's if it's not too late."

They head toward the door, and as they do, I feel a sense of calm. I'm optimistic about our future as a family... I just need to come to terms with Rachel and Raegan's relationship with Rachel's mother.

CHAPTER THIRTY-NINE

Rachel

It's six thirty and Raegan isn't home yet. I've tried calling her and my mother but they're not answering. I keep my phone handy while I clean up around the house. It's mostly clean, I just want to make sure everything is in place for Mike's family. It's not as if I get visitors like that every day. I'm a nervous wreck at the thought of seeing them again. I'm sure they're not happy with me, and who could blame them?

I know Mike's optimistic about this, but it's hard for me. I try to turn the situation around. What if someone had kept a similar secret from me? Or someone I love? I'd be pretty mad about it too. I'm hoping they can see through their anger and try to understand. I'm also hoping that if Mike can forgive me, they can too.

After putting the groceries away, I change out of my work suit and into my bikini and shorts. I step out onto the patio and fluff up the cushions on the patio furniture, then I sweep the pool for fallen leaves. It's hot and the pool looks so inviting. I glance at my phone to see if Raegan's called, but she hasn't. Mostly everything is done besides a little food prep I need to do for tomorrow.

What the hell. I slip out of my shorts and dive in. It's instant relief from the heat. I swim a few laps, appreciating the peace and quiet, using the time and exercise to clear my head. I relish the feel of my muscles working, flexing, and stretching as I push through the water. After my sixth lap, I stop and grip the edge. Before I can turn around, a huge, loud splash sounds behind me and I nearly jump out of my skin. I quickly scramble over to the edge and get out of the pool. I have no idea who it is, but I wasn't expecting anyone and I know Raegan wouldn't make a splash like that.

As I'm getting to my feet, I hear, "Holy shit, did you see that cannonball?"

I literally jump at the sound of his loud voice. "You scared the crap out of me!"

Mike starts laughing as he stares up at me. "I couldn't watch you do another lap in that bikini and not join you. You have a beautiful breaststroke, you know." He waves his hand and says, "Come back. What'd you get out for?"

"Are you kidding? I thought I was alone. Hearing someone jump in the pool behind me nearly stopped my heart. What are you doing here? I thought you were working most of the night."

"I am, but I needed a dinner break." He points to the patio table and says, "I brought you guys dinner. Where's Raegan?"

"She's not home yet and she's not answering her phone."

His brows scrunch together. "What does that mean? Should we be worried?"

"I'm sure she's fine, it just means my mother is trying to get under my skin. Don't move," I say as I dive back in the pool. I surface a foot from him, but it's not far enough to keep him from grabbing me and towing me closer. "Thank you for dinner," I whisper through his kiss.

"I didn't think you had plans. I got a little nervous though when I saw your car in the driveway but you didn't answer. Then I remembered that I still have your key so I let myself in. I hope that's okay."

"If you ever scare me like that again, I'm taking that key back!" I say, gripping his neck as he spins around in the water.

"You can have it back if you want."

"No, I don't want it back." I glance down and say, "Are you in my pool naked?"

This gets a hearty laugh out of him. "No, I have my boxer briefs on. I didn't know you were alone or I might have gotten in naked." He presses me up against the wall of the pool and says, "I've never had sex in a pool before. This could be fun."

"Aha—it could be fun if we weren't expecting our daughter home any minute now."

"Oh, good point." He grinds against me once with a smoldering look and says, "Next time, babe. Right now, we can eat since I need to get back to work." He sinks into me with an achingly slow kiss that makes me wish Raegan wasn't expected.

Then he's gone. Swimming away as if he didn't just set me on fire.

I slowly follow him out of the pool and head to the outdoor linen cabinet and grab us a couple of towels. When I see his boxer briefs are soaking wet and fully tented with his erection, I feel a little better about the state he's left me in. I'm not the only one suffering from it. I grin at this thought as I hand him a towel.

We sit at the patio table together and eat the roasted chicken he picked up on the way over. As we're eating, my phone pings with a text from Raegan. I wipe my hands and pick it up.

Raegan: *Sorry. We went to the movies and Grandma made me turn my phone off.*

Movies? That's insane. I don't think my mother has ever taken me to the movies.

Me: *I wish you'd let me know. I've been worried.*

Raegan: *I tried.*

It's as if I can feel her aggravation through the phone.

Me: *Sorry. I hope Grandma isn't being too much of a pain.*

Raegan: *No. She's been fine, really. We enjoyed the movie. She wants me to spend the night with her and Uncle Mitch.*

"Oh, God! You poor thing."

"What's up?" Mike asks.

"My mom wants Raegan to spend the night over there with her and my Uncle Mitch."

"Is that unusual?"

"Not really. It's just not much fun. My mom is… well, she's my mom." I don't think I need to say more than that. "It's fine though. I can pick her up on my way over to the gym tomorrow. I'll bring her a change of clothes with me."

Me: *Raegan, that's fine with me if you want to stay there. I'm almost done with the cleaning so I don't really need you here. If you don't want to stay, tell me now so I can get you out of it.*

Raegan: *I don't mind. Grandma promised to play Monopoly with me and Uncle Mitch so she's being fun. Not the downer she usually is.*

Me: *Good. I hope that means my talk with her today helped. Mike's here. He came by to see you.*

Raegan: *You're alone together? Are you okay? I can come home if you need me.*

Me: *Why wouldn't I be okay? I told you I don't need you. Everything is mostly done and Mike is going back to work. He stopped by to bring dinner and to see you. Don't worry, you can see him at the grand opening tomorrow.*

Raegan: *Right. Call me if you need me, Mom. I can have Grandma bring me home.*

Me: *I will. Have fun. I love you.*

As I finish my text, Mike stands, wiping his hands on a napkin. "I hate to leave you alone, but I really have to get back to work. I still have so much to do."

"Already?" I stand up and lean against him when he comes around the table to give me a kiss goodbye. "You know, since Raegan isn't here, I could come with you. Maybe help out."

"I love that you want to help, but I was actually thinking that since Raegan isn't here, maybe I could come over when I'm finished."

I grin at the thought. "I fully support that idea." When Mike wraps his warm arms around me, I hold tight, enjoying the warmth of his skin and the way he smells like summer. I wish he could be here all the time, but I know I have to let him go, so I do and get rewarded with a kiss.

When he withdraws from my embrace, he says, "So… what's the move? Should I come in quietly and sneak in bed with you or should I make a bunch of noise so I don't scare you again?"

"You can come in quietly. It won't scare me since I know you're coming. I won't set the alarm so you don't have to worry about disarming it when you get here."

"Okay, but I'm gonna be pissed if you shoot me."

I laugh hard at this. "I'll remember to ask questions first and shoot second."

He throws his shorts on over his wet boxer briefs and tugs on his t-shirt. "I'll see you later." And with a quick peck on the cheek, he's gone.

*

When the cool hand circles my waist, I jerk awake with a gasp. Before I can react further, I hear his whisper in my ear. "It's me, baby. Relax." Then his hand slides up and cups my right breast. It takes me a moment to get my bearings and by the time I realize what's happening, both his hands are on me and his masculine scent is surrounding me.

Is this what it's like? I've never had a man sleep over until this week. I've never felt the sensation of waking up to an erect cock pressed against my bare behind. Knowing Michael would be here tonight and Raegan wouldn't, I purposely went to bed naked—something that's very out of character for me. Always having a child in the house, I've never slept in the nude.

Mike caresses me until I'm fully awake and pushing back against him. I could get used to this… waking up to a horny man touching me until I'm so wet I can barely contain myself. When his hand travels down and grazes my clit, I gasp again. I'm so sensitive and ready, it won't take much for me to lose it. Mike slides a finger inside me and with it, I feel his teeth graze my shoulder.

"I want you so badly, baby. May I have you?" he whispers as his teeth travel to my ear lobe.

I open my eyes to find the room completely black and the house silent except for the sounds of our breaths. "Oh, God, yes, please."

A moment later, he pulls his finger free and presses me, stomach down, into the mattress. His weight covers me and I like it. While his hand is cool, his body is warm, like a heavy blanket. He spreads my legs with his knees, then his weight's gone and he's sliding his hand down between my legs from behind, spreading me. When I feel his cock pressed against me, I lift for him, until he's inside. He doesn't hesitate and I'm so glad when he's filling me completely.

I lift a little further and then he's pressed against me again. His hands cover mine and I cannot move. He's not resting on me, he's somehow supporting his own weight, but he's pressed hard enough that every inch of me is covered by his heat. It's sexy and sensual at the same time. Between his flexing body covering me, his knees between my legs and his hands on top of mine, I'm completely pinned and it's the most arousing thing I've ever felt. He's so big and so strong, I'm completely at his mercy. It's not frightening like I would have thought, no, the opposite. I feel secure and protected… small, even, and it's exactly where I want to be. With each hard thrust, I lose more and more control. I can't touch him, I can't see him, but holy hell, I can feel every inch of him and it's glorious!

I fight to maintain some control so it'll last, but I can't. It's too hard to focus. Too hard to stop myself. Mike's breath is in my ear and with every movement, in and out, in and out, I can hear his faint grunting. It's so hot, so erotic, I can barely make a sound myself. I just want to feel everything, I want to experience him in this carnal moment, losing himself in me.

But I'm the one getting lost in every sensation. My body is tensing, tightening… it's not quick. No, not this time. No flash and bang and I'm coming. This orgasm is from the deep and it's heating every inch of me. He speeds up, pressing harder against me and I'm lifting off the bed. It's agonizing in its intensity, the most beautiful agony I've ever felt, and I'm nearly breathless when I cry out for him before I let go. "Oh, God! Michael!"

It takes me a moment to get my bearings again and then he slows slightly. Pushing all the way inside me, he holds himself there. He's flat against me, and we're both sweating and I'm dying to touch him. I want to feel his skin, taste it, and run my hands all over his body. He lifts and frees my hands as he slides out of me. I groan at the loss, but I'm relieved when he flips me over and his lips land on mine. I take the chance and run my hands down his body, pushing him by the hip until he's on his back, but he doesn't lay down, he sits up, bringing me with him.

"Come here, sit on my lap, Rachel."

I'm straddling his lap and before I know it, he's between my legs and guiding himself inside me again. Oh God… I'm shaking from the pleasure and as soon as I feel his erection spread me, I lower down until I'm fully seated on his cock. We both push out loud moans and with a couple of grinds against him, I'm on the edge of climax again. I'm not sure if it's his hands wrapped around me, or him completely filling me… stretching me, but I'm building toward the edge again and I'm not sure how long I can hold out.

I have my hands wrapped around his shoulders, and feel his scruffy chin between my breasts. Everything about him feels good… and he's so big inside me. I slide up and down with a grinding motion and with each thrust, I cry out a little louder. I don't even care who hears it, I just want him to make me come, now.

"Oh God, Michael… I can't wait. Oh God!"

"Don't wait, baby, let go when you're ready." His hands move down and hold on. His mouth sucks on one taut nipple then switches to the other. "Fuuuck you're hot, Rachel. That feels so good, keep going. I want to watch you come, baby."

I can feel him grow harder inside me, stiffer, and then he says, "Jesus, Rachel, yes, like that." His hands tighten on my hips. "Ride me, baby, just like that. Oh, fuck. I can't wait." The look on his face as he throws his head back is pure satisfaction and it's the most beautiful thing I've ever seen. But when his hand slips between us and the pad of his thumb brushes my clit my eyes slam shut and I completely lose it.

Then Mike's crying out, his arms bracing around me to keep me upright. When we're both spent, I drape myself over his chest and shudder from the release.

"Jesus, Rachel." He brushes the hair away from my face and lands a kiss on my neck, below my lobe. He sighs and says, "I want my hands on you all the time."

"Good," I mumble. His arms are still wrapped around me and he's holding on tight. I am too, I don't want to let go, but eventually, I slide back to the mattress. Mike scoots down next to me and draws me closer, until he's spooning me. His every touch sends little jolts of electricity through me—still—even after all of that. "What a way to wake up. Please feel free to sneak quietly into my house anytime you're in the mood."

I feel his body move with the soundless laugh and I like it. I like this. Him here. Our bodies glued together, but I know there's so much we need to work through. So much exploring to do before we leap into a future together.

I loosen my grip and shift so that I'm facing him.

"Michael…?"

His eyes pop open. "Hum?"

"We need to talk about the fact that we're not using condoms."

His eyes close again but with a nod of acknowledgement. "I know… I assume you're not taking the pill."

"I'm not."

"Is that a bad thing?" he asks.

"It's not a good thing. We're not exactly in the position to have another accident. Especially since our daughter doesn't even know what's happening between us."

He lifts his hand to tuck a strand of hair behind my ear as his eyes ease back open. "I don't care, Rachel. The rest of the world is going to have to get used to this because I'm not going anywhere."

"I hope not. I don't think I could live through losing you again."

"I missed the last time my child grew inside you. I won't miss it again… no matter when that happens. I don't care if it's now, next year, or in five years. I won't miss one single day of it."

My heart flutters at his declaration. I take a good long look at him and I believe him. Knowing I don't have to live another day without him relaxes me. "Okay…"

He drags me closer and kisses me slowly and as he does, I feel his cock twitch against me.

"How are you not exhausted?"

"I am. My dick… not so much."

I laugh at that and I lay my hand on his face. "I love you. Get some rest."

A moment later, he's snoring lightly and it's the sweetest thing I've ever heard. I don't even want to sleep. I just want to lay here and listen to him breathe… next to me.

CHAPTER FORTY

Michael

I hated—and I mean hated—leaving Rachel sleeping this morning, but I had to get to my coaches' meeting in time. She deserves to wake up next to someone every damn day. We'll get there, eventually. But first, I need to get through this grand opening weekend, then I'll have a little more time to spend with her.

She looked so beautiful and content when I got out of bed. And damn, the woman is a heavy sleeper. It was almost scary how far I made it not only inside her house last night, but in bed with her. I had my hands on her before she even stirred.

It was the same this morning. I got up, showered, dressed, and was gone before she even batted an eyelid. I miss her though, and it's only been a few hours. I look around to see what I need to do next. It's quietened down a little and it's the first time I've stood still for more than a minute all day.

Mac's on the patio with his broadcasting crew, with Kelley hovering nearby. Brianna is in the middle of a Pilates demonstration. Gavin is in the middle of a class in the open gym and I've been personally greeting every visitor and explaining what we do. I'm exhausted and tired of talking, but that's okay. At least my fear of not having people show up hasn't come true. We've gotten larger crowds than I was expecting.

I quickly turn when I hear a car door slam just beyond the roll-up doors. It's my parents with Diana and Olivia. They're all smiles and ready to work out in their gym clothes. I almost laugh at the sight of them.

Diana points to me and says, "That smile says it all. Everything must be going well."

"Yes! I couldn't ask for better. Seriously."

She gives me a big hug and whispers, "I take it you didn't sleep *here* last night."

"Aha! No, I didn't." I withdraw and greet Olivia first with a hug that lifts her off her feet. Once she's back on the ground, she goes to play in the bouncy house set up for the kids. Then I hug my parents. They're both focused intently on the class currently working out. I'm so glad I warned everyone to expect to be watched today. Thankfully, nobody seems bothered by it.

My parents start to wander around and head toward the back patio where Mac and Kelley are and that's when my sister pins me down. "Where's Raegan? I thought they'd be here today."

"Raegan spent the night with her grandmother last night and that's why I didn't come home. Rachel should be here with her anytime now. I'm actually a little surprised they're not here yet, but I've been too busy to message them."

"Wow! That many people dropping in?"

"Yes, and I have to explain the membership to each of them. I've gotten several sign-ups though. So many I'm gonna need to hire more coaches." I point to Gavin and say, "Thankfully, Gavin can hang out in Sac for the next few weeks until we get some help."

"How long before he starts searching for the next location?" she asks, eyeing him.

"He's already searching, but the plan is to finalize something in a year. That gives us time to get this place fully settled." I glance over when another car enters the parking lot. "There they are,"

I say, heading out to greet them. Rachel gets out of the car and that's when I realize she's alone. "Where's Raegan?"

She looks upset but calm. "I'm not sure. She wasn't there when I went to pick her up. Uncle Mitch said they went shopping together, but they're not answering my text messages."

"I thought Raegan wanted to be here today. What the hell?" My voice is raised but I can't help it. I'm upset, even a little hurt that she's not here. "I don't understand."

"I'm sorry, Michael. I don't understand either. She was looking forward to today."

I point to her and say, "This is your mother's doing." I pace in a circle, trying to calm my anger. "She's behind this. She's purposely keeping Raegan away from me."

"I'm sorry, Michael." She lifts her keys back out of her purse and says, "I'll go look for her."

I close my eyes and shake my head. "What's the point? If Raegan wanted to be here, she would be. Right?"

Before Rachel has a chance to answer my question, Gavin's class breaks up and people start saying their goodbyes. I shake a few hands as they're leaving, then I walk over to Gavin. "I need twenty minutes. Can you handle shit here for that long?"

He gives me a thumbs-up and says, "Yeah, you're overdue for a break. I got this covered."

I nod a thank you as I turn away and walk back to Rachel. "Let's go into the office and try to call her. Maybe she'll answer if I call."

Diana and Rachel both follow me in and I close the door behind them. I quickly dial Raegan's phone number and wait. She sends me straight to voicemail. I disconnect and shake my head. "I don't get it."

I feel bad for being angry at Rachel, but I can't help but think this is her mom's doing. I was looking forward to today. I was looking forward to sharing it with Raegan and now she's not here and we don't even know why. How do you brush it off when your kid hurts your feelings? I have no idea. I just wish I knew what was going on.

"I'm going to look for her." Rachel tugs the office door open and says, "I'll let you know when I find her."

After she's gone, I plop into my desk chair and put my phone on the desk. "I don't get it, Diana."

"I wish I understood too. I can't imagine why she's ignoring us… but I'm absolutely sure it's not Rachel's fault."

"Fuck. I know. I'm sorry I snapped at her, but I know Raegan's doing this on purpose."

"She might be, but that's still not Rachel's fault."

"I'll apologize when she gets back." I grab my phone and try Raegan again. It goes straight to voicemail so I leave her a message. "I don't understand, Raegan. I thought you wanted to be a part of this grand opening. You worked as hard as I did all week… This isn't just about me. It's about what we did together… and now you're not here. I miss you and I really wanted to share this with you. What's up, kid? What'd I do wrong? I can't fix it if you don't talk to me. Call me back. I love you… I don't know if I've said that yet, but it's true."

I disconnect and lean back in my chair. I take the next ten minutes trying to calm my nerves. I have to coach the next class so I need to get back on task. After several more deep breaths, I get up to walk back out to the open gym but I'm stopped when my phone rings.

"Hello, did you find her?"

"Yeah. Michael, I'm sorry for this."

"I know. I'm sorry too, I shouldn't have snapped at you. I know it's not your fault. What's happening? Are you bringing her here?"

"No, I'm taking her home. She's got a serious attitude and I didn't want to bring her around your parents when she's being such a brat. I'm so sorry. I'm hoping she gets over it before dinner tonight."

"Wow… that sucks, Rachel."

"I know you wanted her there today. I'm so sorry. I don't know what's gotten into her."

I can hear the frustration in her voice and I feel just as frustrated. I shrug, even though I know she can't see it. "All right. I guess we'll see you when we get there this evening."

"I'm not staying home with her. I'm coming back to the gym. Just because she's a jerk doesn't mean I shouldn't be there. I want to support you."

"Thank you. I appreciate that, but I think you should stay with Raegan. Maybe she'll confide in you and tell you what's going on with her." I clear my throat in an effort to hide the disappointment in my voice. "Besides, I have everyone here. I have support, babe. Thank you though."

"Michael… are you sure? It's really okay to leave her here for a few hours alone."

"I'm sure." I walk into my office and sit down. My body is heavy and I need to get off my feet for a few minutes. "There's something up with her. I don't see her acting like this for no reason at all. Until we know what's going on, you should probably be there for her."

CHAPTER FORTY-ONE

Rachel

Dear Michael,

Life is full of surprises. Today, I learn that four-year-olds like to wander off on their own when you're not watching. Do you have any idea how fast kids can disappear? I didn't either. I only looked away for a second, and then she was gone.

Yes, I lost our child today. It's been the scariest day of my entire life. It's okay. We're home now and safe, but she gave me such a fright. I'm so happy she's okay, yet so mad at her for putting me through that. It's crazy, you know? Crazy how you can love someone so much yet be so angry at the same time. It's the strangest feeling. There's no love like the love we have for our children. One day I hope you get to experience it. Maybe one day you'll see Raegan. Maybe one day we'll meet again, and you'll tell me you love me and we'll be a family. Just like we always should have been.

I miss you terribly. My heart aches daily for you and for what you're missing and for what Raegan is missing by not having you in her life. You'd be such a great dad. You always were so caring and loving.

I'm in college, BTW. I started my third year at Sac State. It's not so bad. I'm not like all the other students. I'm twenty, and I already have a four-year-old, but that's okay. I've made a few friends and even been out on a few dates. Of course, they don't usually work out. Once they find out I'm a mom, they suddenly don't have time to date. That's okay, though. I've found that whenever I'm with someone else, all I can do is think about you.

How's the University of Oregon? I hope you're enjoying everything there is to enjoy about college life.

Here's a fun fact: Raegan's favorite color is red.

Here's another fun fact: Raegan is so damn cute, it's hard to be mad at her for very long.

I love you… still,
Rachel

CHAPTER FORTY-TWO

Raegan

I'm been ignoring my mom's text messages. Eventually, I'm gonna have to answer her, but I'm not sure what to say. I'm not sure how to get rid of Mike. At this point, my only plan of action is to be a complete jerk to him in the hope that it scares him off. Nobody wants to deal with bratty teenagers. If he doesn't want to be around me, he won't need to be around Mom. She'll be safe from him and we can go back to the way things were before.

When Grandma comes into the room, she smiles at me and says, "So, what's the plan? Should I take you home, Raegan?"

"No. I'm sure my mom's looking for me but I really don't want to go. I'm not sure what to do. I'm worried about her and I feel like I've pushed her into having to deal with an abuser."

"You have to take it one day at a time, Raegan. He'll show his true colors soon enough, so be careful."

I hear the front door open and I know it's my mom, and I can tell by the sound of her footsteps that she's pissed.

I hear her before I see her. "Raegan, you ready? We need to go." She comes in and says, "What are you playing at, Mother?"

Grandma looks a little shocked, but I know it's my fault. I'm the one who didn't want to go home.

"Mom, Grandma hasn't done anything wrong."

She looks at me and says, "We had plans today. Where have you been?"

"I went to breakfast with Grandma and we did a little shopping. I'm ready so we can go now. You don't have to be all huffy with everyone."

"Raegan Elizabeth, do not speak to me like that. I've been trying to reach you all day and you've ignored me."

"My battery died!"

"The house phone still works. Your grandmother's phone still works."

"Whatever, Mom. Let's just go!" I shout back at her. Jeez, she doesn't need to be so mean to me. I'm doing this for her. She'll be better off once Mike is out of our lives.

My mom doesn't say two words to me on the way home. I know she's mad. I know she's upset that I didn't go to the grand opening, but if she knew why... If she knew I knew about Mike's abuse all those years ago, she'd appreciate my effort.

When we get inside the house, my mom goes to her room to make a call. I know she's calling Mike, but I don't care. I go to my room and slam the door. I need to keep up the act if I'm really going to scare him away. He can't think this is a one-time thing. He needs to know that I'm horrible all the time. Mom's going to hate it. She might even be embarrassed, but she'll get over it once it's just us again.

It's not that hard to act mad. I am so disappointed in Mike. I thought he was a nice guy. I thought he cared about my mom. Now I know he's just a... what was the word Grandma used... narcissist. I get out my computer and Google it. I want to make sure I understand what kind of person I come from. I don't want to turn into him.

I read the definition and I have trouble putting Mike into that category. Yeah, he looks good and he cares about his looks, but mostly, he really cares about his health. But if everything my grandma says is true, he's worse than the typical narcissist.

While I'm looking it up, my mom comes into my room. She really looks upset, but I know I need to stick with this. I can't let my sympathy for her keep me from doing what I need to do… even if it means I don't get to have a father.

She comes in and sits on the end of my bed so I close my laptop. I don't want her to see what I'm looking at. "Raegan, are you going to tell me what's happening?"

"Mom, there is nothing going on. I don't want to go to the gym. Why is it so important for me to be there?"

"It's an important day for Mike. It was important to him for us to be there. He's hurt that you're acting like you don't care."

"I'm not acting. I actually don't care."

"Stop, Raegan, I know you don't mean that."

"I do, Mom."

"Please, please adjust your attitude before the Murphys get here this evening. I need you to behave yourself."

This really makes me feel bad because I was excited about having a large family and cousins too. "What am I doing wrong?"

"Excuse me? Your attitude? Do you not recognize how you're acting?" I think she's waiting for me to say something, but I don't have anything to say. I'll do what I need to do to save her. Even if it hurts.

"I'm just not interested in hanging out at the gym again today."

"Honey, did Grandma do something… or say something to upset you?" She bites on her lip, like she does sometimes when she doesn't want to tell me something. "You know, she's never liked Mike, but that doesn't mean it should affect your relationship with him."

"What about your relationship with him?"

"I'm not sure why you ask that, but my relationship with him shouldn't affect you either. He's your dad and that's not going to change."

I know that's not true. If I have a relationship with him, she has to as well. She can't pretend he doesn't exist. He'll be around… like, a lot. I'm not stupid. I have several friends who come from split homes. Weekends with different parents. Constant fighting. I've seen it. "You're reading too much into this, Mom. It's not about Grandma—and it's not about you. I just don't want to go."

She slaps her hands on her knees and practically jumps up in exacerbation. "Fine, Raegan, but you'd better be on your best behavior when they get here. I'm not kidding. If you act out, you will be punished."

She won't even meet my eyes as she leaves my room. *I'm sorry, Mom.* It's all I can think. I'm sorry for being such a jerk. I'm sorry for pushing you to bring that man into our lives. I'm sorry I have to act out in order to save you from him. I just wish you'd told me before.

If she'd trusted me in the beginning, I wouldn't have pushed. I wouldn't have searched for him. He wouldn't be in our lives and she wouldn't have to deal with trying to keep him at arm's length while also trying to keep me happy.

I fall back on my pillow and try to relax. I didn't sleep at all last night. I was so worried this wouldn't work. What if I'm mean to Mike and he takes it out on my mom? What if I make things worse? Maybe I should tell her that I know. What would be the point, though? We all live in the same city. It's not like we can move away from him… and I know he's here to stay.

I grab my phone to put my music on and see that I have a voicemail. I click the notification… it's from Mike. Gosh! Why won't they leave me alone? I hit the play button and listen to his message. With every word, I feel worse and worse. This cannot be the monster Grandma has portrayed in everything she said. Surely he's not that good an actor?

Is this how abusers work? They lull you into a false sense of security and then turn the tables when you're least expecting it?

I don't know what to think. Now I'm questioning everything I'm doing.

I don't want to be this person. I'm not drama queen material. It's not who I am… but what about Mom? Is she right? Is it possible to have a father-daughter relationship and still protect her? I just don't know how to do that.

CHAPTER FORTY-THREE

Rachel

Mike shows up before his parents and I'm so glad. I can tell he's still not happy and I'm so upset that we've ruined his day. When he comes inside, I can see that he's already been home and cleaned up from being at the gym all day. He's dressed in shorts and a t-shirt, as if ready to swim. He scans the living room, looking for Raegan, but she's still in her room.

"How's it going?" he asks quietly, leaning in to give me a sly peck on the cheek.

"She's been in her room since I got home. I'm not sure what to think. I really don't know what happened."

It's as if he deflates when he hears this. "Maybe we need to confront her about it?"

"And what if it turns into a big fight before your parents get here?" I ask, closing the front door.

"Rachel, we can't be ruled by the emotional outburst of a thirteen-year-old girl. If she blows her top with my parents around, it's on her. She'll only embarrass herself."

"And me, Mike! Listen, I completely agree with you. If this were any other day or any other party, I'd cancel it right now. But it's not. This was supposed to be a big deal. We're supposed to be celebrating you and your gym opening. I don't want her to ruin it."

His eyes drift around and he finally says, "Let's just carry on without her. Leave her in her room and if she wants to meet people, she'll come out. If she doesn't, she won't. We can all still try to enjoy ourselves."

"Good idea." I wave him in the direction of the kitchen where I'm working on the food prep. I peek down the hall before entering the kitchen but her door is shut tight. Whatever. He's right, we need to let her come to terms with this on her own. She's the one acting out and we can't give in to her temper tantrums.

I take out all the fixings for the salad and say, "I still need to tell you about my talk with my mother."

"I really, really don't like Raegan being alone with her. I don't trust her and we don't need her interfering in our lives."

"I made it clear to her that we wouldn't put up with any of her nonsense. She needs to accept that this is happening and we will not allow her to interfere with us being a family."

"How did she take that?"

"At first she didn't take it well at all. I ended up telling her about the rape and about therapy. I told her I how depressed I was after that and how she didn't even notice. I really let her have it. I told her I was done being her victim and that it was her fault that I'd become such a doormat and I wasn't going to be that doormat any longer." I finish washing the veggies and take out a large salad bowl. "I told her a lot and she seem to understand."

"Good. Jesus, Rachel, it's about time."

"I know, but after our talk the other night, I realized I've lived in this void for so long and I'm tired of it. I'm done taking her shit. I'm done taking everyone's shit."

Mike raises his eyebrows at that and it makes me smile. "Rachel Williams, did you just curse?"

"I sure the fuck did," I say, whispering the f word.

He takes the salad bowl from my hand and sets it on the counter before bringing me close. "I'm so proud of you."

"Don't be." I brush him and his praise off. "It's embarrassing. I should have told her off years ago."

"Yes, you should have, but that goes against your nature." He gently tucks a strand of hair behind my ear. "It's not who you are so I understand what a leap this is for you." Playfully poking me with his finger, he takes a step back. "Just don't start that shit on me or I'll have to punish you for back-talking me."

This makes me laugh so hard I nearly snort. I reach out and lightly smack his chest.

"Shut up!"

Mike fakes a deep voice and says, "Watch your mouth, woman!"

We're laughing when the doorbell chimes. Both our backs go straight at the same time and it's funny because we look like we've been caught doing something wrong.

"That's all you. I'm not answering that door."

He laughs as he walks to the door. "So much for being in this together."

I hear him greet his family and everyone sounds so happy and full of smiles. When they come inside, Mike leads them to the back patio. I stay in the kitchen because I'm really not sure what to say. I briefly saw them earlier today at the gym, but I was too preoccupied with Raegan to really say hello.

While Mike comes back inside to get them drinks, I place the prepared salad in the fridge, then grab the marinated tri-tip steak and take it out so it can come to room temperature. I place the shucked corn on the counter, and he says, "You're hiding."

"No, I'm preparing food, not hiding."

"Now you're lying." This makes me smile, despite myself. Okay, yes, he's right. I'm a coward and I'm hiding. "Don't worry," he says. "They're not interested in drilling you. They just want to see you and get to know Raegan."

I try to smile at this, but it's half-hearted. "I wouldn't blame them for hating me."

"I would… but it doesn't matter, they don't. Come on."

I follow him out of the kitchen and into the backyard. I'm immediately hugged by Diana and Olivia and that puts me a little more at ease. "I hope you guys are swimming," I say when Olivia jumps into my arms.

"Yes, yes," she says. "Where's Raegan, is she going to swim too?"

"I think she's planning to join you in a while."

Mike saves me from saying more when he says, "You guys remember Rachel, don't you?"

Mike's mom gives me a big smile as she stands to hug me. "Yes, of course. It's good to see you, Rachel. Thank you for inviting us over for dinner." When Sharon releases me, she says, "And thank you very much for getting us a room at The Sutter. It's such a beautiful place. Mike said you're the manager there. Is that right?"

"Yes, I started as a part-time event planner years ago. When I finished school, I was hired on as the event and wedding manager. And a few years later, I was promoted to hotel manager. I really love it there. The owner group gives me full autonomy so I don't have to answer to anyone really."

"Well, it's a beautiful place and our suite is amazing."

"Good, I'm glad you're enjoying your stay."

Mike and I take a seat at the patio table with them and as I sit, Mike's dad, Edward says, "I'm glad to see you're doing well, Rachel. We were all worried when you disappeared."

I feel instant heat in my cheeks and for a moment, I can't respond. Thankfully, Mike saves me from having to say anything right away.

"Dad, we haven't talked to Raegan about everything yet so please don't bring it up when she's here."

He flashes me an apologetic look and says, "Okay, I just wanted Rachel to know we missed her. Her absence was felt by all of us."

"Thank you for saying that. I missed you all too. It was a very hard time… for everyone. I know."

"Mike mentioned your mom was behind the sudden move—I don't ever remember meeting her when you two were in school."

"It's true," Sharon says. "I don't think we ever did meet her. Do you know what it was that she had against Mike? I even remember him mentioning back then that she never liked him."

"Do we really need to talk about this now, guys?" Mike throws his hands out in irritation and says, "Come on. This is supposed to be a family dinner. I don't want to make Rachel or Raegan feel uncomfortable by talking about the past bullshit."

I lay a hand on his in an effort to relax him. I know he feels the need to defend me, but I don't want his irritation to inflame the situation. I take a deep breath to explain but I'm interrupted by my phone vibrating in my pocket. I grab it to read the display.

Raegan: *Mom, were you raped?*

I'm so surprised reading this, the phone slips from my hand and hits the ground with a smack. Mike quickly snatches it up and glances at the display. His eyes go wide as he hands the phone back. I can see he's as freaked out by the message as I am.

"What's this about?"

"Um… I'm not sure." I smile at everyone and say, "I'm sorry, but I need to go check on something. I'll be back in a few minutes." Then I rush into the house and toward Raegan's room. I push the door open to find her sitting on her bed, waiting for me, and it's clear she's been crying. Her agitation is obvious. Laying around her in piles are all of my notes from high school. She's opened them all and read them. It's as if she's looking for something.

"Raegan, what did Grandma tell you?"

"So, it's true. You were raped?"

"Is that why you're acting out the way you are? Because she told you that."

She rolls her eyes. "Why do you always avoid answering my questions? You told me you'd talk to me—stop treating me like a child. Why can't you be honest?"

"Wait—so, I get victimized and that gives you an excuse to be nasty to me? Is that how this is working now, Rae? Because if it is, I'm leaving. I don't need your attitude. I have people here who actually want to talk to me."

Her gaze falls to the ground and I can tell what I said got to her. She scrubs her nose with the back of her hand and says, "I'm sorry, Mom. I'm just upset. I've read every one of these and I don't see any signs of aggression. I don't see anything wrong."

As I approach her, she sits up and wraps her arms around me.

"What do these old letters have to do with that?"

She squeezes me and says, "I'm so confused."

"Raegan, I'm sorry your grandmother shared that with you, but she shouldn't have. I'm fine, you can see that. It happened a long time ago and everything is okay now. If you want to talk about it, we can, but today isn't the time."

"I started this and I don't know how to fix it." Now she's outright sobbing, her chest pumping in and out as she tries to calm herself.

I'm completely confused now too. "What are you talking about?"

"It's my fault you're having to entertain your rapist. If you'd told me—been honest from the beginning—I wouldn't have pushed you to find him."

I draw back from her and grip her shoulders. "What are you talking about? I'm not entertaining my rapist." Just as I finish saying this, Mike walks into Raegan's room.

"Everything okay?" he asks.

"Why don't you leave?" Raegan shouts at him. "Nobody wants you here!"

Mike's eyebrows raise as he stares at her, obviously hurt by what she has said. "What have I done to suddenly offend you, Raegan?"

"Mike." I reach my hand out to stop him from saying more. "I think there's been a huge misunderstanding."

"I know what you did. I know what you're like. You're a typical narcissist."

As soon as I hear this, I know exactly what's happened and I want to throw up. My mother. How could she?

"Stop!" I shout at her. "Stop talking right now!"

"It's okay, Rachel. She doesn't want me here, I'll go."

"No! You stop too! Stop right there. You're both going to come in here. Shut the damn door and let me talk."

"Mom, let him go. It's okay. We don't need him here."

"Raegan, say another word and I'm going to tape your damn mouth shut. Let me talk!"

She leans back against her headboard and crosses her arms over her chest. Mike closes the door and leans against it, crossing his arms over his chest. My eyes switch between them and it's stunning how alike they are. If this wasn't a very serious moment, I'd get a camera.

"Raegan, you asked me if I was raped. Did Grandma tell you I was raped?"

She nods. "Yes, she told me everything."

"Why would your mother tell her something like that?"

"Aha! Stop talking—both of you." I point to him then to her. "I'm doing the talking right now." I try again. "Raegan, did Grandma tell you who raped me?"

I glance at Mike as I ask this question and his head tilts with confusion. I give him a *be quiet* look and it works, he keeps his mouth shut.

Glaring at Mike, Raegan says, "Yes."

His eyes widen. "Wait a minute… are you telling me—"

"Michael, please, stop. Let me do this."

"Raegan, who did she tell you raped me?"

"Why the song and dance, Mom? We all know it was Mike. Otherwise, we wouldn't be having this conversation."

I'm fighting with everything I have to not lose it. I'm so upset. I cover my mouth with my hand and stand there, staring at her. I seriously do not know what to say. I look over at Mike. He's pale, and actually looks sick too. My eyes are locked on his as I shake my head. "I'm sorry." My voice cracks and that forces me to turn my back on them both so I can get my bearings. I shake it off and turn back toward my daughter and kneel in front of her. I want her to look into my eyes when I tell her this.

"Raegan," my voice wavers so I take a breath and try again. "Your grandmother lied to you. I was raped… but it wasn't Mike. Michael has never hurt me. I was raped by a man I was dating four years ago."

"No, no, Mom. Grandma told me Mike was abusive to you and that he was mean to you and that's why you didn't tell him you were pregnant. That's why you ran away when you found out about me. She said you were scared of him."

I shake my head, and tears drip from my eyes. I'm fighting with everything I have to keep my cool. I'm so embarrassed and ashamed of my mother, now I can't even look in Mike's direction.

"No, Raegan, everything she told you is a complete lie. None of that is true. I was… I was in love with Mike." I place a hand on my chest. "I am still in love with him. He has never… never once hurt me." My voice cracks so I stop to take a cleansing breath. "I left town when I got pregnant because Grandma threatened to put you up for adoption. She threated to have Mike arrested. *She* did all of that. *She* was abusive. *She* did this. Not Mike. She made me promise not to tell him about you. She made a lot of threats… I was afraid of her, not Mike."

CHAPTER FORTY-FOUR

Michael

"I'm so sorry," Rachel says as she gets to her feet. She's obviously mortified by her mother's actions. I walk over and pull her to me. I don't care if Raegan is watching. I don't care if she knows we're together. I don't care if she doesn't like it. I can't see Rachel this upset and not comfort her. I wrap my hands around her and hold her close. She's trembling and as soon as her head hits my chest, she loses all control over her emotions.

I let her cry it out and having her do it in my arms is a relief. I need to be useful, otherwise I'm going to explode. I don't understand why that woman hates me so much. Just as Rachel's crying slows, I feel a set of arms come around us both. Rachel freezes and I do too, then I peek over to see Raegan gripping us both around our waists, her face buried between us.

I lower my left arm to wrap around her and Rachel does too. Now they're both crying and as much as I hate it, I love it at the same time. These are my girls. My family.

After a long time, Rachel withdraws and Raegan clings to me. I lift her off her feet and hold her against me. She's not little, but she's light so it's easy to do. When I hear her whisper, "I'm sorry. I'm so sorry for what I said. I'm so sorry about today. I'm sorry for believing her. I was so confused because… because…"

"Hey, it's okay. This isn't your fault." I set her down and she sits back on the bed. Rachel and I sit on either side of her.

Rachel grabs her hand. "This isn't your fault, Rae. She's manipulative and horrible."

"But why would she tell me that? Why would she want me to believe that..." Raegan's voice cracks and after a pause, she says, "That I was born from that?"

As soon as I hear this, I want to punch a wall. What the fuck is up with that woman? I look over at Rachel, who shakes her head in disgust. "I don't know why, Raegan, but I think we need to ask her." She's still wiping the tears from her face, but her voice is almost back to normal and that makes me feel better.

"Maybe we should," I say. "I think it's time she answers for what she's done—to all of us."

"We're supposed to meet her for brunch tomorrow. Would you like to join us?"

I nod. "Yep. I'll be there."

"Let's invite your entire family. She should be accountable to everyone."

"Jesus, woman, I love the savage in you. I wish you'd show it more often."

This makes Raegan laugh and it's the sweetest sound. I wrap an arm around her shoulders and say, "Your real grandparents are in the backyard waiting for dinner. What do you say we go out there so you can meet them?"

Raegan nods and then grins up at me. "I would like that."

Rachel and I stand and Rachel says, "Take a minute if you need it... put on your swimsuit, then come outside and have some fun with us. Okay?"

Raegan gets up and hugs her mom one more time, then we leave her alone. We both stop in the hall to have a moment to collect ourselves too. We stare at each other and it's as if we're both in shock.

When Rachel starts to apologize again, I lay my finger on her lips. "Stop apologizing for your mother. It's not your fault."

"I can't believe this… I don't know what to say." She closes her eyes and shakes her head. "She completely ruined your day and how absurd of her to tell Raegan that!"

I put my arm around her and lead her toward the kitchen. "Yes, she screwed up the day, but she's shown her true colors. She's given us a gift. Now we know what we're dealing with, we just need to learn why."

She points outside. "And we have to explain it to your family."

"Yes, we do." I let out a long breath. "Let's get that out of the way before Raegan joins us. Maybe that will keep her from feeling embarrassed."

Rachel follows me out and we spend a few minutes explaining what happened… but we leave out the information about her being raped. That's none of their business and not something I want to force her to talk about again. No matter how we tell the story, her mother looks bad.

I get a little excited when they all agree to meet in the lobby of the hotel in the morning. My parents are already staying there so it works out anyway.

We're all going to confront her together. I cannot wait.

Just as we get our plan in place, Raegan walks out onto the patio in her swimsuit. She stands next to her mom and she seems to be avoiding my eyes. I understand why, but it still bums me out. I'll give her a little time, then I'll talk to her about it again.

"Raegan, this is my mom and dad… your grandma and grandpa." Then I say, "Mom, Dad, meet your granddaughter."

Expecting my mom to cry, I'm not surprised to see she's already wiping the tears from her face as she embraces Raegan, who's pretty stiff for a moment but then relaxes into the hug. My mom squeezes her then leans back to get a good look at her. "You look so much like your dad," she says.

"She looks like Olivia," Dad says, and that makes Raegan glance at Olivia, who's getting out of the pool.

Mom releases her and then my dad approaches and says, "Can I give you a hug too?"

Raegan gives him a hesitant smile and nods. My big burly dad wraps his arms around her and holds her for a solid minute. Raegan hugs him back and her arms barely reach all the way around him, but at least she doesn't seem uncomfortable with him.

"It's a pleasure to meet you, Raegan."

"You too," Raegan says with a hesitant smile.

"Me too!" Olivia says, wrapping her arms around Raegan. "Can you swim with me now?"

This breaks up some of the tension and makes all the adults laugh. Raegan lifts a shoulder and says, "Sure."

Thankfully, the rest of the night goes off without a hitch. My parents stay until well after ten, and when they all leave, Olivia is yawning like crazy. Once they're gone, I help Rachel clean up the kitchen while Raegan puts everything away on the patio.

When she comes inside she's quiet and I'm sure she's still feeling bad about earlier. She helps put the dishes away and then she retreats to her room to get out of her swimsuit. Rachel opens a bottle of wine and I'm not sure that's going to be enough to medicate us both after today. When I make the joke to her, she says, "I still have the bourbon, if we need it."

"Yeah, but I have to drive home."

"*Do* you have to drive home?" Raegan asks as she walks back into the kitchen. "Maybe you should stay?"

I nod at that and consider it. "Raegan, if I stay, I'm sleeping in your mom's room and you're gonna have to be okay with that."

Her mouth quirks into a grin. "That's okay."

"Is it?" Rachel asks. "We didn't want to rush it, for your sake."

She nods vigorously. "It makes me happy. I want you to be happy, too, Mom."

Rachel smiles. It's a cautious smile, but obviously genuine. "Your dad makes me happy, Raegan." Then her expression turns sad and she says, "I owe you an apology. You were absolutely right, if I had talked to you, been honest, you would have known Grandma was lying to you. I didn't tell you because I didn't want to hurt you. I didn't want you to know how awful she really is. That's my fault."

"Mom, I'm sorry about… what happened to you." Raegan's face reddens and tears form in her eyes. I can see she's fighting to get the next few words out. "I'm so sorry if I forced you to remember something horrible."

Rachel reaches out and takes her hand. "I'm sorry I didn't share it with you. It's hard to talk about that, it hurts to remember, but thanks to you and Mike, it's getting easier."

"You have to remember to use your voice, Mom. You always tell me that, I wish you would remember it too."

"I will. I promise to be better, and set a better example for you."

"You do set a good example though, Mom. You're a good mom and a really good person. I always ask myself, *what would Mom do in this situation?*" She lifts a shoulder in a shrug. "I don't always do the same thing, but at least I consider it."

I push out a loud laugh when I hear this and it makes me realize that this kid might actually have some of my DNA. We obviously have the same smart mouth. After a drink and a long talk with the girls, I make arrangements with Gavin for him to open the gym tomorrow so I can take the time off to confront Rachel's mom at brunch.

Then I head to bed, with my woman… where I should be. As I'm curling into bed with her, I realize that, even with all that went wrong today, it's still one of the best days of my life.

CHAPTER FORTY-FIVE

Rachel

We're waiting for her in the lobby with a plan. Once we see her walking toward the entrance, Raegan is going to send a text to Mike and he's going to come into the lobby with his family in tow. I'm struggling with the idea of putting my mom on the spot like this, but I'm also reveling in the fact that she has to answer for what she's done. I'm anxious yet so determined. It's the ultimate betrayal. How dare she do this after I warned her not to interfere? How dare she tell me that sob story about her old boyfriend? How stupid of me to fall for it!

Not any longer.

I'm done with her. She'll never see us again. I will never forgive her for what she did to Raegan. To make her believe she was conceived from rape. How could she?

"That's her car, Rae. Give it another minute then send the text. We want her inside before Mike comes in." When I see my mother climb the front steps, I say, "Okay, send it now."

A moment later, she's entering and I sense a slight hesitation, as if she knows she's walking into a trap, but her stride continues as she approaches us. My heart starts racing and I realize she can probably tell by the look on my face that something's not right. I fight to act normal... but I know I suck at it. I'm a bad liar, and I hate putting people on the spot. But as soon as she starts talking, I realize I might enjoy this.

"Honestly, Rachel, why are we meeting in the lobby instead of the restaurant? I thought we had a table reserved."

"We wanted to talk with you about something before we sit down to eat, Mother."

"Why can't we talk while we're sitting? I don't understand…"— her eyes go wide—"What's this?" And I know Mike's just walked up behind me. I sense his presence as soon as he's near, but when I see her face, I know for sure he's there.

"You remember Michael Murphy, don't you, Mother?" I twist to see him and then wrap my arm through his when he steps closer. At this point my mother looks annoyed, but then I see the change. I watch as her color fades and her eyes enlarge and I'm a little fearful she might faint.

"Oh, my God. Barbara, is that you? Barbara Crawford?" Sharon says.

Mike and I glance at each other, confused, then we turn to face Mike's mom and dad.

Edward and Sharon turn toward each other and when their eyes meet, it's as if a silent understanding passes between them and the fog clears. Edward shakes his head. "I can't believe this." Then his voice booms when he says, "Barbara, *you* are Rachel's mother?"

"Wait, you two know each other?" Mike says, and I'm glad he's still got enough sense to ask questions because I'm dumbfounded. "That's impossible."

"Barbara and I were college roommates our freshman year at U of O," Sharon says.

This fact makes me gasp—and it hits me like a ton of bricks. My arm, linked with Mike's, instantly locks in reaction and it takes a few seconds for me to catch my breath. When I can finally talk, my voice is loud, and accusing. "You are joking?" My eyes fix on her face and now my heart is pounding so hard I feel like it might jump right out of my chest. "Mom! Please tell me she's mistaken."

My mother glances at me then back to Sharon and Edward. "It's Barbara Crawford Williams now, not that it matters."

"You conniving, manipulative bitch!" I hear a collective gasp when I say this. "Please tell me you didn't do all of this for revenge. Oh my God! Please tell me you didn't completely screw up my life over an old boyfriend…" I'm equally upset and mad at the same time and this comes through in my thick voice. I'm seriously torn between complete shock and absolute acceptance, because *of course* she did this. "Please, Mother, please tell me this isn't what you did."

"What are you saying, Rach?" Mike asks, with the most confused expression on his face.

"She's saying that her mother and I were a couple in college… then I broke up with her because I fell in love with your mother." Edward's deep voice rumbles over the group, but it doesn't faze my mother at all. She stares at him like she could care less about him or what he's saying. Her stance is confident and I don't know how she does it. I'd wilt under the pressure.

"It's true, your father and Rachel's mother are former sweet-hearts," Sharon explains, dropping her hand on Mike's shoulder. "And here I didn't think she could get any more vindictive. I guess I was wrong… of course, that was nearly thirty-five years ago, but some people are simply that crazy."

At this, my mom lifts her chin higher, looking almost proud of what she's done.

"So, Barb, all the trouble you caused in college wasn't enough? You had to take it further. You had to hide our granddaughter from us? Keep my son from knowing his child?" Edward asks.

"Wait…" Mike says, "You did this to us… you forced Rachel to keep my daughter a secret to get back at my parents for something they did in college? That's crazy."

"Excuse me while I have a private conversation with my daughter," my mother says, trying to take me aside.

"Oh, no!" Mike steps between us. "You no longer get the privilege of private conversations with my family. Whatever you need to say can be said to all of us."

I nudge him aside to face her. I don't need him to fight my battles. I refuse to be the meek little girl my mother taught me to be. I've found my voice and she's going to hear me whether she likes it or not. "I couldn't possibly believe anything you have to say to me. This is completely unforgiveable."

"Rachel, we talked about this. You know why I did what I did. I wanted to protect you. That's all I ever wanted."

"Protect her from whom, exactly?" Diana asks.

I raise my voice over hers, because again, she will hear me even if I have to force her to listen. "What we talked about was how you wouldn't interfere in my relationship with Mike, or Raegan's relationship with Mike... and it was a lie. It was all lies. Just like all the lies you told Raegan about her dad being abusive. Now I understand why you've always been so against Michael—and it has nothing to do with him or me." I point my finger at her bony chest and I'm fighting with everything I have to keep my composure. In the back of my mind, I haven't forgotten that this is my place of business—and that's probably the only thing helping me keep my cool. "The only protection I've ever needed is from you, Mother."

"That's not what this is. If you stop shouting at me... can't we go to your office and talk about this?"

"Absolutely not. I will not go anywhere with you. How could you? How could you tell your granddaughter that she was conceived from rape? How could you use my nightmare against me—against Mike—use that to play on Rae's sympathies, to make her feel guilty for wanting her father? For wanting to see me happy—finally happy." This last part comes out in a whisper of emotion. I just can't believe this. I don't know what to think… I'm not sure how to feel… knowing what she's put me through—put all of us through for all of these years.

"You really are exaggerating, Rachel. If you'll listen to me…"

Edward steps closer. "It's not an exaggeration to say you faked a pregnancy to get back at us thirty-five years ago. That you faked a miscarriage. Was that really not enough revenge for you, Barbara?" My mother looks affected by his words and takes a step back. "When will it be enough?" Her eyes are wide as they bounce from one person to another. When they land on Raegan, she says, "Raegan…"

Diana steps in front of Raegan, as if to shield her from my mother. As she does this, I say, "Do not speak to her. She's heard enough of your lies."

"I think you can go now," Mike says. "And don't let the door hit you in the ass on your way out."

Instead of leaving, my mother stares at me, her back erect and her face pinched into a frown. I have zero sympathy for her and that surprises me, but I'm so incredibly hurt. I gesture toward the door. "Go, Mother. Stay away from me, stay away from Raegan, and stay away from the Murphys."

After another long look, she turns and walks away. I don't move until she's outside and slowly descending the front steps. Even after all of this, she still carries herself with arrogance… she still doesn't show an ounce of shame. As soon as she's gone, I turn to Mike and nearly collapse against him. He wraps an arm around my waist.

"God dammit, I'm sorry, babe," he whispers. "I had no idea."

Edward steps forward and focuses his intense eyes on me. He looks so much like Mike, like Raegan. "I'm sorry, Rachel. I had no idea she was your mother."

"It's… it's not your fault. None of this is any of our faults. She's responsible… entirely." The sentence comes out breathy and I feel like I might be going into shock or something. My limbs feel heavy and I want to lay down.

I must look as bad as I feel because Mike's mom approaches and wraps an arm around me. Very motherly ... yet, so unlike my own mother. "Rachel, let Mike take you home. We'll take Raegan with us for the day and drop her off to you later... I think you guys could use some time alone."

I lift my eyes to look at Raegan and she is obviously upset too. I reach out for her and she hugs me so fiercely I know I need to put on a stronger face for her.

"I'm fine, honey. I can see you're worried, but I'm fine. I want to go home though. Can you spend the rest of the day with your family? Are you okay with that?"

She nods into my shoulder and agrees. "I love you, Mom."

"I love you too. Go spend time with them, get to know them. You deserve real grandparents... But, Raegan, I want you to block Grandma's number on your phone. If she tries to call you, do not talk to her."

"I'll block her. I don't ever want to see her again." She lets me go and says, "I can stay with you, if you need me."

"No, I'm fine. If you're okay, I'm okay, but I'll see you later." I plant a kiss on the top of her head.

She nods and joins Diana and Olivia. I say my goodbyes and let Mike lead me out the front entrance and into the bright, sunny morning. I'm relieved. Relieved to be out from under the sympathetic eyes and relieved to be alone with Mike.

CHAPTER FORTY-SIX

Michael

Rachel doesn't say a word on the way home. I'm not sure what I was expecting, but I know she's hurt beyond anything I've ever experienced. I don't know what to say… and probably shouldn't say anything. It's important to be there for her so that's what I'm doing. I park in her driveway and get out, then walk over to her side of the car and open her door. She slowly gets out, avoiding my eyes. I hope she's not looking for ways to blame herself for this. It'd be just like her.

I unlock the front door and open it for her. Rachel walks to her bedroom. I follow her and watch as she removes her shoes, and curls up on the bed. Nothing, and I mean nothing, could possibly worry me more. I already know she struggles with depression. I don't want her to withdraw from me.

I lay down next to her and haul her to me. She embraces me and that eases my worry some. "I'm here when you're ready to talk."

"Do you think she ever cared about me?" Her voice is heavy but clear and that surprises me.

"I think… in her own sick way she probably did think she was protecting you."

"How is telling her granddaughter a bunch of lies protecting me?"

"Okay, no, that was about revenge, not protection. I meant when she found out you were pregnant. But the truth is, her crimes are numerous and we'll never truly know why she did what she did."

"I feel sorry for her."

I almost sigh in relief when she says this. Again, I don't know what I was expecting, but it wasn't a reasonable woman trying to understand the motives of her monster of a mother. But here she is, staying strong and making sense.

"Maybe she knew we'd never believe her," she reasons. "Maybe she thought once we found out about your parents we'd never believe she had good intentions fourteen years ago when she moved me away."

"So, you think lying to Raegan was a last-ditch effort to keep us from finding out?"

"It was her last-ditch effort to keep us apart... it's the only thing I can believe. Why else would she make up lies that would be so hurtful? She never counted on Raegan talking to me about it."

"I'm sorry. I'm sorry she's hurt you so much over the years. After your talk with her the other day, she had the rare opportunity to turn the past around—to make things right, and she didn't take it."

"I'm not sure how to feel right now. It's an odd sense of grief and relief at the same time. Similar to how I felt after losing my dad. I was terribly sad that he was gone, yet so relieved he was no longer in pain." After saying this, she turns to face me and I'm surprised again by her clear, bright eyes. "Michael, I'm sorry I let her do this to us... and I know you're going to say it wasn't my fault. I might not have been able to change things all those years ago, but I can promise, I will never let anyone come between us ever again."

She leans in and kisses me with the lightest touch and I'm so proud of her. I'm so proud of how she's handled herself today with her mother... and impressed with her resilience. "Rachel, we need to let her go and move forward, okay? We have the rest of our lives together and she can't fuck with us anymore."

She nods and I can see the moisture in her eyes, but I give her a minute to get past it. When she gets up, I'm not sure what's happening but then she starts to strip out of her clothes. "I need this horrible feeling to go away." I strip down too and lay next to her. I want to feel her, skin on skin, and I know it's what we both need. We hold each other for a long time and I realize this is how I medicate now. Rachel is all I need and I'm what she needs. I press my lips to hers and taste her, enjoy her. The longer I kiss her, the more responsive she becomes.

She's emotionally exhausted, I am too, but I need her as close as I can get her. When she's pressed against me, and slips her tongue between my lips, I slide my hand down between her legs and find her wet. It's all the encouragement I need.

I hover over her and watch her. Waiting for what, I don't know. We're quiet and her eyes are soft, but then her voice breaks the silence. "I don't want to know how different things could have been. How we could have had this for all these years."

My body's now aching with the need to be surrounded by her warmth. Pushing inside her, I watch as her expression changes from sad to smoldering and that's exactly what I wanted. "Baby." I hold myself firmly within her and wait as she lifts closer to me. "Don't think about what's lost. Think about what's to come."

She smiles seductively and so do I, now thrusting against her in an effort to make her forget everything but me. Our eyes are locked on each other as I move slowly, but even at this pace it doesn't take long for her need to gain in urgency. That's when her eyes begin to close and her body tightens around me. "I love you, Rachel."

That's all it takes. "Oh, God, Michael..." Her body lifts off the bed, arching closer. Watching her come, I fight not to lose control of my own release. When her gaze is back on mine, that's all I need to let go.

As our racing pulses slow to a normal rhythm, I pull her to me and keep a tight hold on her. She holds tight to me too. It's almost as if we're both afraid the other will disappear.

"I love you too," she finally whispers. "And I like you here."

"I like me here, too."

With a clear and strong voice, she says, "Will you stay?"

I nod against her. "As long as you want me."

"Forever." She lifts her head so that we're nose to nose. "I mean, permanently. I want you to move in with us."

I smile when I hear this. I know it's fast, I know she knows it's fast, but when you put our relationship in perspective, it's really not. I've loved her for more than half of my life.

"Are you sure you want that?"

"I've never been more sure of anything in my life. I don't want to waste another day... another hour."

I plant a kiss on her forehead and say, "I will move in here permanently on one condition."

"Anything, I'd do anything for you."

"Marry me."

Her eyes stretch wide and her mouth breaks into the biggest smile I think I've ever seen on her. But as quickly as her smile spreads, it fades. "Are you sure?"

"You're not?"

"I am!" she says it loudly, as if it's the dumbest question I could have asked her.

"I am too." I stare into her deep blue eyes and say, "So... will you marry me?"

With another big grin, she says, "Yes!"

EPILOGUE

Raegan

My dad's best friend is getting married today. Dad's pretty happy about it. Actually, he's pretty happy all the time these days. I like it. I'm having a fun time with him and my mom. Our house is a happy one and for that, I'm thankful.

I've never seen my mom smile so much in my entire life. I always thought she was just reserved… sort of how my grandma always was. That she liked to keep to herself and she enjoyed quiet time. Now I know she was sad. Not anymore. She's always laughing now, she's always smiling.

I sit in one of the pretty white chairs and wait for my mom to sit next to me. She finally rushes over and takes a seat. She's been helping Isla, but she's also supposed to be a guest. It's a nice day. The east garden at The Sutter is the perfect place this time of day. It's cool in the shade but it's midday in November so the sun isn't that hot. It's bright and warm, perfect for a wedding.

There are flowers everywhere. The trellis over the altar is covered in blooming clematis and the lawn is plush and bright green. Every time I come here, I feel a sense of pride in my mom and her work. She loves this place and it shows in the beauty of it all. I hope I have a job one day that I love as much as she loves hers.

Mac, the groom, is the guy from the radio. He's walking around greeting people, and when he approaches, I hold my breath. He's so good-looking and I always freeze up when I have to talk to him. It's the closest I've ever been to a celebrity and I never know what to say.

He leans in and hugs my mom and thanks her for coming—for the beautiful set-up, and for her work on the wedding.

She smiles widely and, of course, takes zero credit. "Thank you, but it was all Isla's doing. She's so great, isn't she?"

"I know you had a hand in it too and I appreciate it."

"My pleasure, Mac." When the music begins playing, she turns quickly. "You'd better get in place, it sounds like they're starting."

He rushes back up to the altar where his friends are standing. Mac's best man is a woman, which is a little funny, but if she's his best friend, it's understandable. She's his partner on the radio show, and she's super pretty. Probably too pretty for radio, just like Mac.

My dad is Kelley's… I'm not sure what to call it. I guess he's her best man, but I know they've been friends for a long time. He took the job seriously too, helping her with all the arrangements and planning.

It makes me wonder when Mom and Dad are getting married. I reach over and play with my mom's diamond ring. My dad surprised her with it a few weeks ago. They were already talking about getting married, but he made it official with a proposal and everything. My mom cried. When she feels me touch her hand, she glances over with a smile. All she does these days is smile.

"I can't wait until you and Dad get married," I say.

She shifts a little so that she can see me fully. "I can't wait either… and I wanted to ask you something."

"What, Mom?"

"Would you be my Maid of Honor? Stand up for me in our wedding?"

My mouth falls open in surprise and my eyes tear up. "Yes… I would love that, but don't you want to ask Isla?"

"Isla can be a bridesmaid, but I'd love it if you were next to me when I marry your dad."

I nod and hug her really tight. Then the *Wedding March* starts and we jerk away fast so we can watch Kelley walk down the aisle. When she does, I almost gasp at how beautiful she is. I turn quickly to look at Mac and he has a huge smile on his face and he's crying. It makes me choke up again so I turn away and then see my dad, walking behind Kelley.

He's wearing a black suit with a purple tie and he looks so handsome. He looks so happy too, and it makes my heart lighter to see him. When he walks by, he winks at us and that makes me blush for some reason, but I don't care. I'm proud he's my dad, and even prouder that he loves my mom.

A LETTER FROM DANA

Thank you so much for choosing to read *Accidental Secrets*. If you enjoyed it and want to keep up to date with all my latest releases, just sign up at the following link. I promise I won't fill your inbox, but I'll keep you updated on what's happening with my books. Your email address will never be shared, and you can unsubscribe at any time.

www.bookouture.com/dana-mason

Since first writing about Mike in *Accidental Groom*, I knew I wanted to share his story. I love these characters and I'm so glad I've been able to give them their second chance. I really hope you love them too. Thank you for choosing this series and my books. Your support has been amazing and I'll never be able to thank you enough.

I hope you loved reading *Accidental Secrets* as much as I enjoyed writing it and if you did, I'd be very grateful if you could write a review. Just a few words and a star rating go a long way toward helping new readers discover my books for the first time, and I can't wait to hear what you think.

There's nothing better than hearing from my readers! Thank you for all the wonderful messages telling me how much you're enjoying the series. I encourage you to reach out to me anytime you want to chat. You can find me on my Facebook page, through Twitter, Goodreads or my website.

Thanks,
Dana Mason

danamasonromance

@danamason06

danamasonromance.com

ACKNOWLEDGEMENTS

I want to thank all my friends and family for your constant support and understanding. Jim and Trevor, thank you for picking up the slack when I'm working on a deadline. To all of my extended family and friends, I'm sure it gets annoying when my promo posts keep popping up on your Facebook feeds, but you share them anyway. I appreciate you! Thank you so much. Please keep sharing and spreading the word. I couldn't do this without you.

To the ladies who read everything I send them, Lisa, Katie, Nancy T, Paige, Nancy G and Linda, thank you so much for your valuable feedback and for answering my never-ending questions. You ladies are *my* ride or die! I hope you know that. Katie and Lisa, you're both saints for listening to my whining and for soothing my doubts. Thank you for always, always listening, advising, and pushing me.

Thank you, Jennie and Craig Moore and the Benicia CrossFit family, you're a bunch of crazy-ass warriors, and I'm so impressed by what you do. Raegan Moore, you have a beautiful yet fierce spirit, just like your mom. Thank you for sharing it with me.

Christina Demosthenous, and the rest of my Bookouture family, you're amazing! Thank you for your support! Vicky Blunden, thank you for helping me clean this up. It's a better story because of you. Kim and Noelle, you're the best cheerleaders a girl could have. Thank you for always standing on all the rooftops and shouting about my books.